# SOLID GOLD MURDER

**Books by Ellen Byron**

A VERY WOODSY MURDER

SOLID GOLD MURDER

**Books by Ellen Byron writing as Maria DiRico**

HERE COMES THE BODY

LONG ISLAND ICED TINA

IT'S BEGINNING TO LOOK A LOT LIKE MURDER

FOUR PARTIES AND A FUNERAL

THE WITLESS PROTECTION PROGRAM

Published by Kensington Publishing Corp.

# SOLID GOLD MURDER

Ellen BYRON

KENSINGTON PUBLISHING CORP.
kensingtonbooks.com

KENSINGTON BOOKS are published by

Kensington Publishing Corp.
900 Third Ave.
New York, NY 10022



All Kensington titles, imprints, and distributed lines are available at special quantity discounts for bulk purchases for sales promotion, premiums, fund-raising, educational, or institutional use. Special book excerpts or customized printings can also be created to fit specific needs. For details, write or phone the office of the Kensington Special Sales Manager: Attn. Special Sales Department, Kensington Publishing Corp., 900 Third Ave., New York, NY 10022 Phone: 1-800-221-2647.

Library of Congress Control Number: 2025934262



ISBN: 978-1-4967-4538-5

First Kensington Hardcover Edition: August 2025

ISBN: 978-1-4967-4540-8

10 9 8 7 6 5 4 3 2 1

Printed in the United States of America

The authorized representative in the EU for product safety and compliance
is eucomply OU, Parnu mnt 139b-14, Apt 123
Tallinn, Berlin 11317, hello@eucompliancepartner.com

Dedicated to Elisabetta DiVirgilio Seideman, my beloved mama.
You inspired my love of nature and history. I will miss you forever.

# WHO'S WHO

At the Golden Motel

*Dee Stern:* sitcom writer turned budding motelier
*Jeff Cornetta:* data analyst turned budding motelier
*Sam Stern:* Dee's father, a voice actor currently staying at the Golden
*Ma'am:* handywoman who lives off the grid in the backwoods with her husband
*Mister Ma'am:* her mate
*Nugget:* Dee's hound, adopted from the estate of the Golden's late owner, Jasper Gormley

Guests of the Golden

*Sylvan Burr:* a techie so wealthy he's already retired in his late twenties
*Gracie Delacroix:* his girlfriend
*Austin Nyugen:* another wealthy, retired twentysomething techie; Sylvan's frenemy
*Gavin Walsh*: the fourth in Sylvan's "Core Four"; ten years older than the others and a gladhander
*Ed Froelich:* older guest, a struggling accountant
*Trish Froelich:* his wife, an office manager who wishes she could retire
*Assorted others*

In Foundgold

*Elmira Williker:* owner of Williker's All-in-One General Store, which has been in her family since the Gold Rush

*Heloise and -Luca:* her part-time employees

*Serena Finlay-Katz:* ethereal charcuterie artist married to a big Hollywood agent

*Callan Katz:* Serena's husband, a Hollywood agent who's basically up in Goldsgone only on the weekends

*Emmy:* Serena and Callan's infant daughter

*Oscar:* Serena's tiny dog

In Goldsgone

*Verity Donner Gillespie:* proprietor, Goldsgone Mercantile and Emporium. Runs the town.

*Gillie Gillespie:* her nephew and recent hire at the mercantile

*Jonas Jones*: handsome real estate agent

*Pamela Pryor:* proprietor of sexy lingerie shop, Miss Mary's Unmentionables

*Ice Cream Ida:* ornery ice cream purveyor

*Abraham Tanner:* leather goods merchant

*Owen Mudd Jr.*: local jeweler

*Various shopkeepers*

Law Enforcement:

*Raul Aguilar:* deputy sheriff at the Goldsgone substation of the county sheriff agency

*Tom O'Bryant*: chief district ranger, Majestic National Park

*Gerald Tejada*: another deputy sheriff at the Goldsgone substation

# CHAPTER 1

"We had a wonderful stay. I'd even say the Golden Motel exceeded expectations."

The compliment came from a woman named Laurie whose family was among the guests at the recently restored motel's inaugural summer season. "Restored" was a bit of a euphemism. But it went a long way to explaining why the motel still possessed its original décor, down to the 1940s bathroom fixtures. Still, all ten rooms in the Golden's lodge, and nine out of ten cabins—the tenth currently only a concrete slab, thanks to a murderous arsonist—were up and running, albeit with the occasional nerve-wracking clatter from the motel's old pipes.

Newly minted motelier Dee Stern placed a hand on her heart. "I can't tell you how happy I am that you loved your stay with us. I hope you'll make a visit to the Golden a family tradition." She smiled at Laurie's young daughter, Molly. "Until we see you again, here's something to remember us by."

Dee reached into a shelf under the reservations desk, built of redwood like everything else at the rustic Golden, and handed the girl a small stuffed bear wearing a T-shirt emblazoned with the motel logo, along with the tagline, *Go for the Golden!*

The eight-year-old let out a delighted gasp. "Bud!" She took the bear and clutched it to her chest. "I love him. Thank you."

"We're big fans of the Bud the Bear cartoons on your website," her mother said, casting a fond look at her daughter.

"I'm so glad you like him," Dee said. She had spent a good portion of her childhood doodling at the animation studios where her father, a voice actor, recorded cartoon characters. Dee even toyed with becoming an animator before settling on a career as a sitcom writer–producer—a career she'd literally fled, landing in Foundgold, California, and her current adventure as co-owner, manager, and maintenance worker at the Golden, the village's sole lodging. Since shedding one unreliable career for another, Dee had begun drawing again, creating humorous depictions of a lumbering local mammal she'd given a more family-friendly name to than his original moniker of Stoney, bestowed on him by workers at an illegal pot farm.

"In fact," the happy guest continued, "those funny little drawings convinced us to stay at your motel and not in Goldsgone."

The revelation that Foundgold beat out tourist trap Goldsgone made Dee glow like the fake gold nugget paperweight on her desk. "Goldsgone is wonderful," Dee said, choosing to be magnanimous, "but we're glad you chose us."

"And we're glad you didn't live up to your nickname." Laurie leaned over the desk and whispered conspiratorially, "*Murder Motel.*"

And just like that, Dee's glow faded.

"Murder Motel," Jeff repeated. He made a face. "Great. Just great."

Dee and her business partner/best friend/brief former husband stood under a canopy of fir trees, cleaning pine needles out of the dilapidated sluice they'd brought back to life. The sluice was a facsimile of the original Forty-Niners' wooden contraption that utilized water to separate gold from a river's sandy bottom. A big draw for tourists back in the Golden's 1940s heyday, the new moteliers were excited to offer guests a chance, once more, to "pan for gold."

At the moment, however, Dee was focused on griping about her archnemesis, Goldsgone's Verity Donner Gillespie. Dee and Jeff had nicknamed the pushy woman "Yes-*that*- Donner," due to her constant bragging that she was related to the ill-fated members of the eponymously named Donner Party. All the bonnets and gingham skirts in the world couldn't hide Verity's ruthless competitive streak, which led her to view Dee's efforts to promote Foundgold as a threat to her town's decades of dominance. The shop owner and tourism director also happened to publish the local freebie online and print newspaper. After two murders happened to take place on Golden Motel grounds, Verity gleefully dubbed the place "Murder Motel."

"She's determined to make that stupid nickname stick." Dee gave a pine tree branch caught in the sluice an angry yank. "Dag-nab-it."

Jeff waved a finger at her. "Ha! Quarter in the jar."

Determined not to fall into the Goldsgonedian habit of talking like a nineteenth-century miner, Jeff and Dee had turned an empty mayonnaise container into a variation on a swear jar. Instead of dropping a quarter in it every time they let loose with a profanity, they paid up when they used an old-timey word.

"Remind me to pay up when we're back in the office,"

Dee said. "I hope I have change. We may have to do a virtual jar. I wonder if you can send quarters through a money app." Dee dislodged the branch and tossed it in the woods. Nugget, the large, amiable, mangy mutt she'd adopted from the late motel owner's estate, galumphed after it. "Verity is totally set on putting us out of business. It's not like the murders were our fault. We just got stuck being the location for them. We even helped catch the killer. But does she publicize that? *Nooooo*. Do anything that might help us? Not for a doggone minute. Argh!" Frustrated she'd let another miner word slip out, she followed it with a more au courant curse.

"Howdy, you two!"

The greeting came from Sam Stern, Dee's dad, who was staying at the Golden while his home in the Los Angeles neighborhood of Studio City was being treated for termites. He walked toward them, negotiating the hill between the motel's cabins and the sluice. He was dressed to resemble a nineteenth-century miner in jeans, suspenders, a plaid shirt, boots, and a wide-brimmed canvas hat. A woman close to his own age of early seventies was with him. Her straggly gray hair hung long past her shoulders and she wore a dress that not only looked like it was made from old sacks, it was. A man in their age range tagged along behind them. He wore hand-stitched pants and a shirt made from the same brand of flour sacks as the woman.

Dee waved to them. "Hey, Dad. Hey, Ma'am and Mister." In this case, "ma'am" and "mister' weren't appellations, they were names.

"Does your dad's 'Howdy' count for the miner jar?" Jeff asked.

Dee shook her head. "He's in costume for some reason, so no. The 'Howdy' is appropriate . . . marginally."

Sam and the others reached the sluice and exchanged greetings with Dee and Jeff. "Why the new, but old, look, Dad?" Dee asked.

Sam grinned, revealing a blacked-out front tooth. "The termite guys called to say they're done tenting my house. But"—he inhaled a deep breath—"you gotta love this mountain air. And the scent of real pinecones beats the plug-in fresheners I use at home by a mile. I thought I could stick around and make myself useful here by playing Prospector Pete and helping guests pan for gold. If it's okay by you, of course."

Dee glanced at Jeff to gauge his approval for Sam's extended stay. He responded with a smile and a nod. "Welcome aboard, Pete," she said. "Stay as long as you want. But . . . maybe lose the tooth. I mean, keep the tooth, just lose the blackout wax on it."

Sam removed the wax. Ma'am picked up one of the green plastic miner's pans Dee and Jeff had purchased for their guests to use. She gestured for the others to grab pans. "You ready for your lesson?"

Pans in hand, her students nodded.

Ma'am dipped the pan into the sluice, scooping up a handful of rocks. She gave the pan a gentle shake, then dipped the pan slightly to drain the water. She washed what remained in the pan two more times. Dee, Jeff, and Sam copied her moves with their own pans. After the last wash, she showed the others her pan. The rocks were gone, leaving flakes and tiny stones that glistened. "See? The big rocks are gone and the little ones, the pyrite—the fool's gold—are still there. If it was real gold, it'd be easier to keep in the pan because gold is dense. It sinks to the bottom. You'll have to be careful, especially with little kids. They wanna shake like this . . ."

Ma'am gave her pan a few wild shakes, sending whatever was inside flying. A piece of pyrite beaned Jeff. "Ow." He rubbed the spot where the stone connected with his forehead.

"Man up," Dee teased.

"Check your pans," Ma'am instructed. "If you don't see any fool's gold, you shook the pan too hard."

Dee, Jeff, and Sam checked their pans. Dee held hers up triumphantly. "Got some!"

"Not me," Sam said.

"I got a couple of flakes." Jeff pressed his finger to one. "It disintegrated."

"Fool's gold does that. Real gold holds a shape more. Fool's gold also has a duller sheen than real gold, especially once it's dry."

Ma'am removed a tiny chunk from Dee's pan and dried it on her sack dress. She held it up. What had looked like gold in the pan now appeared gray, its luster dimmed.

"I see what you're talking about," Dee said.

Ma'am handed the stone back to Dee. She rinsed her pan and set it back on the stack. "So there ya have it. Placer Mining for Dummies."

"She could have gone with Placer Mining 101," Jeff muttered to Dee.

Mister proudly applauded Ma'am. "Ain't she something? My li'l prospecting missus."

Dee dunked her chunk of pyrite back in the water and it glistened again. "I know some of the local sites use the real stuff. Actual gold flakes. But we can't afford to. At least not yet."

"Wouldn't worry about it," Ma'am said. "Tourists

want the experience, especially the ones with littles. They don't care if it's real or not, as long as they're having fun."

"That's a job for Prospector Pete." Sam snapped his suspenders. "I'm gonna practice panning some more." He stroked his chin. "You know, there's an old cabin up by Little Stream in the woods."

Mister nodded. "Hermit Dan's. Know his place well. Sitting on the edge of Golden Brook. He passed away around aught five. Nice fella, but kept to himself."

"That's pretty much the job description for a hermit," Dee said.

"I'm going to spend the night there," Sam said. "Get my prospector on, as you kids would say." He winked at his daughter.

"Okay," she said. "But if you can finish your method research and get here early in the a.m., we've got guests doing early check-in and I'd love to be able to tell them they can pan in our sluice."

Sam gave her a salute. "You got it." He began singing a made-up ditty. "La di dah, la dee dee, it's a prospector's life for me!" As he sang, Sam hopped back and forth in a dance that was part jig, part Sailor's Hornpipe, and all silly.

"Uh, you might want to ratchet it down a scooch, Pete," Dee said.

"I'll work on it."

Sam headed up the hill and into the woods, leaving Dee to hope she hadn't made a big mistake.

To Dee's relief, her father showed up the next morning sans blackout tooth. "You look refreshed," she said as she scrambled eggs for them on the old stove in the one-bedroom apartment attached to the motel that she called home. Like the rest of the Golden, it boasted the original rustic, carved oak furniture. With its pine-green walls and prints of Majestic's glorious natural wonders, the apartment gave off the feeling of being in a forest glen. "I guess sleeping in abandoned ruins agrees with you."

"To be honest, I didn't have the best sleep of my life. I'm pretty sure our bear friend, Bud, was out for a nocturnal stroll. To get myself going, I bathed in the brook, which is more like a river right now, thanks to the spring rains and heavy snowmelt." Sam patted his curly white hair, still wet from his watery immersion. "Cold as all get-out, but it did the trick."

A bell sounded from the motel lobby behind the door separating it from Dee's quarters. She removed her apron and straightened the navy polo shirt, with the motel logo, she wore underneath it. "Guests. Do you have your phone? I'll text you if they're interested in panning."

"Yes, ma'am." Sam "The Man of a Million Voices" Stern spoke in the reedy twang he'd deemed the voice of Prospector Pete. "You tell them varmints I'm a-dustin' off muh boots 'n puttin' on muh hat and pickin' up muh pan."

*This is going to get old fast,* Dee thought as she left Sam to check in the guests.

She entered the lobby through a door in her apartment that connected to it. The new arrivals were divorced dad Paul and his disaffected tween son, Brandon. "We're on a father-son weekend," Paul explained as Dee handed him a room key, along with a list of attractions in the area she and Jeff had culled. Paul glanced at the list. "There's a lot to do around here, right?"

He sounded slightly desperate. Knowing this probably stemmed from the herculean task the man faced of separating his son from his cell phone, Dee sympathized. "Tons," she assured him. "In addition to the list, we're happy to make recommendations. Also, big news on our front. Today is the first day you can try out our sluice and pan for 'gold.'"

Dee added the air quotes to disavow Paul and son of any notion they'd be panning for real gold. She was happy to see that despite this, Brandon glanced up from his phone. Paul noticed too and jumped on it. "Wow! Awesome, huh, son?"

Brandon mumbled something that might have been "whatevs," but he did seem mildly intrigued. "Why don't you settle into your room," Dee said, "and we'll meet you at the sluice in fifteen minutes?"

"Sounds good," Paul said.

He ushered his son out the door and Dee texted her father: **Prospector Pete, you're up!** She also texted Jeff, then hurried outside and rang the triangle bell dangling from the far end of the motel to summon Ma'am. Given this was the sluice's debut with guests, she wanted an expert on hand in case anything went wrong.

Fifteen minutes later, the Golden group met up with Paul and Brandon at the sluice. Under the watchful eye of Ma'am, Prospector Pete explained the process of placer mining, sharing what she had taught him with only a few added bits of cheesy miner jargon, to Dee's relief. He handed a pan to the father, and then the son. "Before you start, I'd love to film this for our website," Dee said. "You're our first guests to pan."

"Fine with me," Paul said. "But it's up to my son. Brandon, you on board with it?"

Brandon mumbled something that didn't sound like no, so Dee slid her phone to video and the panning commenced.

To the motelier's delight, the event was a success. Paul and Brandon enjoyed the panning process and even joked about one-upping each other with their haul as Sam carefully transferred their findings into tiny glass vials that served as souvenirs.

Paul held up his jar to Dee's camera. "Look, I found gold. I'm rich!"

Everyone laughed . . . except Ma'am. She stared at the vial. "Lemme see that."

Puzzled, Paul handed it to her. She gave the vial a shake. Tiny stones floated to the top, while a few flakes sank to the bottom, where they glistened in the sunlight. "Well, hitch me to a wagon and call me a dray horse."

Dee spoke for everyone when she issued a bewildered, "Huh?"

Ma'am pointed to the flakes, along with a tiny nugget, settled at the bottom of the vial. "This ain't fool's gold. It's *real* gold."

"It can't be," Jeff said. "I didn't order real gold for the sluice."

"Well, it is," Ma'am insisted. "I seen enough of the real thing in my pans to know."

"Um, can I have my vial back?"

Ma'am handed it over and Paul shoved it into his jeans pocket. Brandon held out his vial to Ma'am. "Do I have real gold?" he asked, forming the first full sentence he'd uttered since arriving at the Golden.

Ma'am took the vial and shook it. Again, a small, shiny stone rose and golden flakes sank. "You do, son." She handed the vial back to the boy. Like his father, he quickly shoved it into his jeans pocket.

"How did the gold get in there?" Dee wondered. "Could

some have accidentally been mixed in with the pyrite you ordered, Jeff?"

He looked perplexed. "Maybe, but I doubt it."

"It sure is a mystery," Sam said.

Her father took off his hat and ran a hand over his still-damp hair. Dee noticed a sparkle on the edge of his sleeve. "Dad, freeze!"

Confusion colored Sam's face, but he did as ordered. Ma'am carefully studied his shirt sleeve. She gently removed a flake from his sleeve and examined it. "Gold."

The others murmured various expression of awe and disbelief. "The stream," Sam suddenly blurted. "When I took a plunge, flakes must've gotten on me. Then when I dunked my hands in the sluice, it washed off."

"That means . . ." Jeff trailed off.

"I heard rumors that the heavy spring rains exposed gold in places where no one's found it for years," Ma'am said. "But I thought it was rumors. Sam, show me where you plunged. No one say anything about this until I check out the site and confirm the find."

Paul grabbed Brandon's arm and they started running to their car. "Wait!" Dee yelled to them. "Where are you going?!"

"To town to buy mining equipment," he yelled back. "Best father-son weekend ever!"

"So much for keeping this on the down-low," Jeff said.

"I wouldn't worry about them," Ma'am said. "They'll wanna keep the secret to themselves so they can mine whatever they can." She gestured to Dee's phone. "But you best delete that video."

"Right. I forgot I was recording." Unnerved by the momentous discovery, Dee's hands shook as she fumbled with her phone. "Agh!" she cried out. "I accidentally shared it!

I need to get into the site and delete it." Panicked, she fumbled with her phone. "Argh! I can't figure out how to do it from the mobile version."

"I built the site," Jeff said. He opened the Golden website on his cell. "I'll do it."

"You better," Ma'am warned. "Or you're gonna start another Gold Rush."

Jeff stared at his phone screen in disbelief. "Whoa. We just got a booking. Make that two. No, four." He looked up. "I think the rush already started."

# CHAPTER 2

Jeff was right. The Golden booked up for the next week within minutes. But instead of celebrating, Dee couldn't shake a sense of foreboding.

"I'm so mad at myself for sharing that video," she griped to Jeff the next morning. The two were going from room to room, and cabin to cabin, double- and triple-checking to make sure they were ready for the onslaught of guests. "I mean, it's great we're sold out. But I keep feeling it's for the wrong reason: greed. People are only coming to see if they can cash in on the gold."

"Hey, you did us a favor," her friend/business partner replied. "And specifically, me. First off, we *are* sold out, which, greed or not, is a good and very necessary thing for motel finances. And secondly, I'm usually the one doing stupid stuff, like accidentally sharing the wrong thing." He peered into the cabin bathroom. "Extra roll of toilet paper."

Dee handed him one from her cart. "We should learn more about the original Gold Rush so we know what to expect. The basics are the same. There's gold and people want it. Dad was recording a show in New York during fourth grade, so I got their state history and not California's. Did you know twenty to thirty men died while building the Brooklyn Bridge?"

"No, and now I'm sad. Humane mousetrap, please."

Dee handed him an animal-friendly trap. "Can you keep an eye on things here for an hour? I'm going to make a run to the All-in-One. Elmira might have a book on the Gold Rush in her tourist section. I also have to pick up our fake order of scones."

Elmira Williker, proprietor of Foundgold's only store, prided herself on her baking skills. But she'd lost her sense of taste to a virus and the locals couldn't bring themselves to tell the beloved proprietor that everything she pulled out of her oven was inedible. Dee and Jeff had a standing order for breakfast pastries, which they promptly discarded the minute they returned to the motel.

The moteliers finished prepping the last cabin. Dee leashed up Nugget and the two took off for the store. Nugget leaped over the middle seats to the way back and spread out, making himself comfortable. Dee had traded in her Honda Civic for a Subaru Forester, knowing the compact crossover SUV provided more room, and the four-wheel drive would prove critical in the winter months. *Another box checked off in my transition from Valley Girl to Mountain Girl,* she thought as she navigated the winding two-lane mountain road.

The All-in-One parking lot was full, with overflow parking taking up the side of the road. Considering employees—of which there were three, with only Elmira full-time—usually outnumbered shoppers, this came as a surprise. Fortunately, someone was pulling out. Dee zipped into the spot, beating a driver heading in the All-in-One's direction from down the road.

Dee got out and retrieved Nugget. They headed to the store's entrance at the original section of the store, which dated back to 1849. Additions fanned out from both sides of the core, creating a mash-up of architectural styles representative of their differing time periods, but all crafted from the same stone and redwood used to build the picturesque historic homes of Foundgold.

Dee entered the general store. She stood stock-still, gaping at what she saw. The place was packed. A line to check out snaked past worn wooden shelves almost picked bare. A customer grabbed the last shade hat, earning glares from two other customers who'd reached for it. Another customer snagged the last shovel.

Nugget whimpered, attracting the attention of Elmira, who was behind the wooden sales counter ringing up a customer on an ancient cash register. Her face lit up at the sight of Dee. "Well, if it isn't my favorite citizen of Goldsgone. Heloise, Luca, look who's here."

Elmira's part-time employees stopped restocking the shelves to join her in a round of applause, embarrassing a perplexed Dee. "No idea what I did to earn that. But hey, I'll take it."

Elmira motioned to Heloise. "Cover the register for me."

Heloise did so, freeing Elmira to join Dee and Nugget at the souvenir section of the shop, which sat next to the combination bar and café. The store proprietor gifted an appreciative Nugget with a rawhide chew, then declared to Dee, "You're my hero." She followed this with a hug that threw Dee off-balance, literally and figuratively. Elmira was a tough, sturdy widow in her mid-forties, and Dee counted on her for no-holds-barred honesty, not effusive warmth.

"How am I your hero?" Dee asked, relieved the woman had turned her attention to petting Nugget.

"Williker's hasn't seen so much action since the first Gold Rush. My thrice-great-grandfather sure did call it when he decided he'd make more money selling to miners than mining."

Elmira's ancestors were rare birds: Black miners who'd made their way to the region almost a century and three-quarters earlier to try their luck at panning, thought better of it, and stuck around to help found Foundgold. Williker descendants had been there ever since, with the All-in-One handed down through generations until it landed in Elmira's lap. A single mom with a son and daughter who'd grown and flown, Elmira managed to keep many of the historical touches that made Williker's a local landmark, while coaxing it into the modern age. The All-in-One now counted a coffee bar among its many offerings, allowing customers to grab a cappuccino while they shopped for buckshot.

"I'm glad you're happy about this," Dee said. "I'm conflicted. On the one hand, it's exciting to sell out the motel so soon after we reopened it." She was distracted by two shoppers grabbing for the last plastic mining pan. A tug-of-war quickly escalated into a war of words, which threatened to move up the ladder of arguments to a full-on brawl. "On the other hand, it's kind of scary."

"I'll take scary when it comes to the ringing of my register."

Elmira excused herself to deal with the dustup. Dee thumbed through the books on display, digging through a shelf of guidebooks and self-published memoirs from local citizens who fancied themselves important enough to write about. Finally she found what she was looking for: *There's Gold in Them Thar Hills: A History.* "It's all about the Gold Rush in this county. That should be helpful," she told Nugget.

Dee got on the end of the line to pay for her purchase. Elmira, who was back to manning the register, called to her, "You don't have to stand there. I'll put it on your tab." She pulled a bakery box out from below the counter. "Along with the scones. Two dozen, made with fresh-picked blueberries."

"Yay," Dee responded weakly, feeling sorry for the blueberries.

"Tell your dad to stop by when he can," Elmira said, her tone suddenly coy. "I made a batch of his favorite, Solid Gold Blondies."

"I will, " Dee said. Sam's crush on Elmira began the day Dee sent him to All-in-One to pick up a bottle of bathroom mildew cleaner. Dee's mother, Sybil, had suffered a fatal heart attack in her sleep the previous year, and Dee feared her father might never recover from losing her. She was happy to see him taking the smallest steps toward a new relationship, especially with one of the best friends she'd made since moving to Foundgold. *If Dad's declared any of Elmira's baked goods to be a favorite, this must be getting serious*, she thought.

Dee left with the scones, Nugget, and her book—which would soon go unread because Williker's parking lot was emblematic of the madness about to erupt.

By the following day, every motel and B and B for miles was booked by prospectors, wannabes, families, and curiosity seekers, resulting in the first traffic jam in the area's history. Those who couldn't find lodging slept in their cars wherever they could find parking. On the upside, Elmira wasn't the only one who hailed Dee as a hero. The motelier's unintentional video release led to her earning accolades from a lot of local merchants, all of whom quickly adopted a side hustle of selling prospecting equipment. Dee had struggled for acceptance since her move to Gold County, but she now found herself with no time to enjoy it. She was either checking in guests, turning them away, or booting squatters trying to set up camp on the Golden's property.

A couple named Trish and Ed Froelich, the last guests booked for the night, showed around ten p.m. "I thought we'd never get here," Trish said as Dee swiped her credit card. Somewhere in her mid-sixties, Trish had a bubble of dirty blond hair and a soft midsection doing its best to hide under leggings and a long, short-sleeved black tunic top. "I started to panic when it got dark. Ed and I don't have the best night vision."

"Well, we're glad you made it." Dee flashed what she deemed her signature "Welcome to the Golden!" smile. "Are you here for vacation, panning, or both?"

"Only panning." Trish rubbed her eyes. Dee could see remnants of makeup that had faded during the hours it took for the Froelichs to make the trek from San Bernardino County to Foundgold.

"If you're panning, we sell kits for the lowest price you'll find in town." Rather than see a potential revenue stream float by them, Dee and Jeff had adopted a Gold Rush side hustle of their own, creating kits to sell their guests. The kits contained black pans, which made it easier to spot gold, sifters, tweezers, glass vials, foam shade visors, and a small plastic shovel. They'd also included a printout they'd created with a map of their property, including details about the brooks and creeks that meandered in the woods above the motel, and a list of safety instructions.

"Sure. We'll take one."

"You got it." Dee reached under the desk to retrieve the kit.

Trish leaned an elbow on the counter and rested her chin on it. "We need the money from whatever gold we find. I thought I'd finally get to retire—I'm the office manager for an advertising agency—and have time for my hobbies. I love gardening and genealogy and I want to take up pickleball. But we had to spend a fortune on my late mother-in-law's memory care facility. We budgeted for two years. She ended up being there for seven, which almost wiped us out. And Ed's accounting business is falling apart. His client base is shrinking. His older regulars are dying off and he's not getting new ones. People would rather go with the latest online tax service or app. So, no retirement for me. If things keep up the way they're going, Lord knows what's gonna happen."

Trish reached for the bag containing the panning kit. Dee hesitated, then handed it over. "You know what . . . it's on the house."

"Oh, thank you. That's so kind and generous. Eddie, look. Our very own panning equipment."

She held up the bag to show the man who'd just entered the lobby. Ed was about the same age as his wife, but where she was soft, he was taut to the point of being bony. Bald and bespectacled, he was clad in a T-shirt decorated with a Loyola Marymount University logo. It hung loosely over his khaki Bermuda shorts. Dee noticed the couple wore matching orthopedic sandals.

"Terrific. I'm looking forward to putting it to use." Ed limped toward them, breathing heavily as he walked. The lobby was up a small hill from the parking area and the incline appeared to have gotten to him. "The nice young man who works here put our luggage in our room. I'm still stiff from the car ride here. Arthritis is a mean mistress."

"You must be Mr. Froelich. Welcome to the Golden." Dee flashed her smile.

"I'm Ed. Mr. Froelich was my father."

Dee laughed politely at a dad joke she wouldn't be surprised to find on a cave painting. "Are you planning to start panning early?" she asked. The couple nodded in unison. "No problem. Prospector Pete, our resident panning expert, will meet you at the sluice to give you a lesson on how to do it." Dee picked up her copy of the safety instructions she handed out to every guest, whether they bought a kit from her or not. "Right now, I want to go over some important safety concerns. Take the sheet out of your kit so you can follow along with me."

The Froelichs did so.

"Be very careful in all waterways," Dee warned. "Their depth can be deceiving. The heavy winter rain swelled every water source around here. You can take a single step and find yourself going from a spot that's a foot deep to one that's eight feet deep. This is definitely true of Dry Creek. Its name is the definition of irony right now because it's closer to a raging river. Stick to Little Stream, or better yet Golden Brook, which is also flowing heavily, but not as bad as the creek. We don't want any of our guests drowning on us."

"We're gonna be extra careful," Trish said. "I'm a bad swimmer to begin with, and on top of his arthritis, Ed has tendonitis in both shoulders, so he can't swim at all anymore."

Ed raised his arms to prove her point and winced. "Ouch. Aging is not for the faint of heart. But nothing a kid like you has to worry about."

Dee, who would begin her fortieth trip around the sun in December, didn't feel like a kid. But she appreciated the compliment. "The land around here is littered with old mines. Some are abandoned, some are still privately owned, so obey every Do Not Enter sign you see. Ignore rumors that the winter rains exposed new veins of gold in the old mines. They're only rumors and the mines are too dangerous to risk exploring. Lastly, just so you know, there's great cell reception here and in the village, but little to none in the woods." She double-checked her list. "Okay, that's it. You're in room 1, which is closest to our little parking lot. If you have any questions or problems with your accommodations, text me or Jeff." She flashed her signature smile a third time. "Like we say on our website and our new line of merchandise, thanks to our 'Gold Rush' of guests, we want 'every stay with us to be pure gold.'"

"That's what we're here for," Ed said. "And if panning doesn't work, we may have to sneak past the Do Not Enter signs and check out those old mines. Kidding, of course."

Dee faked another laugh. But she had a worrisome feeling this wasn't a joke.

# CHAPTER 3

With their guests left to their own somewhat-dubious devices, Dee and Jeff turned their attention to other tasks. An excited Dee applied for a crafts fair being sponsored by the Goldsgone Business Association. With the influx of tourists, the fair would be the perfect sales venue for her Bud the Bear merchandise. Knowing this second Gold Rush would eventually end like all rushes do, Jeff was on a mission to add activities besides the sluice to the motel's offerings.

Dee found her fellow motelier about to mount an electric bicycle in the circular gravel drive fronting the motel. She eyed Jeff with skepticism. "Where did you get that and why?"

"I got it slightly used from an online marketplace. Electric bikes are popular right now. We could buy a couple and charge our guests a small fee to rent them by the hour."

"It looks like an accident waiting to happen."

"They're safe, as long as you ride at a slow speed."

Jeff fired up the bike. He hopped on and took off. It only took a few feet for him to lose control and topple over.

Dee helped him up. "Are you okay?"

Jeff dusted himself off. "Yeah, except for a couple of small scrapes. I don't think they're meant to be ridden on gravel."

"Considering that's all we have around the Golden, maybe look for a different activity."

"I already have a possible alternative." He limped over to his backpack and pulled out a package. "Slingshots." He took one out of the package, along with a tube of wooden balls. "We can set up soda cans and have contests to see who can knock the most down."

Dee gave him a look. "And there's no way a guest won't try and use the slingshot against some poor defenseless squirrel, is there?"

"I didn't think of that," Jeff admitted, embarrassed. "Forget the slingshots. Too bad, they're cool."

He loaded a ball into the slingshot and released it. The ball went flying out of sight. There was the sound of breaking glass, followed by the sound of something shattering. "Uh-oh."

Dee craned her neck to check out the damage. "Wow, that made a perfect hole the exact size of the ball. Luckily, it was in the window of your cabin and not one of our guests. You better check and see where the ammo landed. For your sake, I hope it didn't take out your computer screen."

Jeff groaned.

Dee extracted her keys from her fanny pack. "I'm going into Goldsgone. I haven't heard anything back about my crafts fair application, so I'm going to check in person. You need anything?"

"Nah, I'm good." Jeff examined a scrape on his arm caused by the fall from the electric bicycle. "Maybe some antibiotic ointment."

Dee left Jeff figuring out what to do with his ill-fated, nonreturnable purchase and took off for Goldsgone. No cars were allowed inside the historic site, so she parked in a lot on the outskirts and entered the equivalent of a time tunnel.

Tiny Foundgold, home to the Golden Motel, barely dodged being lost to the mists of time. When its settlers found gold in the mid-1800s, they quickly left to spend it. The destitute citizens of Goldsgone didn't have that option—which, ironically, led to its current prosperity. A perfectly preserved miner's village, it was the biggest draw in Gold Rush Country. Compact nineteenth-century buildings made of brick and wood lined the hard-packed dirt streets. A stagecoach clip-clopped by every fifteen minutes, trading one group of tourists for another. Shopkeepers and tour guides, dressed in pioneer garb, traded howdies when they crossed each other's paths. Dee always found the whole scene simultaneously entertaining and off-putting.

She steeled herself for a visit to Goldsgone shopkeeper-mayor-tourism director/self-anointed power broker Verity Gillespie, who'd added head of the business association to her résumé and iron grip on the town. Dee's spirits were buoyed when she got a wave and hello from Liza Chen, the lovely restauranteur behind the Golden Grub Café, which was the village's close-to-trendy eatery. Dee returned the greeting. She pointed to Verity's place of business, the Goldsgone Mercantile and Emporium, and made a face. Liza laughed and mouthed, "Good luck."

Dee climbed up a few steps from the street to the wooden sidewalk fronting a row of shops. She took a deep breath and pulled open one of the mercantile's double doors. The

minute she stepped inside, she was assaulted by the overpowering scent of sarsaparilla. She restrained herself from gagging and searched the shop for Verity, avoiding identical twins Angel and Addison Rose Trapp, who were working at the store under the guise of interns. With their flaxen hair, perfect features, and piercing blue eyes, which were far too cold for sixteen-year-olds, the girls reminded Dee of characters from a gothic horror film.

A young man Dee had never seen before approached her. Tall and gangly, he was dressed like a nineteenth-century store clerk, but had a mop of brown hair cut anachronistically with a fade in the back. Colorful markings peeking out from his shirtsleeves indicated arms laced with tattoos. "Hi there," he said. "Can I help you?"

"Thank you, but I'm just looking for Verity."

An expression Dee couldn't decipher crossed the clerk's face. It seemed to combine amusement with annoyance. "My aunt is over there," he said, pointing to the middle of the shop. Dee raised an eyebrow at the revelation that the clerk was related to Verity.

"No child ever leaves Goldsgone without a hobbyhorse," Verity's voice fluted.

Dee followed the sound of the voice, navigating aisles filled with wooden display cases of old-timey souvenirs. She bumped into a mannequin dressed like a character from *Little House on the Prairie* and caught the thing before it toppled over. Unfortunately, the incident also caught Verity's attention. Seeing the businesswoman was tending to a family with a young girl, Dee tried to salvage the moment. "This is such a pretty dress," she said, caressing the dull gray calico garment. "Perfect for a pretty little girl."

"It is cute," the mother said. "How much is it?"

Dee checked the price tag. "One hundred fifty dollars?!" Unable to keep the shock from her voice, she sheepishly added, "What a steal."

"We'll stick with the hobbyhorse," the dad said.

"Wonderful!" Verity couldn't have sounded happier if he'd announced he was buying the mercantile's entire inventory. "Gillie," she called to the store clerk, giving her nephew a name, "ring up this nice family, please." She turned her attention back to them. "Make sure to take a look at our penny-candy display," she said with a wink and a smile. "It's the best in town."

The instant the family left to make their purchase, Verity dropped the act. She glared at Dee. "What?"

Verity's folksy nineteenth-century pink gingham costume, complete with lacy white bonnet perched on top of a mass of blond curls, belied the fact she was a formidable woman and ruthless competitor. Her lace-up booties made her tower over Dee's petite height, which didn't help. Dee fought back against the urge to shrink in the woman's presence. "I just wanted to check and see if you got my application for the crafts fair. I'm super excited about it."

"Oh yes. Sorry I didn't get back to you." A blond curl came loose. Verity pushed it back with one of her anachronistically long nails. She often decorated them with old-fashioned images. Today they sported tiny bonnets that matched her cap. "I'm afraid your application was denied. The crafts fair is only open to Goldsgone residents."

"It is?" Dee was disappointed. She was also suspicious. "It didn't say that anywhere on the website."

"It's in the title. The *Goldsgone* Crafts Fair. We didn't think we'd have to spell it out for people."

Dee narrowed her eyes. "Interesting. Because I saw peo-

ple on the list of exhibitors who definitely don't live here. Like the cheesemonger from Fresno."

"I'm sorry," Verity said, not sounding the least bit apologetic. "I don't make the rules."

"Oh, I think you do. But you know what? Rules are made to be broken."

"Not this one."

The women stared each other down. A bell above the door jingled, alerting Verity to a group of potential marks entering the shop. She instantly dumped Dee and scurried to them. Fuming, Dee stalked out of the store, making sure to slam the aged door behind her. As she slammed, her eyes caught nephew Gillie's. He subtly cocked his head toward Verity and made a sour face in an unexpected show of solidarity with Dee.

Dee stomped down the road toward her car. Pamela Pryor, the proprietor of Miss Mary's Unmentionables, waved to her from the porch in front of her shop, where she was adjusting a lacy black corset on the porch's display mannequin. The corset was similar to the one Pamela currently wore to promote her wares. An attractive woman in her late forties, she was a former website swimsuit model who'd held on to her figure and looks, thanks to some work that was teetering on the edge of too much. "Hi there, Dee. You all right? You look like you could deliver a haymaker to a nest of hornets."

"I'm fine." Not in the mood for Goldsgonedian miner jargon, Dee responded in a curt tone, but mindful of creating more enemies in town, she added with fake cheeriness, "Thanks so much for asking!" before quickly moving on.

Dee continued to stew on the drive home. On impulse, instead of staying on the road toward the Golden, she made a left onto an even narrower and more winding road. Eventually the road transitioned from paved asphalt to bumpy dirt, making Dee grateful for her Subaru's four-wheel drive.

She parked at the trailhead of a hike she'd discovered on her first visit to the area and exited the car. Dee followed the trail, climbing through a dense forest of black oak, cedar, white fir, ponderosa pines, and sugar pines. The scent from the pine trees was intoxicating and she found herself relaxing.

The forest gave way to a meadow. The summer heat had turned its green grass golden, and only a few hardy wildflowers still bloomed. In the middle of the vast meadow, a crystal-clear lake reflected the famed craggy granite peaks of Majestic National Park. This was Dee's refuge, a place to block out all stressors and drink in the beauty that had motivated her move to the rural county.

She plopped down on the golden grass and closed her eyes. The only sounds came from chirping birds and a slight breeze rustling the trees in the woods. After indulging in a bit of daydreaming about all the ways she could get revenge on Verity, Dee focused on coming up with a plot to do an end run around her formidable nemesis. However, the *whuppa-whuppa* noise of a helicopter distracted her. She tried to ignore it, but the roar grew louder and louder, signaling an approach.

Dee sat up and looked skyward, shading her eyes with her hand. "What the—"

The copter hovered over the meadow. Dee scrambled to her feet and backed away as it set down, its rotors creating a stiff wind that whipped her chestnut hair back from her face. The copter door opened. A twentysomething, wearing a hoodie and hipster chin stubble, hopped out of the copter, sticking the landing onto the meadow grass. Three others similarly attired disembarked. One of the new arrivals pushed back the hood on their hoodie, revealing themselves to be a girl.

The lead guy turned to the copter pilot and nodded. The copter rose and roared off. The foursome saw Dee and headed to her. "You scheduled our rideshare to meet us here?" Hoodie #1 said to the girl. "Nice."

Dee glanced around, then realized he was talking about her. "I'm not a rideshare," she said, feeling testy. The obvious leader of the pack exuded a cocky arrogance that made her take an instant dislike to him.

"I'm Sylvan Burr." He said this in a way that indicated she should be impressed. The name sounded vaguely familiar, but Dee reacted with a blank look, not wanting to give him the pleasure of recognition. It didn't matter. Whoever Sylvan Burr was, he thought enough of himself not to need her fawning over him.

"We're from Palo Alto." He gestured to the others. "These are my friends Austin, Gavin, and Gracie. We're the Core Four."

Unsure how she was supposed to respond to this, Dee simply answered, "Hello."

"Gracie read about the second Gold Rush and we thought it'd be a kick to check it out," Sylvan said.

"And I once worked with someone who moved here," Gavin said. "A guy named Jeff Cornetta. He bought some place called the Golden Motel. You know it?"

The connection to Jeff confirmed Dee's instincts the four were Silicon Valley techies—the kind of people Jeff had fled from. "I own it. The Golden. With my business partner, Jeff Cornetta."

"Cool," Gavin said. "We're gonna be staying there."

"I'm afraid not." Dee kept her tone pleasant, but cool. "We're sold out. Our last guests checked in this afternoon."

"Not anymore." Sylvan held up his hands. He rubbed his thumb to his index and middle finger, making the universal sign for money. "I paid some of your guests a nice chunk of change to make other plans." He flashed a cocky "gotcha" grin. "Looks like you're our rideshare driver, after all."

# CHAPTER 4

Dee led the four and their carry-on bags through the woods to her car. As opposed to the usual Golden guests' habit of peppering her for recommendations of eateries and activities in the area, they chatted among themselves. *Not interested in engaging with the help,* she grumbled to herself.

Since they weren't paying attention to her, she snuck out her phone and typed in Sylvan Burr's name. The first headline that popped up jogged her memory: TAX HAX APP MINTS A NEW BRO-LLIONAIRE. Keeping an old motel afloat didn't leave Dee with much time to peruse the news, but she now recalled an awestruck Jeff mentioning Sylvan's stupendous success.

They reached her car. Dee unlocked it and opened the rear door. The four deposited their luggage by her feet and climbed into the car, leaving Dee to load the bags into the back of the SUV. Annoyed, she roughly hefted them in, then climbed into the driver's seat. She wasn't surprised to see Sylvan had claimed the front seat, while his cohorts squished together on the middle seat behind him. Eager to make fast work of the drive, she gunned the engine and they took off.

She surreptitiously eyed her charges. Sylvan, the sun that the other Core Four members revolved around, was slight, around five-seven. His features were bland, and his eyes almost the same color as his medium-brown hair, which he wore short. He was what a friend of Dee's who worked as a celebrity publicity agent in L.A. called "money sexy," meaning that if he wasn't rich, no one would pick him out of a crowd.

Austin, on the other hand, was genuinely handsome, with thick black hair, chiseled cheekbones, and a tall, slim frame. Gavin, who appeared about ten years older than the others, had the kind of WASP-y blond looks that reminded Dee of frat guys at her alma mater, UCLA. Gracie had a wispy frame, delicate features, and stick-straight light brown hair that hung in a bob to her shoulders. A tiny diamond twinkled from a left nostril piercing. Dee could hear her late grandmother saying, "She'd be so pretty if she wore a little makeup."

Sylvan deigned to speak to her. The conversation quickly made Dee long for being ignored again. "I had my assistant do a search for you. You wrote on a lot of sitcoms."

"I did," Dee said. While her previous career had been checkered, she was proud of her decent run in an incredibly competitive field—a field notoriously ageist and sexist, which eventually led to dwindling job offers as Dee stared down the barrel of middle age. Her last job on a squeamishly bad Kidz Channel show called *Duh!* provided the motivation to get out of the business.

"I don't watch sitcoms. They suck." After delivering this review of an entire genre, Sylvan moved his seat back. From Dee's perspective, it looked like he already had plenty of leg room.

"Can you move the seat up?" Austin asked. "My knees are in my chest."

"Deal with it."

"You should be able to move your seat back a couple of inches," Dee, firmly Team Austin, told him over her shoulder.

He did so. "Thanks."

Sylvan glanced her way, a corner of his lips curved up in a smirk. "My assistant dug up some good dirt on you. You're the inspiration for Lee Flern in *Vengeance: Year 3004*. It's a pleasure to meet the chick who inspired the most evil character in TV history."

Dee gritted her teeth. "I think that's a big exaggeration."

*Vengeance: Year 3004* was the bane of her existence. Ian Akerman, her ex-husband—second ex, factoring in the brief marriage between Dee and Jeff postcollege that they'd agreed to forget—was also a television writer. When the two married, Dee's career was on the upswing, while Ian struggled to find work. He channeled his jealousy into a sci-fi drama pilot about a heroic Space Force commander fighting back against his evil ex-wife, Lee Flern. Now Ian ran a hugely successful streamer, while Dee ran a motel in the mountains and shuttled obnoxious rich techies to it. Oh, how the tables had turned.

"Hey, I think it's cool." Sylvan turned to the back seat. "Don't you, guys?"

All three echoed his sentiment. Dee guessed they did this on a regular basis.

"I have a question," Gracie said.

"Great," Dee said, relieved by the change of subject and happy to hear a voice besides Sylvan's.

"Are there any resale shops around here?"

"Good question," Sylvan said, commandeering the conversation. "I'm into thrifting. You know, upcycling and helping the planet. I hate when the other one-percenters throw their money around on stuff like labels."

Dee registered the word "other" in the sentence and managed not to groan with disgust.

"I *only* wear labels," Gavin said. He held up a foot. "Even my socks come from a designer." Normally, Dee would have written him off as an elitist, but his good-humored tone in comparison to Sylvan's pomposity made his materialism refreshing. "And I'm guessing our friend Dee here noticed we arrived via your helicopter. Pretty much the definition of a one-percenter."

Dee glanced in the rearview mirror and Gavin winked at her. She stifled a laugh.

"You're so bougie," Sylvan said. "I hate bougie. That's why the Golden looked good to me. It's not bougie. Or twee. I hate twee too. Like, we checked out this B and B in Goldsgone. It had a fake wishing well." He wrinkled his nose in distaste. Dee got a modicum of pleasure from the negative review, since she knew the B and B in question belonged to Verity.

"To answer your question, Gracie"—Dee made a point of pivoting the focus back to the girl—"there isn't a thrift store in Goldsgone. The shops there cater more to tourists. But there are a couple in West Camp, the county seat."

"Sounds good," Sylvan said, depriving Gracie of the chance to respond. He threaded his fingers together and placed his hands behind his head. "You'll be interested to know I have a history with Gold County. My ancestors were prospectors in the '49 Gold Rush. They excavated enough gold to buy real estate in San Francisco and kick off the family fortune."

"That's what really motivated the trip," Austin said.

"Sylvan wants to pick up where his great-great-greats left off and see if he can pillage the land for more gold." He said this as a joke, but Dee picked up an underlying hostility she found curious for a group that considered itself tight enough to have the nickname of "Core Four."

They reached the Golden and Dee swung her car into the graveled circle fronting the motel. She parked and the Golden guests disembarked just in time to see Jeff fall off a paddleboard into the motel pool. She headed to him, the Core Four in tow.

"You okay?" she asked as he climbed up the ladder and out of the pool.

"Yeah." He shook himself like a wet dog, earning a yelp of dissatisfaction from an actual dog as water drops flew off his ginger hair and hit Nugget, who was lounging poolside. "I thought paddleboarding at one of the lakes around here would be a good activity for guests."

"Maybe for them," Gavin said. "Not so much for you."

"Gavin?" Jeff's face lit up. "Hey. Long time, no see."

Jeff grabbed a towel, dried his hands, and extended one. The men shook. "Nice to meet up again," Gavin said. He introduced the rest of the Core Four, only using a last name with Sylvan, implying his was the only one that mattered.

"Welcome, all," Jeff said. "And it's a true honor to meet you, Sylvan. If you need anything, say the word. I'll give you my cell."

He pulled out his phone. Sylvan held out a hand to rebuff him. "No need. I'm good."

"You should have both our cell numbers," Dee said, feeling defensive on Jeff's behalf. "For emergencies."

"Sure," Sylvan said. "Give them to one of the others. Where do we check in?"

"The lobby," Dee said. "Follow me."

"Hey, Gavin, let's have a drink later and catch up," Jeff said.

"Yeah, maybe."

Gavin delivered this without turning around. To Dee's ire, he clearly calibrated his connection to Jeff so that it synced with Sylvan's dismissal of her partner and friend.

With all the motel guests checked in and their rooms tended to, Dee found herself with a rare half hour of free time before going to bed. She used it to find out more about Sylvan Burr.

Entering his name in a search engine generated pages of references. He was a tech entrepreneur who came up with the idea for a program called Tax Hax and brought in his friend Austin Nyugen to code it into life. Tax Hax built on current online tax programs by offering an AI virtual accountant who was genius at finding loopholes and end runs around the IRS, for way less money than a real-life accountant would cost.

Gavin Walsh was the company's former chief financial officer, while Gracie Delacroix was a former senior vice president of marketing. The "former" in their titles was thanks to Sylvan selling Tax Hax to the world's largest global tax firm, earning retirement at the ripe old age of not-even-thirty for three out of the Core Four. Thirty-seven-year-old Gavin was the outlier geriatric of the group.

But interspersed with the basic facts of Tax Hax's genesis and phenomenal success were a phalanx of articles detailing Burr's macro and micro aggressions. The young billionaire had been accused of everything from racism and sexual harassment to sending a gift-wrapped box of feces to a reporter whose profile on him he disliked.

Dee shut down her computer. She had a bad feeling about Sylvan. She thought about how he brought up *Vengeance: Year 3004,* obviously hoping to provoke a reaction from her. He reminded her of the worst kind of writers she'd worked with, the ones who couldn't simply enjoy their own success, instead getting off on stirring up trouble and then sitting back to watch the fallout. As one of them once said to her, "It's not enough that I succeed, others must fail."

Dee sensed that Sylvan Burr was one of those pot stirrers.

And that made her nervous.

# CHAPTER 5

Early the next morning, Dee woke up to the sound of someone gently knocking on her door. She stumbled out of bed and grabbed her eyeglasses from the nightstand, then threw on shorts and a T-shirt decorated with the logo of a winking toilet bowl under the TV show title *On the John*. Like most of her wardrobe, the shirt was swag from a short-lived sitcom she'd worked on, this one having starred a comedian conveniently named John Plumber.

She opened her door to Serena Finlay-Katz. Serena, a self-proclaimed charcuterie artist, was married to Callan Katz, a powerhouse Hollywood agent. During the pandemic, they'd escaped to a stunning house on a nearby lake. Now Callan split his time between Los Angeles and Foundgold, while Serena stuck to the lake house, where she operated her small business of creating a variety of food boards for local events.

Serena had a large board covered with breakfast items with her, which she held below the baby carrier strapped to her chest. The question of whether the carrier contained infant daughter Emmy or tiny Morkie dog Oscar was answered when Oscar stuck his head out to sniff the board.

"Morning," Serena said. "I've come bearing your weekly breakfast board." The ethereal woman glided into the room, her naturally blond hair falling in soft waves below her shoulders. She wore simple leather thong sandals and a gauzy white dress. The dress hung perfectly on a frame made slim without the aid of the weight loss drugs celebrities stampeded to. Dee debated taking them herself to lose the twenty-five pounds she'd gained throughout her career, thanks to a revolving menu of food delivered to writing staffs that spent upward of twenty hours a day banging out scripts.

"Awesome," Dee said, admiring Serena's sleight of hand with foodstuffs. "It's such a fun treat for our guests. Let's put it out."

Serena followed Dee into the lobby, where they laid out the board, which was packed with mini bagels, smoked salmon, and a variety of fixings. "Congratulations," Serena said as she snapped on plastic gloves to give the spread a last-minute decorative zhuzh. "I heard you're sold out."

"Yup. We're packed with aspiring miners. A hearty shout-out to the original get-rich-quick scheme. Some of our guests aren't bothering with breakfast, they're just heading straight to the brooks and streams to pan. Although they may change their minds when they see this awesome brekkie smorgie."

Serena artfully built a tower of mini bagels. She lingered as Dee double-checked to make sure there was plenty of coffee and tea for guests. "I heard Sylvan Burr is staying here."

Dee glanced at her, surprised. "That was fast. He and his friends only got here yesterday afternoon."

"There's not a lot to do around here besides gossip and have sex."

Dee raised an eyebrow. "You'd think that would kick up the Foundgold population past two hundred."

Serena glanced around, then whispered, "Callan says Sylvan Burr is controversial. He's a bad guy. Of course, when Burr announced he was writing his autobiography, Callan wooed him and lost out to CAA, so he's a little biased."

"A little." Dee didn't bother to hide the sarcasm. She knew Callan would have claimed Sylvan as his new best friend if the billionaire techie had signed with him.

Dee laid out compostable plates, napkins, cups, and utensils next to the platters on the reservations counter, then went to the refrigerator to pull out yogurt containers and juice boxes. "As long as Sylvan and company stay in their guest lane, I'm not going to worry about them. Our guests are pretty much settled in, so my priority is figuring out how to finagle a stall at the Goldsgone Crafts Fair. Apparently, there's a residency requirement."

"Really? I've got a stall for my business and Verity never mentioned that to me."

"Of course she didn't." The confirmation that Verity manufactured the residency requirement simply to thwart Dee raised her ire. She slammed the fridge door shut, causing bottles inside to rattle.

"In my case, it wouldn't have mattered." Serena rearranged a few hard-boiled egg halves that had tumbled into each other. "There's an edge of our property that borders Goldsgone. We think of the town as just being the historical village, but it's way more spread out than that. My real estate agent showed me a map. Goldsgone's borders are all over the place." She pulled off her gloves and tossed them in the trash.

An idea came to Dee and her mood instantly improved. "Serena, if I can pull off what I think I can pull off, I'll owe it all to you."

"Oooh." Serena placed a hand on her heart. "That means so much to me."

Despite her beauty, wealth, and famous husband, Dee knew Serena suffered from an insecurity of being demeaned as a WAG, an acronym that stood for Wives and Girlfriends. Coined to describe—and dismiss—the partners of NFL players, it also encapsulated the position women like Serena found themselves relegated to in Hollywood. To Dee's shame, she'd written Serena off as a WAG when they'd first met. She'd come to respect the aspiring entrepreneur and consider her a close friend.

Dee and Serena exchanged a hug, then the charcuterie artist and Oscar left to retrieve infant Emmy from the babysitter.

Eager to put her plan in motion, Dee hunted around the lobby for her cell phone, which she found lying under a stack of flyers promoting a local fly-fishing business. She texted a message, then prepared to welcome guests for breakfast.

By eight a.m., the boards were empty, despite the fact the Core Four never showed, which came as no surprise to Dee. She'd noticed a truck from Fresno's one farm-to-table restaurant pull up and deliver to Sylvan's cabin, sparing him from commingling with guests Dee was sure he considered beneath his lofty perch as a Silicon Valley mucky-muck.

The lobby door opened and Jonas Jones, Dee's quasi boyfriend, stepped into the room. "Hello there."

Dee giggled. "Sorry, but you sound like a soul station

DJ. 'Next up, we have Luther Vandross with "Always and Forever".'"

"Maybe I should look into that. Has to be more lucrative than selling old houses in Gold County."

Dee and the handsome real estate agent exchanged a kiss. They were on the cusp of transitioning from casual to official couple, but with three divorces between them, both were committed to not rushing the relationship.

Jonas pulled a blueprint from the cylinder he carried under his arm and unrolled it. "I got your text. This is the most accurate map of your motel property. If any of it can be designated as within Goldsgone's borders, it'll be on here."

He pulled out two magnifying glasses from his briefcase and handed one to Dee. They scoured the map in silence. Dee was losing hope, when Jonas cried out, "Aha!"

"What? What?"

Jonas removed the pen he'd tucked behind his ear and pointed to a spot on the map. "See that?"

Dee squinted. "Barely."

"Barely is enough. The plot's the size of an area rug, but it's in Goldsgone, and within the boundaries of your motel property."

"Yaassss!" Dee did a triumphant Rocky dance. "I have now met my residency requirement. You're the best."

She threw her arms around Jonas and kissed him. The kiss took on a life of its own and would have led to more amorous doings—if Jeff hadn't clomped into the lobby.

"Hey." Jeff ignored the couple, who'd reluctantly broken apart. He made a straight shot to the breakfast boards. "There's nothing left?" he asked, disappointed.

Dee shook her head. "You should have gotten here earlier."

"I would have, except Sylvan invited me to join the Core Four for breakfast, but then forgot to order for me."

Dee pursed her lips. "Really."

"Yeah. I figured I'd grab something here before we hiked to the stream. But Sylvan just texted he didn't need me. He's hiring a professional prospector. He's meeting with Ma'am and Mister now."

Jeff went behind the desk and pulled a yogurt from the lobby's small backup refrigerator, missing the look Dee and Jonas exchanged. Both suspected the tech mogul of purposely baiting Jeff.

"Whatever," Dee said, tired of hearing about the oh-so-wondrous Sylvan. "I have to make a call."

She hopped onto a café barstool and tapped Verity's number into her phone. She put the call on speaker so the others could hear her triumph. "Verity, hi, it's Dee Stern."

"I'm very busy right now. We've marked down the hobby-horses and they're selling like hot cakes. Which we're also selling as a pancake box mix."

"I'll keep this quick. I accessed a map of our property and it turns out a portion of the motel land is actually in Goldsgone. So I've met the residency requirement for a stall at the crafts fair."

"Having a spit of land that happens to fall within our borders doesn't count. You have to live here."

Dee managed to hold back the stream of profanity at the tip of her tongue. She swallowed, then said, "Then I'll live there."

But Verity wasn't ready to admit defeat. "I'll need visual proof."

"And you shall have it." Dee delivered this in a cheery tone, while indulging in an extremely satisfying fantasy of consigning Verity to the fiery bowels of hell.

There was a long pause. "Fine," Verity finally muttered. "When I get the visual, I'll approve your stall at the crafts fair."

"I'll get it to you as soon as I can. Thank you so much." Dee ended the call. "Argh. I have to prove I'm living in Goldsgone. Jonas, what's the fastest someone can build a tiny house?"

"Hmm . . . well, first you gotta get the permits—"

Dee held up a hand. "Stop right there. The word 'permit' is pretty much a synonym for 'slow walk.' Next idea."

"There's the tent I bought for guests who might want to camp out," Jeff suggested.

Dee pulled a face. "My people are not a camping people. We're a midpriced-motel-with-a-decent-free-breakfast people. Like what we're trying to do here at the Golden."

"You could sleep outside on a chaise longue," Jonas offered.

"I might as well wear a Free Eats for Bears sign," Dee said. She glanced down at the map, stalling for time. "The truth is," she said, "I'm kind of scared of the outdoors."

Jonas pressed his lips together, trying to contain a laugh. "Darlin'," he said, "look around you." He gestured to bucolic scenery outside the apartment window. "We're in the country. It ain't nuthin' but the outdoors."

"I know, I know." Dee released a long sigh. "Tent it is. I'm moving"—she pointed to the map dot—"here. At least until after the fair."

Jeff peered at the map. "Huh. I know where that is. You better do a sweep of it and bring bear spray. I've seen Bud take a poop there at least twice."

"Honestly, at this point, I'd sleep on a bed of bear scat if it meant sticking it to Verity. Let's go check out my new home."

Dee, Jeff, and Jonas headed to the storage closet at the far end of the motel.

"I think I hear people arguing," Dee said, glancing around the wooded area.

"You do?" Jonas asked.

Jeff pointed to a small cluster of people. As the three drew closer, they saw Ma'am yelling at Sylvan, backed up by Mister, as the rest of the Core Four watched, discomfited. Ma'am got in Sylvan's face. Dee gave him grudging credit for not flinching.

"You dumb, sexist SOB! For the last time, I am the prospector, not him." She gestured to Mister with her thumb and his head nodded up and down in agreement with the spring of a bobblehead doll. "I ain't takin' you nowhere. You can fall into one of them abandoned mines, for all I care. Into all *of* them."

Mister glared at Sylvan. "If I were you, I'd make it my business never to insult my wife again. She's twice the person you are. Notice I said 'person,' and not 'man,' because I have respect and admiration for my wife. I recommend you start showing her – and all women - the same." He and Ma'am stomped away.

"Okay, okay, I'm sorry," Sylvan said to their backs. "I genuinely apologize. I just want to take my girlfriend on a private hike to a mine." Ma'am and Mister kept walking. He called after them, "I'll give you ten thousand dollars for a half-day tour." They stopped and turned around. "I'm guessing that'd go a long way for the lawyer you need to overturn or at least shorten your son's jail sentence."

Ma'am gasped. Her eyes grew flinty. "How'd you know about that?"

Sylvan shrugged. "I'm in tech. It's my job to either know everything, or know how and where to find it. Information is power, right?"

"Would you guys mind if I punched him?" Dee muttered to Jeff and Jonas.

"Not if I get to go after you," Jonas said.

"You guys don't know Silicon Valley," Jeff said under his breath. "A lot of guys are like Sylvan."

"Stop defending him!" Dee spoke to Jeff in a sharp whisper. "He's not going to turn the Core Four into the Core Five or hire you to manage his websites. You're a toy to him, something he can play with until he breaks it." Seeing the expressions on both Jonas's and Jeff's faces, Dee immediately regretted her words. "I'm sorry. Don't listen to anything I said. It's not about you, Jeff. He just pushes my buttons."

"No, you're probably right. I'm kidding myself if I think I can level up to someone like him."

Dee felt terrible. She'd never heard Jeff sound so despondent. "Don't say that. It's not true. You're so much more than Sylvan or any of his broligarch buddies could ever dream of being."

"Dee didn't mean anything bad," Jonas added. "You know she can speak without thinking first."

"Yes, but also *ouch*," Dee said, a little annoyed.

Dee's dearest friend didn't seem to hear them. "I'll get the tent," Jeff said.

He trudged off, head down, leaving Dee to debate who she was more angry at: herself or Sylvan Burr.

# CHAPTER 6

Foundgold was too small a community to throw off much, if any, ambient light, so nighttime at the Golden was dark enough for the motel to qualify as one of the dark-sky parks beginning to dot the country.

Dee took a few photos of the tent with her phone to provide Verity with the required visual proof of residency. She sent the photos to the Goldsgone martinet, resisting the urge to add a poop emoji in the subject line. Dee then climbed inside the tent and into her sleeping bag, where she shot a few selfies to prove she "lived" there. The ridiculous task completed, she reached for her air horn and can of bear spray, clutching one in each hand. Much as she cherished the beauty of Foundgold, Dee didn't trust it. The unexplained noises and rustlings from mysterious and possibly ominous woodland creatures still terrified her, especially at night.

She tried to get comfortable, which wasn't easy—even with a foam mat beneath the sleeping bag. It didn't help that every time she turned, Nugget readjusted himself to ensure he was smashed up against her. Dee made a vain attempt to sleep, but when she closed her eyes, all she saw was Sylvan's smug expression as the Ma'ams reluctantly accepted the financial carrot he'd dangled in front of them.

Ma'am's son and Mister's stepson, Huck, was a sweet, affable lunk who'd gotten involved with the sketchy stoners behind an illegal marijuana farm in the deepest recesses of Majestic National Park. Huck only had a year to go on his jail sentence, and had even earned the honor to be chosen as a firefighter with the California Department of Defense firefighting crew. But the Ma'ams would do anything to see him released sooner . . . even make a deal with the devil that was Sylvan Burr.

Dee rolled over. Nugget did the same. She was about to give closing her eyes another try, but she heard what sounded like a large bee buzzing. She cursed and pulled the pillow over her ears, but the buzzing grew louder. "What the . . ."

She wiggled out of the sleeping bag and lifted a flap of the small tent. A drone hovered over the cabin Sylvan shared with Gracie, now ID'd as his girlfriend. The two had spent the afternoon hiking alone, reducing the Core Four to Core Two at the Golden, and with it lowering the tension to negligible.

The drone lowered, dropped a yellow bag from a food delivery service on the cabin's doorstep, then flew off. "Seriously?" Dee called to it as the drone zipped by overhead. She gave the finger to the techie's toy, then crawled back inside the tent and into the sleeping bag. As she readjusted herself, Nugget snorted and his back legs tremored. "Shh," Dee whispered. "Don't worry, buddy. You're okay."

Dee dozed off, wishing the same could be said for her.

She woke up in the morning and emitted a series of grunts as she tried to bring her stiff body to standing. After achieving this, she limped out of the tent. Nugget bounded ahead, barking happily when he spotted Jeff heading for the motel lobby, his arms laden with what looked like old board games.

"Morning," Jeff greeted Dee in an upbeat voice. She was happy to see his mood much improved from the night before.

"Are those vintage board games?" she said, falling in step with him.

"Yup. I was the first person at a garage sale in West Camp and snapped up all of them." He and Dee had made a habit out of hitting the garage sales in the area to acquire items for the motel. "Outstanding haul, huh? Simple, affordable fun for our guests."

They entered the lobby. Jeff set the board games on top of the room's rustic Ranch Oak coffee table, which featured an indestructible slate top. A couch and two side chairs upholstered in green Naugahyde formed a half circle around the coffee table.

Dee took a deep breath and released it. "I want to apologize again for what I said yesterday."

Jeff waved off the apology. "Don't. You did me a favor. Not gonna lie, I did feel bad when I got back to my cabin, so I texted a friend in the city about how Sylvan is staying here and what an SOB he is. My friend texted more people and it exploded into a giant group chat. No joke, fifty people must've jumped on to shred him." Jeff smiled a satisfied smile. "By the time I jumped off the chat, I had three invitations for drinks next time I'm in town, and one guy who's launching a start-up wants to talk to me about building his website."

"That's . . . great? I put it as a question, only because I feel bad it took an 'enemy of my enemy is my friend' scenario to make you feel better."

"If it doesn't bother me, it shouldn't bother you."

"Okay, then," Dee said, relieved. Still, she feared Sylvan might come up with new ways to needle her best friend. He seemed like that kind of guy.

A quick check of the motel snack inventory led to a Wil……liker's run for supplies. Dee's parking luck held, allowing her to grab the last spot in the lot. She noticed her car neighbor was a brand-new black Rivian SUV, the car du jour among those who could afford the most high-end electric vehicles.

She entered the store and commandeered a grocery cart. "Hi, sweetie," her father called to her from the top of a ladder. He held a lightbulb in his hand.

Dee pushed her cart toward him. "Hi, Dad. Whatcha up to?"

"Doing a few odd jobs around the store to help out Elmira."

He glanced at the store proprietor with affection. Elmira sensed his gaze and looked up from the cash register to favor him with a warm smile. The obvious affection between the two made Dee's day.

After filling her cart with a variety of snack packs, Dee pushed it to the checkout counter. She found motel guests Sylvan and his cohorts were already there. *That explains the Rivian,* Dee thought. She'd noted paper license plates on the car and wondered how much the billionaire had forked over to guarantee quick delivery of the gleaming vehicle. *God forbid he should rent a car like a normal human being*, she thought to herself, annoyed.

"Hi there," she said to the foursome, faking a smile. "You discovered Gold County's favorite store."

Sylvan held up a scone with a single bite missing. "Which sells the worst baked goods any of us have ever eaten."

The store fell silent. Shoppers froze. A lightbulb fell from Sam's hand and shattered on the wooden floor.

Dee flailed as she searched for a response, finally landing on a toothless "How can you say that?"

"Because it's true. It's not like I got a scone from a bad batch. We all got different things and they all suck." He turned to the others. "Right?"

Austin, Grace, and Gavin nodded in unison, if somewhat reluctantly. Grace, embarrassed, fiddled with the diamond stud in her nostril. "I'm sorry," she had the decency to add to Elmira.

Elmira fixed a cold look on all of them. "I'll be happy to refund your money."

Sylvan shook his head. "Not necessary. But I thought you should know. I'm surprised none of your friends ever mentioned it." He directed this at Dee. "I guess in a misguided way they thought they were doing you a favor." He dropped the scone into a trash bin. "We gotta go. I need to find a charging station for the Rivian."

The four departed. "Ignore them," Dee said, trying to defuse the tension hanging in the air. "They're horrible people."

Elmira folded her arms in front of her chest. "Is it true?" she asked in an icy, clipped tone.

Dee glanced around, desperately hoping for backup. She debated lying, but knew Elmira wouldn't buy it. "Taste is subjective," she said.

"Those kids have no idea what they're talking about," Sam chimed in, holding a dustpan of lightbulb shards.

"Is it true?" Elmira repeated.

Dee winced. She held out as long as she could, then murmured a pained . . . "Yes."

Elmira spoke slowly and deliberately. "So all my . . .

supposed friends have been . . . lying to me . . . all this time."

"We didn't want to hurt your feelings," Dee said, feeling awful.

"Instead, you hurt my business. " She addressed the regulars in the shop in a frigid tone. "I think you should go. Every single one of you. *Now.*"

Sam cast a pleading look at the shopkeeper. "Ellie—"

She held up a hand and turned away from him. "You too."

Despondent, Dee, Sam, and the other customers shuffled out of the store. "If that Sylvan Burr doesn't fall into a mine, I wouldn't mind pushing him into one," Sam said through gritted teeth.

"I can't think of a more bonding father-daughter activity," Dee replied through her own gritted teeth.

While Jeff made a run into Fresno for supplies, Dee spent the morning turning over rooms for the next batch of guests, while obsessing over how to make things right with her treasured friend. Much as Dee despised Sylvan in general, and specifically for outing Elmira's inedibles, she had to admit he was right in pointing out that lying to the store owner had been a mistake.

She took a break from housekeeping for lunch, which she ate on one of the benches fronting the motel rooms. From her vantage point, Dee could see Prospector Pete helping a family pan in the sluice. She could tell her father was simply going through the motions and felt for him. He'd put a tentative toe in the dating waters for the first time since her mother's death and suffered for it.

The Rivian pulled into the motel's graveled drive. Ma'am jumped out before the car came to a full stop, which Dee assumed was motivated by her eagerness to rid herself of the Core Four's company. "How'd it go?" Dee asked the backwoods person as she stomped by.

"They're all here and not at the bottom of a mine," Ma'am threw over her shoulder, not breaking stride. "That's the best I can say."

She disappeared into the woods.

Laughter drew Dee's attention to the techies, who seemed to be enjoying themselves for a change. In fact, for the first time since arriving at the Golden, they looked like what Sylvan Burr claimed they were: four close friends.

"Those mines were epic," Austin enthused to the others, who echoed agreement.

"The tour lady was *so* ticked when we snuck past the Do Not Enter sign on the last one," Gracie said. "I felt bad for her."

"It was worth it," Gavin said. "I swear, we saw into Middle Earth when we got inside and looked down. You really missed something, Syl."

Sylvan shook his head. "No way. Just looking at the entrance to that thing set off my claustrophobia." He mock-shuddered. "I'm having a flashback. Hold me."

He put an arm around Gracie's waist. She responded in kind. They exchanged a lustful glance. Dee noticed Austin react to the sexual tension between the two with a much darker expression, and the group's bonhomie evaporated.

"Miss? Hello . . . Hello!"

Dee realized someone was calling to her. She got up and craned her neck and saw the Froelichs making their way down the hill from the woods. Their T-shirts were soaked with perspiration, and their sneakers and jeans soaked to the knees.

Dee went to them. "You two look like you had a day."

"We panned for hours," Trish sounded disconsolate.

"The only thing we came up with, besides river bottom, was an old button, probably from the first Gold Rush."

Ed leaned against a tree to catch his breath, then bent over and put his hands on his knees to stretch his back. "Could you by any chance grab us a couple of water bottles? We went through ours. You can put them on our bill."

"Don't worry about it. They're on the house."

Ed slowly stood up. "Thanks. If there's a chiropractor on the house, I wouldn't mind that either, ha—" He stopped midsentence and held a hand over his eyes to shade them from the sun. "Is that . . . It can't be."

Ed took a creaky walk over to the Core Four. "Excuse me, but are you Sylvan Burr? The money behind Tax Hax?"

Sylvan shrugged and held up his hands. "Guilty as charged," he said, doing his best to sound modest.

Ed let out a roar. "You ruined me! You ruined my family!"

He then let out another, even more ferocious roar and lunged at Sylvan.

Gracie screamed as the men fell to the ground, grappling with each other. Dee and Trish raced over, almost colliding with Gavin and Austin, who were trying to separate the two—with little luck.

"I'll kill you!" Ed yelled, his hands around Sylvan's throat. "I'll strangle you to death and I'll be a hero to every accountant in America!"

"Eddie, for God's sake, stop!" Trish fell onto her husband's back and wrapped her arms around his waist to pull him off Sylvan.

The distraction allowed Gavin and Austin to yank Sylvan away from him. Dee helped Trish and Ed to their feet, keeping a tight hold on the accountant.

"I'm so sorry," Trish said tearfully. "But you have no

idea what you've done to people like us with your program."

Sylvan, furious, strained to be released from Austin and Gavin's grip. "You think you have problems now? Wait until I sue you for battery."

Ed took a step toward Sylvan. "Sue away, you—"

"Whoa." Dee pulled him back, which wasn't easy. He might be bony, but he was also strong. "Both of you, dial it back."

"If you'd bother to do your homework, you'd know you were going after the wrong guy." Sylvan rubbed a red welt where Ed's fist had connected with his cheek. "Next time, take a swing at him." He tilted his head toward Austin. "He's the one who created Tax Hax. All I did was come up with the idea and the money."

Austin stared at him, fury coloring his face. "Really?" He dropped his hold on the tech mogul. "You steal the attention. You steal my *girlfriend*. And now it's all on me?" Austin's face grew mottled with anger. He clenched his fists. "You—"

"Hey! *Enough*." Fearing an inter–Four Core brawl was about to break out, Dee delivered this in her sternest voice, the one she'd used during the brief time she'd worked as a public school substitute teacher after a show she wrote for was canceled. "I think it's time for everyone to return to their corners. *Now*."

Stern Teacher Voice proved effective. The Froelichs stormed off in one direction, Sylvan in another, Gracie and Gavin in tow. Austin hung back, glowering. "I swear to God," he said, "sometimes I full-on hate him."

*You've got plenty of company,* Dee thought. She wanted to say it out loud, but didn't, knowing Austin was talking to himself and not to her.

Disturbed by the altercation, Dee left Austin to his brooding. She needed to put some space between herself and her guests, the techies in particular. She was about to retreat to her living quarters when her phone pinged an all-caps text from Serena: **WHAT HAPPENED W/ELMIRA????!!!! NOT TALKING TO ANY OF US!!!!**

Dee sighed. The dustup between her guests had driven the Elmira debacle from its front and center position in her brain. She was about to write back and explain the situation to Serena when another text came through. This one was from Verity: **You are eligible for a stall at the Goldsgone Crafts Fair. You have until 1 p.m. today to claim it.**

Dee checked the time on her phone. It was 12:45, giving her exactly fifteen minutes to pack up her car and get to Goldsgone. She knew the short window of opportunity was no accident and shook her phone at the heavens. "Curse you, Verity 'Yes-*that*-Donner' Gillespie! But you will not win!"

# CHAPTER 7

Dee ran down the main drag of Goldsgone, pulling boxes of sales goods stacked on a folding luggage cart behind her. She zipped past the stagecoach, which was off-loading tourists. "Hey, it's our favorite citiot," the stagecoach driver called to her in a joking tone.

"Ha, that never gets old, Barnabas," Dee called back, hoping he didn't notice the sarcastic edge to her voice. She hated the nickname, which combined "city" with "idiot."

Dee kept going. She spotted Verity chatting with her cabal of interns, including the eerie Trapp twins, at the festival stand outside her store. "Verity!" Dee called, out of breath. "Yoo-hoo!"

Verity turned to see Dee. She scowled, then checked a watch she pulled out of the pocket of her cotton apron. "You've got one min—"

Dee and her cart pulled up alongside the town alpha female. "Made it," Dee said, panting.

"So you did," Verity was forced to admit. "Follow me."

She led Dee down the street, which was lined with shaded wooden stalls selling a range of appealing crafts, foods, and home products. Dee inhaled the enticing scent of apple pie as they passed by Ma Bailey's Homemade Fruit Tarts. They reached the end of the road. The stalls petered out, as did the scent of apple pie, replaced by a smell far more noxious.

"Here you go." Verity pointed to a beat-up plastic table almost buckling under the sun's glare.

"It's a table, not a stall. There's no shade." Dee wrinkled her nose. "And it smells like poo."

"It's the old outhouse."

Dee glanced at the building behind her table and realized with a sinking feeling that Verity had positioned her directly in front of Goldsgone's least appealing historical site, which sat next to a more current bank of equally foul-smelling restrooms.

"Don't worry," her nemesis said. "It only gives off that scent on a hot day."

"It's summer," Dee pointed out. "Every day is hot."

"I know," Verity said with a malicious smile, and flounced off.

Dee directed a few choice profanities to Verity's back. Then she sucked in a deep breath, which she immediately regretted, thanks to the odoriferous surroundings, and got to work setting up her wares.

"It's not a bad location. We get visitors who park at the lot on this end of Main Street."

Dee looked up from setting out tea towels, teddy bears, and mugs decorated with her Bud the Bear cartoons. To her surprise, the friendly comment came from Majestic National Park ranger Tom O'Bryant. A couple of months prior, a Golden guest had been murdered in the woods behind the motel. Since the victim's body straddled both the motel and the national park property, the investigation necessitated a joint effort on behalf of local and park law enforcement.

Dee had found the stocky park ranger suffused with his own importance, causing the two to butt heads when she and Jeff were compelled to do some investigating of their own. But considering her current stinky circumstances, she decided to put the past behind her and accept Ranger Tom's friendly overture.

"Hi, Tom. Nice to see you. Are you checking out the fair?"

"Nope. Got my own table. I make sculptures with found objects from the park."

Dee looked over to see an old folding table like hers, topped with a collection of odd sculptures. A hubcap painted with the image of Majestic Rock at sunset sat mounted atop a set of barbeque tools. A wall hanging featured a wide range of reading glasses, all spray-painted gold. "Very creative," she said, not really lying.

"Thanks. You wouldn't believe what people leave behind at the park. Including their own children sometimes. But those get claimed. Usually." The ranger picked up one of Dee's mugs decorated with an image of Bud peering into the refrigerator of a cabin and calling back to the terrified residents: "*We're out of guac.*"

Tom chuckled. "Funny. You got Bud down pat."

"Thanks. I have to ask, though. How did you end up at this end of the fair? I would have thought you rated a less outhouse-y location."

"I made the mistake of dating Verity," Tom said. "Then I made a bigger mistake and broke up with her." He glanced up the street where tourists were milling around the more prominent stalls. "Although the way folks around here are sniping at each other these days, I don't mind being out of the loop."

He took a seat behind his table, the flimsy chair creaking perilously under his ample weight, leaving Dee to wonder what he meant. Not wanting to risk the rapprochement between them, she didn't press. Dee welcomed having someone to commiserate with over their shared smelly outsider status.

A lack of shoppers on the fragrant end of the fair allowed Dee time to text Jeff details of the fight between the Froelichs and Sylvan Burr. He responded he'd be back by evening and had a few ideas on how to keep the fractious parties separated during their stay.

Relieved that dealing with this particular problem was out of her hands, she checked in with the Ma'ams, who ran the front desk when Dee and Jeff were off the premises. Relieved to get an all-quiet-on-the-motel-front update from them, she focused on coming up with a way to make amends with Elmira. The Bud the Bear swag surrounding her led to an idea. She'd draw a giant poster board illustration of Bud holding a sign that read: WE'RE *BEARY* SORRY, and have all of Elmira's friends sign it. TV writers generally considered puns the lowest form of humor—although it didn't bother the creator of *On the John*, a bemused Dee thought. In this case, she considered it cute and warranted.

Verity sauntered over to them. "How's it going down here, you two?"

"Slow and sweaty," Ranger Tom said.

"If you're not comfortable, I recommend you reconsider your participation in the fair," Verity said, an evil glint in her eye.

Dee eyed Verity with a glint of her own. "Verity, it's too bad you can't grow a mustache. You would have *so* much fun twirling it."

"Ha!" Tom chortled. "Good one."

Verity opened her mouth to respond, but the Core Four strolled over and she snapped it shut. Their appearance also silenced Dee. She hadn't expected to see them at the fair, especially acting as if the hostility between Sylvan and Austin never happened. "It's too bad we can't close off the fair to certain people," Verity muttered, glaring at the techies.

Dee gaped at her. "Are you talking about who I think you're talking about?" she asked sotto voce. "Because if you are, we actually have something we can agree on."

She was dying to press Verity for the exact reason she seemed to despise the four, but Miss Mary's Unmentionables owner Pamela sashayed their way, handing out coupons to anyone who didn't dodge her. "Stop by my shop before you leave the fair today," she said to a couple, then added with a wink, "Free panties with purchase." She next eyeballed the three male techies. "You cuties must have girls in your lives you wanna pick up something sexy for, " she cooed in a flirtatious tone.

"No thank you, *ma'am,*" Sylvan responded. His tone somehow managed to be polite and yet demeaning, thanks to his intentionally heavy emphasis on the word "ma'am."

*"Owie,"* Pamela said. "It's a sad day when a gal goes from 'miss' to 'ma'am.'" She delivered this humorously, but Dee could tell she was hurt and felt for her.

"No offense," Sylvan responded, "but I've got a girlfriend, and even if I didn't, I'm not into cougars."

"Honestly, Sylvan." Grace, who'd been browsing Ranger Tom's sculptures, turned around to scold her boyfriend. "That was so insulting. You should—"

She froze, her eyes on Pamela, who had moved on to hand out more coupons. "No. It can't . . ." She paused, then blurted, "We should go."

Grace took off at a fast clip. Her friends jogged after her, exchanging looks of bewilderment, which were echoed by Dee, Tom, and even Verity.

"What just happened?" the ranger asked, staring after the techies.

"I have no idea," Dee said, "but I'm really burned out on the drama that comes with those four."

Eventually the sun lowered in the sky, dropping the temperature by a few blessed degrees, which made Dee's sales stand more bearable. She even sold a handful of gift items. Exhausted by the difficult and stinky day, Dee quickly packed up and headed home when the fair closed at six p.m. She nuked a frozen meal in her apartment and sketched the poster board card for Elmira before crawling into her temporary tent home with Nugget, along with the can of bear spray and air horn. She replayed Gracie's odd reaction to the sight of Pamela, wondering what could have engendered such a strong reaction to the lingerie shop owner. She also wondered what prompted Verity's hostile attitude toward the four Silicon Valley dwellers. Dee came to no conclusions before drifting off to sleep.

"Dee. *Dee.* Wake up."

"Go away." The order came out muffled as Dee turned her back on whoever was trying to rouse her.

"I can't. We have a problem."

Dee turtled her head out of the sleeping bag and saw Jeff peeking through the flaps. She slowly hoisted herself to a sitting position, body aching from sleeping on the hard ground. "On a scale of one to ten, how big a problem?"

"Off-the-charts big. On a scale of one to ten, a trillion." Jeff, usually so good-natured, sounded grim. "Sylvan Burr has disappeared."

# CHAPTER 8

Jeff filled Dee in as they hurried to her apartment, where he'd stashed a distraught Gracie. "She came banging on my door around six a.m. She woke up and Sylvan wasn't there. His side of the bed hadn't been slept in."

"Did they have a fight?"

Jeff shook his head. "No. The opposite of a fight."

Dee got what he was insinuating and made a face. "Ugh. TMI."

"Grace said that after their not-fight yesterday afternoon, she fell asleep and she didn't get up until around six this morning."

"That's a nice night of sleep," Dee said. "Speaks well to the new mattresses that cost us a fortune."

"I checked their room before I texted Raul," Jeff said, referencing Raul Aguilar, the deputy sheriff who covered Goldsgone, Foundgold, and surrounding environs. "I didn't see anything indicating Sylvan came home and then went out again or something."

"Have you talked to Gavin or Austin? Maybe he went somewhere with them."

"Gracie got in touch with them before she came to me. They don't know any more than she does."

Dee rubbed her temples. She'd had a premonition that something terrible might happen, thanks to the blatant greed and avarice unleashed by the second Gold Rush. *But why does it have to happen at the Golden?*

Law enforcement vehicles filled the few empty spaces in the Golden's parking area. Inside Dee's apartment, Deputy Sheriff Raul Aguilar sat in one of the space's original oak dining chairs. Raul's youthful age belied his important position. He was all of twenty-eight, in the same ballpark as two of the three techies huddled together on the couch opposite him, looking like students being called to the principal's office.

The apartment's living area had an open floor plan, allowing Dee and Jeff to observe the action from where they hovered behind the kitchen counter. So tense was the mood that none of the Silicon Valleyites seemed to notice that the law enforcement officer wore the uniform of a nineteenth-century sheriff, a choice forced on him by the Goldsgone Business Association—aka Verity Gillespie.

Raul took a small pad out of his lawman's duster jacket interior pocket. "When was the last time each of you saw your friend?" he asked.

"Around four o'clock," Gracie said. "In the afternoon, not the morning." Her cheeks were pale and tearstained. She looked exhausted, despite her night's sleep.

"Around three in the afternoon for us," Gavin said. He turned toward Austin. "Right?"

"Sounds about right," Austin said. "We came back from that fair in Goldsgone, and Gavin and I decided to pan in the stream up in the woods behind the motel, the one where they first found gold. We texted Sylvan to see if he wanted to come with us, but never heard back."

Raul jotted notes on his pad. "Did you notice any changes in his mood?"

"You mean like, was he depressed?" Austin asked. "No. If anything he was more of a cocky SOB than ever."

"Austin, please." Gracie's lower lip quivered. "This is hard enough."

"I'm sorry, Gracie. I know that hurts, but it's true." Austin did his best to imply he was merely being honest, but judging by Raul's raised eyebrow, she assumed she wasn't the only one who picked up on the undercurrent of hostility in the techie's tone.

Raul ran a few more questions by them, which didn't elicit any additional helpful information. He stood up. "Most likely, he went out for a walk and got lost," he said, offering a semblance of reassurance. "I put out a call for officers from all over the county. We'll find him."

Dee found Raul's matter-of-fact confidence comforting, but Gracie seemed doubtful. "He's already been gone hours. There are wild animals out there. We need to look for him too."

"I know you're worried about your friend," Raul said, "but that's not a good idea. None of you know the area. The last thing we need is to have to muster up a second search party."

"He's got a point." Gavin placed a sympathetic arm around Gracie's shoulder, then addressed Dee. "Is it okay if we wait here?"

"Of course," she said. "Consider it Command Central."

Raul walked to the door. He subtly motioned to Dee and Jeff and they followed him outside. "I want to talk to your other guests. See if they saw or heard anything that might be helpful."

"It's early," Dee said. "Everyone should still be around."

"Why don't you go with Raul?" Jeff suggested. "I'll hang out here. Since I know Gavin, I might be able to get some intel out of him."

Jeff went back inside and Dee led Raul to the lobby, where guests were waiting for breakfast. She explained the delay as she made coffee and put out pastries Jeff had brought back from the Bay Area. While people ate, Raul went from table to table, putting the same questions to them that he'd put to the Core Four minus one. The closest he got to new information was the Froelichs sharing they'd seen two techies panning in the stream not far from the area the couple had staked out. "But Burr wasn't with them," Ed said. His face darkened. "Believe me, if he'd been there, I would've made sure he took a cold bath in that stream. Maybe his last—"

"Ed!" Trish, alarmed, motioned for him to be quiet. "Stop talking, you're gonna get us arrested."

"He's missing, not dead," Ed said, dismissing his wife's concerns.

The word "dead' sent a shiver up Dee's spine. *Please—oh, please—don't let him be the D-word,* she prayed silently. The prayer did nothing to calm her increasing anxiety.

Once Raul was done questioning the guests in the lobby's dining area, Dee took him to a few rooms to catch anyone he'd missed. By the time they finished, it was almost noon. "I wish that had been more fruitful," the sheriff said, helping himself to a leftover croissant. They'd come full circle and were back in the lobby.

"At least the Froelichs confirmed Gavin and Austin were where they said they were." Dee hesitated. "You don't think that Ed . . ."

"Nah." Raul shook his head. "He's the definition of all talk and no action."

"I don't know. He did go after Sylvan yesterday." She detailed the incident.

"Huh." Raul mulled this over. "Anger may have propelled Froelich to take a swing at Burr, but it's hard to picture him winning a fight with a guy almost forty years younger. I'll keep it in mind, though." Raul wiped the crumbs from the button-down vest that was part of his old-fashioned uniform. "Now that I finished the interviews, I need to rejoin the search party. I haven't received any updates, which is concerning."

Dee nervously shred the napkin she'd picked up to throw away. "I wish I could do something. I'm supposed to be at the fair, but it feels so callous to be hawking my wares when one of our guests is in trouble. Ugh, me not showing up will make Verity's day. She'll probably use it as an excuse to boot me from it."

"Go to the fair," Raul said. "Sell your wares. On behalf of all of us, do whatever you can to make Verity's life a living hell."

"Yes, Officer," Dee said, managing a small smile.

With her apartment occupied, Dee showered in Jeff's cabin, then slathered on sunscreen, grabbed an umbrella for shade, and headed to the crafts fair. She set up shop at her table, then took a seat behind it. Tom's table was empty and she found herself wishing he was there so they could dump on Verity together. She wondered if he'd been called to join the search party for Sylvan.

Dee was so deep in her own thoughts she didn't notice Goldsgone's most powerful citizen approach until the woman was standing directly in front of her table. "You're here," Verity said, not bothering to mask her disappointment. "One would think you'd be back at the motel showing concern for your missing guest."

"You know about that?" Dee asked, not happy, but also not surprised the word was out.

"It's all over the news. National news because of Sylvan. He's a name. I fielded a few calls from reporters myself."

She handed her phone to Dee, sunlight reflecting off the tiny butter churns painted in gold on her fake nails. The glee in Verity's voice set off an alarm for Dee. She glanced at the cell phone and saw what appeared to be an endless thread of posts about Sylvan's disappearance. She saw the Murder Motel reference pop up on a couple of them and silently cursed the probable source, whose cell phone she happened to be holding.

Refusing to give Verity the satisfaction of letting this get to her, Dee returned the phone. "Sylvan is world-famous. Of course it's going to be a big story. Frankly, I'm glad his disappearance is being publicized. It could help find him." A family strolled by. Grabbing the chance to end the unpleasant conversation, Dee held up one of her bears. "Hello, hi there! Free bear with purchase today."

The bears were Dee's most expensive items, which meant that if the family didn't pony up for mugs and tea towels, she'd be taking a loss on the sale. It was a sacrifice Dee was happy to make if it meant ridding herself of Yes-*that*-Donner. She waved the bear up and down and back and forth, making it dance. "Howdy, I'm Bud and I wanna go home with you," Dee said in her best bear voice. The ruse worked. The family's young children zoomed over to Dee's table, dragging their parents with them. Thwarted, Verity left to annoy someone else.

Dee stayed at the crafts fair until it ended for the day, then raced to her car. On her way home, she called Jeff. "Any news?"

"No. Raul brought in Tom O'Bryant and a group of rangers to help with the search."

"I thought he might have, because Tom wasn't at the fair today. Wow, those two don't get along at all. If Raul asked for Tom's help, he must really need it."

"It makes sense. Nobody knows the land around here like O'Bryant. He's a green blood." Jeff used the nickname "green blood," which was given to people born and raised within the boundaries of a national park. "If Sylvan got lost in Majestic or anywhere near it, O'Bryant will find him . . ." Jeff paused.

"What?" Dee pressed.

"I heard Raul and him talking. Tom brought up the possibility . . . that Sylvan fell into one of the abandoned gold mines."

Dee gasped. "No." The thought was untenable. She hated to think of a guest trapped and injured in a dark, dank mine. And aside from the personal angle, the Golden didn't need the damaging publicity the incident might prompt. She made a decision. "We're joining the search. I know some locals have. I saw a few empty tables at the fair today. Raul trusts us. We'll stick close to him. I think he'd appreciate the support."

"Okay. I'll let him know."

Dee drove fast, eager to do something besides worry. When she pulled into the Golden's circular drive, Jeff was waiting for her. "The search crew is deep into the woods behind our property."

"Where we back up against the Majestic?"

"No. West of there. Come on."

Jeff led Dee through the woods. They pushed aside overgrown brush and scrambled over boulders. Jeff almost lost his footing crossing Golden Brook, but Dee grabbed him before he toppled into the drink. "When we find Burr," he said, shaking water out of his sneaker, "he owes us."

"Shh." Dee put a finger to her lips. "I hear them. This way."

They wended their way through the dense forest, following the sound of voices that grew louder as they drew closer. Jeff helped Dee climb over the trunk of a giant ponderosa pine lying prostrate on the forest floor, blocking their path. Right beyond the tree was a small clearing. Raul and Tom, along with a half-dozen other law enforcement officials, stood in front of a rock outcropping.

Dee and Jeff approached the officers. Dee noticed an opening in the largest rock, framed by remnants of wood. "This is the entrance to a mine, isn't it?"

"Yup," Tom said. "Rich Diggins. That's its name. The shaft's a little ways inside." He pointed to a small piece of black T-shirt fabric snagged on a splintered piece of wood. "And I got a bad feeling your motel guest is lying at the bottom of it."

# CHAPTER 9

Dee's heart thumped as she watched a park ranger whose hobby happened to be cave exploration rappel into the mine's recesses. "We got lucky," said Ranger Tom, who stood next to her. "These mines can be hundreds of feet deep. This one takes a bend at around twenty feet."

Dee didn't find this comforting. "That's still a long way to fall. Like, two stories long."

"Just trying to find a bright side," Tom said.

A rustling came from the woods. Jeff had gone back to the Golden to report the sobering development to Sylvan's crew. He now pushed aside branches and stepped into the clearing, followed by Gracie, Gavin, and Austin.

Gracie separated from the others and hurried to Tom and Raul. "Did you find him?" she asked, wringing her hands. "Is he down there? Is he okay?"

"We're waiting to find out." Raul kept his tone level, but Dee picked up on a sober note that didn't bode well.

Tom's walkie-talkie crackled. Knowing there would be no cell reception in the mine's lower depths, the rangers had gone old-school with their means of communication.

Tom pressed a button to talk. "Jenkins, you find anything?"

"Yes, sir."

The response sparked a frisson of tension among the observers. Dee, Jeff, and the others moved closer to the ranger.

"Hold on," Tom said into the walkie-talkie. He gestured to Raul, and the two law enforcement officers disappeared into the woods to hear whatever news Ranger Jenkins had to share in privacy. Dee, Jeff, and the techies, along with the growing number of law enforcement officials milling around the site, waited in silence.

A moment later, the ranger and sheriff reemerged with somber expressions. They approached Gracie, Gavin, and Austin. Everyone else respectfully stepped away. Dee didn't need to hear Tom and Raul break the bad news. The techies' distraught reactions said it all.

With hope of rescue gone, the mission turned into one of recovery. Dee and Jeff followed Raul's recommendation and led Gracie, Austin, and Gavin away from the site back to Dee's apartment. By now, it was late evening. Lacking appetites, everyone had either passed on dinner or opted for a liquid one.

Gavin downed a shot of whiskey. Noting his empty glass, Dee refilled it. "What was Sylvan thinking, going out on his own like that?"

Austin downed his own shot. Dee refilled his as well. "He probably thought he had a lead on gold and wasn't ready to share it."

Gavin gave a nod. "Sounds about right."

"*No!*" The ferocious delivery coming from the generally wan Gracie startled everyone. "Hunting for gold wasn't about money for Sylvan. You both know he didn't need it. He wanted to learn more about his family's history here. That's what brought him to Gold County. To connect with it." Gracie's voice was thick with tears. "Show some respect. Seriously."

"You're right," Gavin said. He had the decency to sound remorseful. "Sorry, Gracie. I think we're all trying to figure out exactly what happened and make some kind of sense of it."

Sylvan's girlfriend didn't seem ready to accept an apology. "And you both know he was claustrophobic," she insisted angrily. "He never would have even *looked* into the mine shaft, unless there was a really good reason for it. Or he thought there was one."

Austin eyed her. "What exactly are you implying? That he was lured to the mine?"

"Yes. No. I don't know."

Her voice raised in pitch until it bordered on hysteria. Worried, Dee jumped up and filled a glass from a pitcher of water. She handed the glass to Gracie. "Here. This is an awful time for you. For all of you. Gracie, do you want me to call someone? A relative? A friend?"

Gracie shook her head. Austin placed a protective arm around her. "She has her friends."

"Then ya might wanna start acting that way, dude," Jeff said.

Austin looked abashed. "You're right." He stood up and helped Gracie to her feet. "My bad for acting like a jerk. I'm taking you back to my cabin. You need rest."

"Why don't you all stay here tonight?" Dee said. "I have to sleep in the tent. Gracie can stay in my room. The living-room couch folds out and we can open a cot for one of you."

"I'd like that." Gracie sounded calmer, but understandably still teary. "Thank you."

Gavin's phone pinged a text. He read it and then spoke. "A little bit of good news. The cryonics facility is coordinating with the coroner's office. Sylvan will be placed on ice and on his way to the facility as soon as the coroner gives the go-ahead."

"He's being . . . cryogenically frozen?" Dee wanted to be sure she heard this correctly.

"Yes." Gracie choked up. "And not just his head. His whole body. It's what he wanted."

Gracie began to blubber and Austin led her away to the bedroom as Dee and Jeff exchanged a look.

After making sure the techies had everything they needed, Dee reluctantly trudged down the hill to her "home" in Goldsgone. Nugget stayed behind at the apartment, providing emotional support in exchange for a much more comfortable bed and an excess of treats.

Stuck in the tent for another miserable evening, Dee rolled over for about the tenth time in the fruitless quest for a comfortable position in her sleeping bag. She closed her eyes, then popped them open, unable to shake the image of the grim, derelict mine where Sylvan Burr met his fate. She couldn't stop pondering the mystery of how the tech billionaire wound up alone at the remote and dangerous location. *Hopefully, he simply went for a hike with the arrogance of the uber rich, who never think anything is going to happen to them,* Dee thought. During her prior Hollywood career, she'd met several phenomenally successful showrunners and even a studio head who exuded a strong belief in their own immortality.

She heard splashing coming from the motel pool and sat

up, heart racing. Technically, the pool closed at ten p.m., but Dee and Jeff allowed a grace period up until midnight. If their guests wanted to enjoy a late-night swim, they were welcome to, as long as they didn't swim alone, policed their own safety, and kept their bathing suits on. After midnight, however, the pool was off-limits.

Dee crawled over to the tent flap and peeked out. The guest in the pool wasn't a motel patron. Instead, Bud the Bear was treating himself to a bath, rolling around and splashing with what appeared to be a smile on his face. Dee grabbed her bear spray and air horn and assumed a defensive position. But after a few minutes, Bud climbed out of the pool, shook himself off, sending water flying, then lumbered back into the woods.

Dee crawled back into the tent and pulled a pencil and pad from the backpack of supplies she'd brought with her. Using the flashlight on her phone to illuminate the tent, she sketched a Bud cartoon:

"Come on in, the water's fine!"

She gave her work a once-over and realized she'd made a mistake. Instead of drawing Bud in the pool, she'd placed him in the stream where gold had first been rediscovered, thanks to her dad and the cold bath he took to get into character for Prospector Pete. *I've got gold on the brain,* she thought. As she floated off to sleep, she mused how a similar preoccupation with the precious metal seemed to have doomed Sylvan Burr to an early demise.

The next morning, after a few stretches that didn't provide much help for her sore body, Dee made her way up the small hill from the tent's perch in Goldsgone to her apartment. She imagined the now–Core Three had had a rough night and wanted to offer support. She found Austin manning a frying pan at her stove, while a listless Gracie played with scrambled eggs on her plate.

"I helped myself to a few eggs," Austin said. "I hope that's okay."

"Of course. Anyone want a cup of tea?" Austin and Gracie declined. "Should I bother to ask Gavin? He doesn't strike me as a tea guy."

"He's not." Austin scooped eggs from the pan and dropped them onto a plate. "But he's not here anyway. He went to Palo Alto to work with the Tax Hax communications team on how to handle Sylvan's dea . . ."—Austin stopped and glanced at Gracie—"the thing with Sylvan."

Dee filled a mug with water, added a tea bag, and stuck it in the microwave for a minute. "If there's anything Jeff or I can do to help in any way, just say the word. You said he was interested in his family's history in the county. We can do some research on his behalf and share it with his family."

"He was estranged from them," Gracie said. "They resented how successful he was and only tried to mooch off him. We were his family."

The microwave dinged and Dee retrieved her tea. Austin had taken the counter stool next to Gracie, so she sat down on the stool next to him. "How did you all meet?"

"College," Austin said. "At least me, Sylvan, and Gracie. UC Berkeley. Sylvan and I got assigned as roommates freshman year. I was a dual major in computer science and electrical engineering, and he was in the business school studying entrepreneurship and technology. Gracie was in the media studies program. Gavin came along after."

Dee picked up a hint of disparagement in Austin's mention of the company's former CFO—almost as if Gavin was an afterthought. Or an addition to the Core Four that Austin wasn't too happy about. Then again, she wasn't sure how Austin felt about his late college buddy Sylvan either, especially at the moment, when the glances he snuck at Gracie telegraphed he was still in love with his ex-girlfriend.

Gracie's phone rang. She put down the fork she wasn't using and answered. Dee saw Gavin's face pop up on the screen. "Hey, I'm with the Tax Hax communications team," he said. "We're good to go with the online memorial. They can set it up for a global reach."

"Okay." Gracie's response sounded rote and leaden.

Austin leaned into frame. "Hey, Gavin, you do know how to do a conference video call, don't you?"

"Yeah, sorry. I spaced. It's been insane here. The press is all over the communications team about Sylvan. Speaking of which, I think we should stay put at the Golden for a while. Security's scraped the internet clean of anything related to our trip and Sylvan's passing, so it'll be easier to lay low until all the publicity dies down."

"I'm not ready to go back," Gracie said. "To our place. Figuring out what to do with what we shared. I can't."

"There's no rush," Gavin said. "Besides, we should see the whole gold thing through. For Sylvan."

Austin, who'd given up trying to stay in frame, snorted.

"I heard that, Austin," Gavin said. "I'd recommend an attitude check, friend. Now's not the time for cynicism."

Austin started to respond, then glanced at Gracie, and restrained himself.

Gavin ended the call. Austin got off his stool and put his plate in the sink. "If you're up for it," he said to Gracie, "we can start a guest list for the memorial."

"Okay." Gracie sounded even more lifeless than she had with her previous "okay."

Austin helped the girl off her stool. To Dee's eyes, she'd gone from wispy to almost emaciated in a couple of days. "I need a minute alone with Gracie," she said.

Austin started to balk, but Gracie stopped him. "It's okay. I'll meet you at your cabin in a few."

As soon as he was gone, Dee opened the refrigerator and pulled out a small bottle. She handed it to Sylvan's bereaved girlfriend. "Muscle Milk. From when I was on a diet that failed because I loved this and drank too much of it to lose any weight. You're not leaving here until you drink it. You need nutrition."

Gracie hesitated.

Dee walked over to the front door and stood in front of it, arms crossed in front of her chest. "I'm not kidding."

"Fine." Gracie opened the bottle and swallowed its contents. "It's good. Chocolatey."

"Why do you think I couldn't stop drinking it?"

This almost elicited a smile from the protein drink recipient. She handed Dee the bottle. "Thank you. I did need that."

"I've got two dozen bottles of it, and they're all yours. I'll have Jeff bring them by your cabin."

Dee stepped away from the door. Gracie opened it and then paused. "I know everyone thinks I was with Sylvan because he was rich. I mean, that was great and all, but I meet a lot of rich guys in the tech world."

"Including Austin."

"Yes," Gracie acknowledged with an undercurrent of emotion Dee couldn't quite place. "I know Sylvan could be awful sometimes. I called him on it whenever I could. But there was something about him. A kind of confidence I've never seen in anyone else." She drifted for a moment, lost in a memory. "He was very seductive."

An unexpected cloudburst led to the canceling of the Goldsgone Crafts Fair, which freed Dee up to share the news about Sylvan's death with her other guests. She used it as a cautionary tale of the dangers gold hunters risked when they ignored the safety warnings on abandoned mines. By the time she met up with her father to clean out the sluice at the end of the day, she was exhausted.

"I'm plumb tired, right down to my bones," she said as she used a pool skimmer to remove pine needles from the sluice. "Argh, I used miner talk. Remind me to put a quarter in the jar."

"You've had a lot to deal with." Sam finished drying the sluice pans and stacked them. "It's sad when anyone passes away, particularly someone young like Burr. But he was not a nice guy."

Dee sprinkled fool's gold into the sluice. "Have you made up with Elmira? With everything that's happened, I haven't had a chance to."

Sam took a rake and began cleaning the ground around

the sluice. "She's not talking to me. Or Serena. Or any of her 'so-called' friends."

He raked with increased ferocity. "Dad, easy," Dee said. "That's a cheap piece of equipment. It's not designed for anger raking."

Dee heard the crunch of gravel and glanced toward the parking area. She felt an unpleasant sensation in the pit of her stomach when she saw who'd pulled in.

Raul exited his sheriff department's SUV and made his way to Dee and Sam. "Are Sylvan Burr's pals around?" he asked, skipping a greeting.

"Two are," Dee said. "Gavin Walsh is in the city. Why?"

"Harry Liu found something during his examination of Burr," Raul said, referencing the sheriff coroner. "He was stabbed in the back."

"Literally?"

Raul looked at Dee like she'd lost her mind. "Of course *literally.*"

"Sorry," Dee said, flailing as she tried to wrap her mind around the awful news. "It's just that 'stabbed in the back' is a classic expression and he was in a very competitive business, and I was really hoping you meant it in the metaphorical way, because otherwise—"

"Sylvan Burr was murdered."

# CHAPTER 10

The chaos of the second Gold Rush paled in comparison to the pandemonium unleashed by the news that Sylvan Burr had been murdered. It took a private security team hired by Tax Hax to keep the press at a distance from the Golden Motel, even though Burr's death technically didn't occur on their property. Once again, moteliers Dee and Jeff found themselves fearing that events beyond their control would scare off guests and the Golden would forever be known as Murder Motel. But . . .

"I now thank the universe for greed," Dee said to Jeff midmorning the next day when she returned to the lobby lounge after showing a half-dozen eager gold-panning guests to their rooms.

"It's disconcerting how little people are bothered by the murder." Jeff gazed out the large glass lobby window to where two security team members patrolled the perimeter. They were clad in black, from their storm trooper–type boots to the gaiters covering their faces, and kept both hands on the assault rifles strapped across their chests. "You'd think those guys would freak people out."

"The couple who drove here from Arizona said they

made them feel safer." Dee left her station behind the reservations counter and joined Jeff staring out the window. "I'm convinced those guys are mercenaries in a rogue country when they're not here."

"Oh, a hundred percent."

Dee and Jeff watched in silence. "Long term, this isn't good," Dee finally said. "In TV, when a show was in trouble, we'd say it had a stink on it. If Sylvan's murder isn't solved, and *soon,* the Golden will have a stink on it. When this happens to a show, it's the beginning of the end."

"That can't happen to the Golden. To us." Jeff stroked the stubble on his chin, his go-to tic when anxious. Dee noticed a couple of gray hairs had sprouted among the tufts of ginger. "We'll lose everything."

"I know. *I know.* Plus, who will want to stay here if there's a killer still on the loose? I'm not sure we'd want to—and we live here."

Dee left the window for the breakfast station. She snagged an errant half of a cheese Danish from a sympathy breakfast board Serena had dropped off. "Have you heard if they found the murder weapon?"

Jeff shook his head. "They haven't. When I asked Raul, he said the killer could have dropped it in any one of a ton of abandoned mines, or thrown it in one of the streams or brooks, or buried it. They'll keep looking, but I don't get that he's optimistic about finding it."

"So that's useless," Dee said, aggravated. "Do they have an estimated time of death?"

"All Raul would tell me is Sylvan had been . . . gone . . . awhile when they found him."

"Not too vague." Dee placed a hand on her heart, which was beating way too rapidly. "I'm a wreck from all of this. I need to calm down. I'm making a cup of tea. You want one?"

"You and your tea," Jeff said, shaking his head.

"Right now, it's that or medicate myself." She opened a cabinet door and took out a bag of loose-leaf jasmine green tea. "Back to my original question." She held the bag up to him. "Want some?"

"Only if it's tea made out of booze." Jeff tore himself away from the window and sat down on one of the old oak chairs at a two-top table. "It's going to take a few belts to get me through today."

Dee picked up on a tone in his voice that concerned her. "What's wrong?"

Jeff toyed with a paper napkin someone had left on the table. "Nothing," he mumbled, staring at the floor.

Dee abandoned her tea and sat down across from him. "Jeff, look at me. *Look at me.*"

Jeff didn't lift his head, but he glanced up.

"You're my best friend in the world. My ride or die. You have to let me in on whatever's bothering you."

Jeff released a long, sad sigh. "You know the text group chat I was on with people who hated Sylvan? I . . . I wrote some things that weren't good."

"Like what?" Dee asked, tamping down a rising fear.

"We went on a long rant about different ways we'd like to see Sylvan die. And one of the ways I pitched was him having an 'accident' in an abandoned gold mine."

Dee's eyes widened. "Oh boy."

"I know." Jeff nervously shredded the napkin. "I'm such an idiot. A citiot idiot."

"No! Do *not* say that." Dee fought to calm him—and herself. "The mines are on top of the list of things on our minds lately. When Ma'am got back from taking Sylvan and the others on a tour, she made a crack about how the only good thing about it was that none of them ended up at the bottom of a mine. My dad was so upset about Sylvan outing Elmira's bad baking that he even made a threat about pushing Sylvan down one."

"Uh-oh."

*"Nooo!"* Dee cried out, now in a full-blown panic. "You didn't kill him, and Ma'am didn't, and my dad didn't. There are so many other suspects. Austin, for one. I can tell that he never forgave Sylvan for moving in on Gracie, even though he tried to get over it. And even though Gracie insists she wasn't in a relationship with Sylvan for the money, maybe she was. Raul can check with Sylvan's attorney to see if she's in the will. That would be major motivation. And what's the deal with Gavin? Why is he palling around with people ten years younger than him? You know he's totally doing it for the money. Maybe Sylvan got sick of his sucking up and was going to boot him from the Core Four, so Gavin got rid of him before he got cut out."

Dee rattled on, barely taking a breath. "And Ed Froelich—he full-on attacked Sylvan in front of all of us. Sylvan ruined his life. Talk about a motive. His wife's got one too. Trish was going to retire and learn how to play pickleball, but thanks to Tax Hax, no pickleball for her. Or the killer could be a complete stranger, another gold hunter who ran into Sylvan at the mine, got into a fight over who'd get to explore it, and wound up stabbing him." Dee grabbed Jeff's hands and looked him right in the eyes. "The one thing I know for absolute sure is that you did *not* kill him. I don't care if you wrote in the stupid group chat that you'd push him down a thousand mines."

"Hello."

Dee and Jeff turned their heads to see Raul Aguilar standing in the doorway. "I finished interviewing all your guests again, now that we know Sylvan's death wasn't an accident, and I was going to hit you up for a cup of coffee." Raul eyed Jeff. "But it looks like I have one more interview left to do. Something about a text group chat . . . and ways to kill a certain murder victim?"

"*Noooo!* How is this happening again?" Jeff, who'd been a suspect in the first murder to take place at the Golden, groaned. He stood up. "We can talk in my cabin."

He and the sheriff left. Dee picked up the napkin her friend and partner had dropped. As she watched him trudge to his cabin with the sheriff, she began shredding the napkin herself.

Her phone rang. She recognized Ranger Tom O'Bryant's telephone number. Hoping he was calling with a "We caught Sylvan Burr's killer" update, she quickly answered the call. "Hi, Tom. Any news?"

"About Burr? No."

"Oh," Dee said, deflated.

"I'm calling from the fair. I'm packing up my sculptures because it looks like I've been drafted to help Aguilar in the Burr investigation, and I saw Verity put a Crafts Fair Space Available sign on your table. I thought that given what's going on right now, you might have bailed on the fair, but since Verity looked way too pleased with herself, I thought I'd check."

"Thank you so much," Dee said, steaming. Truth be told, she had considered dropping out of the fair. If Jeff and possibly her father were truly considered suspects in Sylvan's murder, they'd need her help clearing their names. But now, there was zero way she'd give Verity the satisfaction. "I haven't dropped out of the fair," she told Tom. "In fact, I'm on my way there now."

Dee avoided eye contact with the other vendors as she pulled her wagon of goods down the path between the two rows of fair stalls, but the stares of either curiosity or judgment bored into her.

"Dee . . . Dee?"

She lifted her head slightly. Serena waved to her. Dee relaxed and detoured over to her friend's stall, where a stunning array of cutting boards for charcuterie and other spreads was displayed. The waiflike food artist had taken up woodworking as a hobby, and Dee had a feeling Serena channeled her occasional frustration with her charismatic but self-involved husband, Callan, into her table saw.

Serena crooked a finger at her and Dee bent down to hear Serena whisper, "I heard Sylvan was *murdered.* It's horrible."

Dee straightened up. "We don't have to whisper. It's all over the news. And not just in America, but everywhere. Jeff showed me a post from a website in Kuala Lumpur."

"Still," Serena said in her normal voice, "it's scary. And sad. I feel for his loved ones."

"I'm getting the feeling that's a pretty small circle."

"And it has to be hard on you and Jeff. If we can help in any way, please let me know."

"Thank you so much." Feeling unexpectedly emotional, Dee reached over the display and hugged Serena, who returned the hug.

They let go and Serena said, "We also have to solve the Elmira problem. She was my closest friend in Foundgold until you moved here. And now she won't even speak to me." Serena teared up. She removed a napkin from one of her displays and wiped her eyes.

"We'll fix it, I promise," Dee said. "I'm already working on something. But one crisis at a time."

"I just hope we can make up with Elmira soon. I miss her—and the All-in-One. I can't stand the thought of giving Yes-*that*-Donner's store any business." She gestured to Verity, who was three stalls away and appeared to be holding a giant lollipop hostage until the parent of the little boy who wanted it forked over the necessary cash.

"Amen." Dee watched the boy's parents cave to Verity and pay for the overpriced candy. "The thing I don't understand is, how has no one complained about Elmira's baked goods before? You think the fact they're inedible would have come up sooner."

"She's only been baking a year or so," Serena said. "Tourists basically buy and run. They're on the road by the time they bite into one." She paused, then added, "A couple have complained, but we dismissed them to Elmira. We told her they didn't know what they were talking about." There was a catch in her voice. "We thought we were being good friends."

"Hey, babe."

Callan Katz, Hollywood powerhouse agent and Serena's husband, appeared at the stall. Except for baby Emmy strapped to his chest, he was attired in classic off-duty agent mufti of jeans and a T-shirt decorated with the logo from one of his A-list client's production companies.

He came around the table to give his wife a kiss. "Hi, sweetie," Serena said. "Aw, did you bring Emmy to visit Mommy?" She cooed at her baby, who giggled as Serena covered her tiny face with kisses.

"You betcha. Also, she wet her diaper and needs a change."

Callan began to unbuckle the baby carrier. Selena grabbed his hand. "Oh, no you don't. Mommy is working. This is daddy-daughter time and that includes the changing of diapers."

"But you're so much better at it." Callan flashed the

smile that had wooed many a star to his agency. Serena stared Callan down. "Fine," he said, buckling under her glare. "Is there a changing table around here?"

"In that bathroom." Serena pointed to a sign that read RESTROOMS, with an arrow pointing to the facilities near the town's old jail.

"Alrighty." He kissed Emmy on the top of her head. "Looks like you and me are going on an adventure, kid." He noticed Dee. "Hey. Bad news about your motel guest, huh?"

Dee shot him a look. "I know you, Callan. You love that CAA is now out a client who turned you down."

Callan gave a good-natured shrug. "Schadenfreude, my friend. Nothing like getting pleasure from someone else's pain when that someone is your biggest competitor." He grew serious. "But I'd never wish what happened to Burr on anyone. Not even a CAA client. Maybe one of their agents . . . but not a client."

He and Emmy took off for the restroom and Dee headed to her table. When she reached it, she saw the sign Tom had warned her about. But someone had turned it around and written on the other side: *Be Back Soon!* Mystified, she looked around for a clue to who had saved her spot. She saw Gillie Gillespie exchanging money for a hobby-horse pony at the stand outside Verity's shop. He finished the transaction and glanced her way. Dee held up the sign and pointed to it. He nodded with a wily expression. She mouthed, "Thank you." He responded with a thumbs-up.

Dee removed the sign, grateful to have an ally in Verity's camp, even if Gillie had to operate like an undercover agent to protect his own hide. She set up her goods for display and sat down to wait for customers. But Dee's heart wasn't in it. She had to admit to herself that she'd only shown up to spite Verity. *Which doesn't make me much better than her.*

She opened the umbrella she'd brought to ward off the sun. To her delight, Dee saw her friend Owen Mudd Jr., owner of the local jewelry store, had taken up residence at Tom O'Bryant's table. She waved to him and he returned the wave with a warm smile. "I'm glad you're the new Tom," she said.

"Only while he's helping the sheriff solve Sylvan Burr's murder." Owen's smile disappeared. "I'm sorry that happened again."

Smarting at the word "again," Dee gave a slight nod, then changed the subject. "Is that a digital scale?"

"Yep." Owen held it up. "The most accurate portable one on the market. I burned out my old scale measuring people's findings. This scale wasn't cheap, but it's already paid for itself." He held up a small vial that glimmered gold. "I paid a tourist miner ten bucks for this. It's worth twice that to me."

Dee settled back to wait for customers. A paucity of them gave her time to muse about Sylvan's murder. Given the tech giant's claustrophobia, his very presence at the mine where he died was a mystery. Gracie was on point when she posited someone must have lured him there. But who? And what exactly was the lure?

Patience had never been one of Dee's virtues, which meant that simply waiting for law enforcement to figure out who killed Sylvan was a nonstarter. Dee pulled her phone out of her fanny pack. With Sam banished from the All-in-One like the rest of them, and their guests more interested in panning for real gold rather than playing at it in the sluice, Prospector Pete was at loose ends. She texted her father a message: **Up for doing some research?** He texted back a thumbs-up followed by a question mark. **See what you can uncover about the history of the mine where Sylvan died,** Dee wrote. He responded with a line of exclamation marks, followed by another thumbs-up.

Dee put away her phone. She noticed Callan browsing a nearby stall sans baby. He glanced her way, then wandered over. "Where's Emmy?" she asked. "Please don't tell me Serena gave up and changed her for you."

"Nope. The lady who owns the underwear store offered to help me out."

"You mean Pamela? It's a lingerie shop, not an 'underwear store,' and I can't believe you manipulated the poor woman into doing your dirty diaper work. Oh, wait, I can."

Callan, who was absorbed in checking out Dee's merchandise, didn't respond. He chuckled and held up one of the towels featuring a cartoon of Bud peering into a cabin refrigerator to the terror of the human homeowner:

"Where's the mayo for my turkey leg?"

Callan chuckled. "This is funny stuff. Are there other cartoons?"

"A bunch, but I've only turned a few into merch." She handed Callan a mug where Bud wore an annoyed expression as he walked away from a campsite he'd trashed. The caption under the image read: *Ugh, Vegan campers. I might as well eat tree bark.*

"Ha. It's funny because it's true. Most vegan stuff tastes so bad it might as well be tree bark." Callan made a small pile of Dee's goods with the mug, a couple of towels, and a bear. "I'll take all of this. How much?"

"Nothing. With the deal Serena cuts me on the weekly breakfast board, it's the least I can do. That's why I only serve up the board once a week. If I let her make us a board every day, you'd go broke."

"Excellent. Thanks." He waved to Pamela, who was walking toward them. She was holding Emmy close to her chest, which was clad in a black-and-red saloon girl corset. "I can put everything in Emmy's diaper bag," he said.

"Good," Dee responded, relieved. "Because I just realized I left my gift bags at home."

Callan retrieved Emmy from Pamela and departed with his merch and daughter. In need of gift bags in case she made an actual sale, Dee scoped out the stalls to see who she could bum a few from, landing on the stall for Ye Olde Soapery.

She walked over to the stall, where the floral scents from the soaps provided a welcome change from the odors of the bathrooms near Dee's table. She exchanged greetings with soap maker Jenny Baxter, a retired schoolteacher who was a lifelong resident of Goldsgone. "Can I impose on you for a few gift bags?" Dee asked. "If I don't make a sale, I'll return them. If I do, I'll replace them from my own stock tomorrow."

"I'll trade gift bags for one of your tea towels so I can wipe away my tears." Jenny delivered this in a tone more sardonic than emotional.

"Uh-oh. What's going on?"

"I made a sweet handshake deal to sell my business and building to that Sylvan Burr, but now he's dead and it looks like so's the deal. No offense to him and his loved ones, of course. But dang."

"You were going to sell *everything* to Sylvan?" Dee was taken aback by what Jenny shared. In her experience, the average Goldsgonedian's attachment to their town and property spanned generations, both backward and forward. It seemed inconceivable that they'd part with a brick of the place.

The unexpected news triggered a memory of something Tom O'Bryant had said when he and Dee were first manning their fair stations. He'd mentioned the locals had been at odds—"sniping at each other"—lately. She put a question to the soap maker. "Just wondering, did Sylvan make a deal like this with other shop or building owners?"

"Oh yeah. His people put out feelers about a month ago to a bunch of us, on the down-low. Sylvan got into it himself and ratcheted up the pressure by pitting neighbors against each other. Like, if he was making a deal with one of us and the person next door wasn't interested in selling, he'd threaten to cancel the first deal." She called to the stall across the street, where the aptly named Abraham Tanner was selling handcrafted leather goods. "Abe, didn't you get into it with Steve Garrison when he wanted to sell to Sylvan Burr and you didn't?"

Abe gave a grim nod. "I can't blame Garrison for wanting to give up the smithy business. Not much call for blacksmiths anymore and there's only so many cutesy horseshoes he can sell to tourists. But I got no plans to go anywhere, and I didn't appreciate him and that tech guy putting the screws to me, trying to force me into selling. None of us met Burr in person until now. I'm sure the S.O.B. showed up just to intimidate us holdouts. "

"He didn't make me an offer," pouted Pamela, who was passing by with her coupons.

"Probably because he hadn't gotten around to you yet," Jenny said.

"He weren't gonna get nothing from me." This declaration came from the ancient woman known as Ice Cream Ida, the proprietor of Sweet Licks Ice Cream Parlor and Soda Fountain. She had the stall next to Abe, where she sold her much-loved homemade ice cream sandwiches. "My ancestors founded this town, and if I go anywhere, it'll be in a pine box. That sneaky little rat, coming in here and throwing his money around. He was like to ruin Goldsgone." She cracked the knuckles of her gnarled fingers. "I'm not gonna lie. I'm glad he died."

"I'm not," Jenny shot back at her. "I was gonna move to San Diego."

"So go," Ida shot back. "No one's stoppin' ya."

From there, the conversation devolved into an argument involving more Goldsgonedians. Verity rushed out of her shop to try and calm things down before the noise chased away customers. "Focus on the fair, people, focus on the fair!"

Fearful of the consequences if Verity learned she was responsible for the ruckus, Dee snuck away from the scene and returned to her table. But instead of the fair, she focused on something far more chilling.

Real estate was the equivalent of twenty-first-century gold in California, and the buying and selling of it could get ugly, especially in communities where the residents were divided on whether to stay or take the money and flee.

To Dee's thinking, Burr's mysterious real estate machinations had just created a passel of new suspects in the case of his murder.

# CHAPTER 11

Dee texted what she'd learned to Raul, then waited out the clock until she felt she could leave without risking Verity snatching away her location.

As she packed up her goods, Dee heard familiar voices. She looked up and saw Austin and Gavin, who'd returned from Palo Alto, browsing at Owen's table. She stopped packing and went to them. 'Hey," she said, voice laced with sympathy. "I'm glad you're taking a break from being at the motel. How are you holding up?"

"Okay." Gavin held up a tiny vial. "The police can't make us stay, but they strongly suggested we stick around for a while."

"We were going to anyway," Austin said. "It's like Gracie said. We can't just go back home like nothing happened."

"Anyway," Gavin said, "we went panning in the stream and scored some gold."

"Twenty dollars' worth," Owen said.

"Two tens, please," Austin said. "We're splitting the take."

Gavin held up a hoodie Owen was selling that was emblazoned with THE GOLDFATHER across its front. "Put my ten toward this." Owen wrote up both transactions and Gavin pulled on the hoodie. "I *am* The Goldfather," he announced in a deep voice, then broke character and snickered.

"Come on, Goldfather," Austin said. "We should get back to Gracie."

The tech bros departed. Dee stared after them. Owen did the same. "Those are—were—Burr's friends, right?"

"Half of the Core Four," Dee responded.

The jeweler scrunched his face, perplexed. "They don't exactly seem grief-stricken."

"I know," Dee said, frowning. "I really don't get them."

Dee finished packing up her merchandise and left for home, where she shared the techies' behavior with Jeff over a dinner of beer and frozen pizza in her apartment.

"I'm not surprised," Jeff said. "In the tech world, when you're as rich and successful as a Sylvan Burr, everyone wants a piece of you and it's almost impossible to have a relationship that isn't transactional. Gavin's only connection to Sylvan was through the business, so it was absolutely transactional, even if they appeared to be friends. Austin and Gracie's relationships with Sylvan may have dated back to college—"

"Which was all of six years ago," Dee pointed out. "They're not even up to their ten-year reunion."

"Doesn't matter," Jeff said. "Six years might as well be sixty in tech years, considering where they are now versus where they were then. And considering Sylvan was the alpha dog, there was a transactional aspect to their relationship too, despite their past."

"True. Except they both seem to have plenty of their

own money." Dee took a swig of beer. "On to the other big story of the day." She filled Jeff in on Sylvan's dubious real estate dealings in Goldsgone.

"Raul was about to leave when he got your text," Jeff said. "He'd heard rumblings about someone trying to buy up the town, but people were closemouthed about it and at the time, it didn't tie to any criminal investigation, so there was nothing to look into. Now he's looking into Sylvan's Goldsgone game plan to see if there are any clues that would help reveal what got him killed. He's also trying to find out if there were any problems between Sylvan and his fellow Silicon Valley moguls that could have led to his murder, but he's being blocked by their gatekeepers claiming privacy concerns. On top of all this, Raul's dealing with all the crime being generated by the new Gold Rush—fistfights, claim jumping, people stealing each other's gold."

"Wow," Dee said. "It might as well be the OG Gold Rush."

"I know, right?"

Dee gestured to the last slice of pizza. Jeff shook his head, so she took it. "It explains why Verity wasn't a fan of Sylvan's. If he bought up Goldsgone, she'd be deposed as town dictator." This elicited a chuckle from Jeff. "Jonas must know something about this land grab," Dee continued after swallowing the last bite of her slice. "He's one of exactly two real estate agents in town."

"It looks like Sylvan was trying to keep the whole plan under the radar. But I'd be surprised if Jonas didn't at least pick up on a rumor. I told Raul I'd see what I can uncover from the tech end, which puts me in the unique position of being both a suspect and a volunteer for the sheriff's department."

"Jeffrey"—Dee used his full name as a term of endearment—"you're only a suspect because I accidentally alerted Raul to the text group chat you were on, and you weren't the only one pitching ways Sylvan should kick the bucket. Does 'kick the bucket' count as old-timey?"

"You're saying nice things so I'll give you a pass on the miner jar."

"Thanks." Dee sat up. "I've racked up some bill by now. I better pay it off. I don't like living under a cloud of debt."

Dee retrieved her wallet from the fanny pack she'd taken to wearing and dropped a few dollars into the jar. She and Jeff finished dinner, and Jeff went off to plunge a guest's toilet. Dee stayed behind to straighten up the lobby. She was happy to see guests had availed themselves of the board games Jeff scored at the West Camp garage sale. He'd found a thousand-piece puzzle featuring a photograph of Majestic's spectacular Piute Waterfall at another sale and had set it up on a bridge table. Dee saw guests had already assembled three-quarters of the outer edges.

Overwhelmed by emotion, Dee dropped into a chair and let herself have a brief cry. The motel had become more than a business venture. It was the launch of her second act, a career she'd never remotely envisioned, but now felt like destiny. Aside from the trauma of a lost life, each murder—and three had touched the Golden already—felt like a sucker punch to her dream of turning the motel into an iconic regional destination.

Nugget padded up to her. He sat on his haunches, placed a paw on her knee, and made a few guttural sounds Dee was able to translate. "I know, buddy." She wiped her eyes. "A walk and a treat—then it's beddy-bye time for both of us."

After accomplishing the first two tasks, she and Nugget tromped through the woods to the tent she'd been forced to call home for too many nights. Nugget curled up on his doggy bed and soon his doggy snores filled the air. Dee wriggled around inside her sleeping bag, unable to sleep, thanks to the methodical march of the heavy-booted Tax Hax security guards patrolling the grounds. Giving up, she began a mental list of who among the citizens of Goldsgone would be driven to kill Sylvan to protect their property. It proved to be a short list: Ice Cream Ida, Abe Tanner, and even Verity were obvious choices. Adding other names to the list would require more sleuthing.

Bone-tired after what amounted to three hours of sleep at the most, Dee dragged herself to the lobby in the morning to lay out a continental breakfast for the Golden guests. None of the remaining Core Four showed up, so Dee texted each of them to see if they wanted a breakfast basket dropped off. Gavin and Austin replied in the affirmative, but Gracie didn't respond at all, which concerned Dee. She decided to assemble a basket anyway and use it as an excuse to check on the girl.

First, Dee saw to the motel's other guests. She and Jeff had opted for a utilitarian coffee machine rather than pods, which they agreed were environmentally antithetical to their goals for a relatively green motel. Dee made a fresh pot of coffee and went from table to table to refresh people's cups. She finished with the Froelichs and noticed they both appeared depressed.

"Coffee?"

"No thanks," came from Trish as Ed said, "Sure."

Dee bypassed Trish's mug and topped off Ed's. "You

two look down. Anything the Golden can do to perk up your spirits?"

"Afraid not," Ed said, sounding glum. "We panned for hours yesterday and I was pretty excited by our haul. But when we had it weighed, it only came out to seven dollars' worth."

"I'm trying to stay positive and think to myself, well, it's seven dollars we didn't have yesterday." Trish attempted an upbeat delivery, then gave up. "But honestly, it's hard to keep up our spirits."

Dee felt for the couple. She'd noticed their aging sedan had unrepaired fender dents that indicated deferred maintenance. She'd always assumed accounting was one of life's more sensible professions. But technology disrupters like Tax Hax were up-ending a lot of professions once assumed safe.

"I do have a little bit of good news for you," she said, making it up as she spoke. "Jeff and I have started a special program called Gold Rush Guests, where we draw one of our guests' names and their bill gets comped. And you're our first winners. Congratulations."

Seeing the Froelichs' faces light up made the financial hit worth it.

"That's wonderful," Ed enthused.

Trish clapped her hands joyfully. "This *is* good news. Thank you so much."

"By the way, extracting seven dollars' worth of gold isn't bad. It could be a sign there's more where it came from."

"You're right," Ed said, now beaming. "We'll give that location another shot."

Dee left the couple, now happy and energized, as they made plans for the day. She texted Jeff, **Remind me to tell u**

**about Gold Rush Guests.** Ignoring the string of question marks he texted back, she put together three breakfast baskets and rolled them out of the lobby on the library cart she'd found earmarked for oversized pickup on the curb outside the West Camp library. Instead, Dee nabbed the cart and repurposed it for the motel's use.

She left baskets at Austin's and Gavin's cabin doors, texting them reminders to grab the baskets before Bud the Bear got a whiff of them. Then she headed to Gracie's cabin, where Gracie had returned after her brief stay in Dee's apartment. "Hello?" Dee said, knocking on the door.

Gracie opened the door. Dee had expected to find the only relatively grief-stricken techie unwashed and still in her pajamas. Instead, she appeared to be dressed for a hike, except for the knee-high wading boots. "Um, hi," Dee said, thrown. "I texted you about a breakfast basket and got a little worried when I didn't hear from you, so I went ahead and brought one over."

She handed the basket to Gracie, who placed it on the room's desk. "Thanks so much. I was in the shower and haven't looked at my phone. Syl's online memorial is tonight."

Dee marked this as only the second time she'd heard anyone call Sylvan by a nickname. She took a closer look at Gracie. Her eyes were shadowed and her skin grew paler every day. She might be washed and dressed, but she was in pain. "Just so you know," Gracie said, "I'm not leaving here until the police arrest whoever murdered Sylvan."

"I totally get it," Dee responded. "Stay with us as long as you need to. But I hope for your sake, they catch the killer fast. It's awful for you to have to go through this."

"I'm so stressed and tense," Gracie said, her voice raw. "I hired Ma'am to take me panning in the stream. I'm hoping it'll help me relax before the memorial. This is going to sound strange, but I find panning for gold relaxing."

"I can see that. It's like fishing, but for gold."

Dee heard herself and winced at what sounded to her like a ridiculous analogy, but Gracie nodded. "Exactly. Anyway, I'm meeting with her in a few minutes."

"Just you and Ma'am?"

Gracie nodded.

Dee saw an opportunity for quasi–one-on-one time with Sylvan's girlfriend and seized the opportunity. "That sounds like such a good idea. I've been really tense lately myself. I'll come with you."

She zoomed away with the cart before Gracie could object.

Dee quickly changed into sturdier gear. She strapped on a backpack and met up with Gracie and Ma'am under the motel's triangular bell. Keeping in mind Gracie's goal was relaxation, Dee respected this and kept silent on the hike. As they traipsed through the forest, the only sounds came from birdsong and the crunch of twigs and leaves underfoot. Dee found herself relaxing, an added benefit she didn't expect.

The gentle babbling of the stream grew louder as the three women neared it. They reached a small outcropping of mossy rocks at the bottom of a three-tiered waterfall. "Here we are," Ma'am announced. The backwoods woman pulled pans out of the sack she'd made from the same burlap sacks she'd used to hand-sew her dress and handed them to Gracie and Dee. "Pan away."

Dee and Gracie dipped their pans into the water and

scooped up the sandy stream bottom. They shook their pans, then dipped again to wash away sediment, repeating the process two more times. Dee peered into her pan. "I've got something," she said, excited.

Gracie checked her pan "Me too."

Ma'am examined Dee's pan first. "Fool's gold." She dumped the pan's contents back into the stream, then cast an eye at Gracie's pan. "Real gold. Nice." She gave Gracie an appreciative nod.

"And the rich get richer," Dee muttered, annoyed.

Gracie eyed her. "What was that?"

"Nothing," Dee said, quickly backtracking. "Real gold. Yay, you!"

Ma'am used a snuffer bottle to suck up Gracie's gold flakes and transfer them to a vial, after which the women resumed panning. Dee waited until they'd achieved a rhythm to their panning; then said in a casual tone, "So Austin and Gavin came by the crafts fair yesterday. They seemed in good spirits, considering." Gracie didn't respond. Dee tried again. "To be honest, I was kind of surprised." Still, no response. Dee pushed harder. "I thought they'd be more upset about losing such a close friend, especially to murder."

Gracie held up her pan to Ma'am. "I think I've got more gold."

Ma'am eyed it. "You sure do." She slapped Gracie on the back. "You got the knack, girl."

Dee shoved down her frustration at her own empty pan and made one last attempt to engage Gracie. "Back to what we were talking about—"

"*We* weren't talking about anything," Gracie said. "*You* were talking. I was panning. Which I'd like to keep doing without *anyone* talking."

Ma'am waved a scolding finger at Dee. "You heard her. Let the girl pan in peace."

"Sure," Dee said, giving up. "Sorry."

Gracie panned for another hour, accumulating flakes with each scoop of the streambed. Thwarted in her goal of pulling useful information out of the young woman, Dee grew bored. She pulled a pad and pencils out of her backpack and sketched a cartoon of Bud triumphantly yelling "Gold!" as he held a large, fat salmon over his head, and a panicked hiker reacted:

"Gold!"

Finally Gracie waded out of the stream, to Dee's relief. "I'm done for today." She shook the water off her boots, then towel-dried her pan and handed it back to Ma'am.

"You did real well." Ma'am held up Gracie's vial, which sparkled with gold. "Must be a hundred bucks' worth of flakes here." She held out the vial to Gracie, who refused delivery. "Keep it."

Ma'am grinned, generating rows of wrinkles in her sunburned cheeks. "Not gonna say no to that. Thanks."

She stuck the vial in the deepest recesses of her sack and started toward the motel. Gracie purposely lagged behind. Sensing she wanted to open up, Dee kept pace with her.

"I need to tell you something," Gracie said.

"I'm listening," Dee said, giving herself props for a well-played plan.

Gracie stopped so suddenly, Dee bumped into her. She lost her balance and stumbled, grabbing a tree branch to keep from falling. Unfortunately, it was a dead branch and came off in Dee's hand. She helplessly waved her arms in the air as she fell to the ground, landing hard on her backside.

Gracie looked daggers at Dee. "You're trying to get me to incriminate my friends. Or myself. You need to stop. *Now.*"

Dee slowly rose to her feet. She rubbed her lower back. "Ugh, I landed on my tailbone. That really hurt." She dusted off the back of her pants and faced Gracie. "I'm sorry. I didn't mean to upset you. But I have to say, I find Gavin's and Austin's attitudes questionable. You all lost someone who was so integral to your lives that you called yourselves, the Core Four. I hope neither of your friends killed Sylvan. I doubt you did, because you're the only person who seems to be genuinely suffering his loss. But someone did kill him. And I don't think anyone is safe until they're captured."

Dee hoped this would get through to Gracie. Instead,

she narrowed her eyes even more. "You might want to snoop closer to home for my boyfriend's killer. Sylvan was trying to buy up Goldsgone and Foundgold."

"I know."

"Well, what you don't know is, when he made an offer to the lady who owns the All-in-One store, the one who bakes the awful baked stuff, she didn't take it well. Like I told your friend the local sheriff, the lady got in Sylvan's face and said, 'If you don't stop trying to buy out myself and my friends and ruin our towns, I promise that you're gonna find yourself at the bottom of a mine shaft.'"

# CHAPTER 12

Exasperated, Dee paced her living room. The minute she returned home from her outing with Gracie, she'd texted Jeff to meet her there. "Is there anyone in Foundgold who didn't threaten to throw Sylvan Burr down a mine shaft?"

"You, I guess," Jeff said from his perch on a kitchen stool.

Dee stopped pacing and collapsed onto the couch. "I thought about it," she admitted. "But at least I never said it out loud, like Dad. Or put it in writing, like you. Or said it to Sylvan's face, like Ma'am or Elmira."

"Did Gracie tell Raul what Elmira said?"

Dee gave an unhappy nod. She grabbed her car keys. "I tried to reach Elmira to warn her she's been marked as a suspect, but she won't return my texts or calls, so I'm driving over to the All-in-One to talk to her in person."

Jeff held up the poster board apology Dee had finished drawing. "I signed the card and got Serena to sign it when she stopped by to pick up the empty breakfast board. Nice work, by the way. Bud looks *beary* sorry." He gave an exaggerated wink and chuckled.

Dee took the poster board from him. "Hopefully, Elmira will be as amused by cheesy puns as you are."

The gold craze had dissipated slightly, allowing for less traffic on the rural two-lane roads and a mere five-minute drive from the Golden to Williker's. Dee entered the store with the poster board tucked under her arm. The first thing she noticed was an empty space where the baked-goods display case once sat.

"Yes, it's gone."

Elmira announced this from where she stood in the doorframe that separated the shop, café, and bar from the laundromat at the west end of the All-in-One.

"It doesn't have to be." Dee cursed herself for the vague and vapid response.

"Yes, it does. Why would I ever bake again? To give my so-called friends more chances to lie to my face while talking smack about my baked goods behind my back?"

"Elmira, we all feel terrible about what happened. We love you. We want you to find your baking mojo again. With a few small adjustments."

"Like making my goods edible?" The shopkeeper and former baker delivered this with a massive amount of side eye.

Dee held up the poster board card in an attempt to redeem herself. "Look, we made you a card. To show how *beary* sorry we are." She mimicked Jeff's wink, adding a hopeful smile.

"Not a fan of puns," Elmira said, unmoved. "But I'll give you credit for the cute take on Bud."

"Marking that as a small step forward." Dee put down the poster board. "I'm ready to apologize to you for however long I need, but I came about something else. There's a chance you're on the sheriff's list of suspects in Sylvan's murder."

Elmira raised her eyebrows. "Mark that as a big step backward."

She turned and strode down the hallway to the All-in-One's laundromat, a more recent addition to the store's offerings. Dee trailed her. "The last thing I wanted to do was deliver more bad news, but since Gracie already told Raul what she heard you say to Sylvan, I wanted you to be prepared for when he shows up to interview you about it, because you know he will."

They reached the laundromat, which was excessively warm from the heat being generated by the machines. The swishing of laundry and thumping of dryers provided a sound background to the women's conversation. Elmira opened a dryer and took out bed linens. "What does Gracie say I said?"

"She told Raul that you basically threatened to throw Sylvan down a mine shaft."

Elmira stopped what she was doing. She jutted out a hip and placed a hand on it. "Did she, now." Her voice was laced with sarcasm. She dropped her hand from her hip and resumed emptying the dryer. "I'll tell you what I'll tell Raul if he ever darkens my door with this nonsense. I *did not* threaten to toss our visiting billionaire into a mine shaft. What I did do was warn him that he best be careful with all his real estate tomfoolery and playing people against each other, or someone on the receiving end of his greed might drop him down a shaft. If you don't believe me, I have a witness. Heloise was making the entitled foursome their fancy coffee drinks while he and I were having this conversation."

"Of course I believe you. But for your own sake, I'm glad Heloise can back up the conversation." Dee leaned against a washing machine, pondering Elmira's version of the exchange with Sylvan. When she spoke, her voice vibrated thanks to the machine, which had begun its spin cycle. "I wonder if Gracie genuinely misheard you, or if she made up a version of the conversation that points the finger at a suspect who isn't in her inner circle."

"Don't know and don't care." Elmira yanked a fitted sheet from the dryer. "But I'll tell you this. With me losing my friends and my favorite hobby, if one of those Richie Rich techies made me an offer to buy this place today, I'd take it."

Dee gasped. "No! That can never, ever happen." Elmira replied with a grunt as she wrestled with the sheet. Seeing her friend struggle, Dee reached for a corner. "Let me help you."

"I don't need help."

"Elmira, be serious. Everyone needs help folding a fitted sheet."

"Not me." The All-in-One owner pulled the sheet out of Dee's reach. "If you need anything from the store, Heloise'll ring you up. When you leave, please take one of the mini charcuterie boards Serena keeps dropping off as apology gifts. I need them out of the store before the meat turns."

Dee left, disappointed she hadn't made amends with Elmira. *At least the boards will be my lunch at the fair today,* she thought, placing the two she'd taken from the store on the passenger seat. As she drove to Goldsgone, she thought about what Gracie claimed Elmira said to Sylvan. Had the grief-stricken young woman misspoken? Did Dee hear her wrong? Dee replayed her exchange with Gracie in her head, word by word. She came to the conclusion she'd heard Gracie correctly. And while there was a chance Gracie paraphrased the argument between Elmira and her boyfriend, Dee's instincts told her that casting suspicion on Elmira was no accident.

* * *

The crafts fair had its busiest day yet, thanks to a couple of tour buses filled with seniors from assisted-living facilities in the Central Valley. Dee sold enough merchandise to merit a reorder, which she placed upon returning to the Golden around dinnertime. She'd just pressed the send button, when Jeff texted a reminder about the online memorial for Sylvan. They'd agreed they should show their respect for their late guest by signing on for it. At least that would be their excuse if anyone questioned why they were watching—the real reason being that it offered a chance to snoop on the mourners while blending in with them.

Dee settled down in front of her laptop and called up the video platform hosting the event. It opened with a short homage to Burr's life made up mostly of press clips and videos set to a somber soundtrack. Dee noted a paucity of personal snapshots. She acknowledged this might be by design. The uber rich tended to keep a stranglehold on their image, a paranoid gesture often extended past their time as a sentient being. This seemed especially true of Sylvan, considering his commitment to cryogenics and being reconstituted at some point in the future.

The memorial, which Gavin ran in his hail-fellow-well-met way, mostly consisted of Tax Hax employees trying to top each other with unctuous tributes to Sylvan. The attendees skewed male, with a small smattering of twenty-something women, which was on par with most Silicon Valley companies. The sense Dee got from the anecdotes shared was that Sylvan was more of an ATM than human, and the mourners were more hangers-on than friends. Dee didn't count a single relative, immediate or distant, among the group, giving credence to Gracie's claim that he was estranged from his family.

The memorial dragged on for two hours. Gavin finally,

blessedly, brought it to a close. "Sylvan once told me that the only fear he had about being brought back to life is not having the people who meant the most to him around anymore. So, in his honor, Tax Hax will gift all of you with a coupon for five hundred dollars toward your very own cryogenics package."

He ended the event, but not before Dee caught the disgruntled expressions on the attendees' faces and heard one say, "Those cost, like, two hundred thousand—" before he was cut off.

Dee sat back in her chair, thinking. She noted that the gift came from Sylvan's company, not the billionaire himself, which led her to wonder where his personal fortune was destined to land. She put a call in to Raul. "Hi. I'm assuming the black image on the screen with just the name Raul was you."

"Yup," the sheriff said. "Virtual or not, I had to be there. Burr's killer could easily be one of the mourners."

"Anyone stand out?"

"Not really. But I got all the names and we'll do a deep dive into their backgrounds."

"I have a question. Are you at liberty to tell me anything about Sylvan's will?"

"All I can say is that if he had one, no one's found it yet."

"Really? Huh. You'd think he wouldn't want his money floating around in the ether."

"It's not so surprising. I can't think of a twentysomething who doesn't assume they'll live forever—including me—and I just dodged a bullet from an idiot playing with a vintage nineteenth-century Winchester Model 1873, which he didn't check to see if it was loaded."

Raul signed off. Dee yawned and Nugget placed a paw

on her knee. "I know, buddy. It's been a long day." She gave the top of his large head a pet. "Let's hit the sack. Is that an old-timey term? Ugh, I'm too tired to care."

Dee washed up and changed into her sleep tee and pants. She slipped on her backpack and pressed the button on her flashlight, then forlornly traipsed down the hill and through the woods to trade the comforts of her apartment for the Goldsgone tent.

Nugget promptly fell asleep. As usual, Dee had a tougher time. "I feel like I'm sleeping in an actual sack," she muttered. She made a few adjustments to her position, which proved useless, then tried distracting herself by scrolling through the news app on her cell phone. A story popped up about a bear breaking into a bakery. Dee sat up. She pulled a pencil and pad from her backpack and dashed off a sketch.

Bud sat on the floor of a bakery next to a pile of empty cupcake wrappers, while the baker, who'd run outside, freaked out:

"Coconut, ya either love it or hate it."

Pleased with herself, she replaced the pad and pencil and wriggled back into the sleeping bag.

Dee closed her eyes to take another stab at falling asleep. She turned over and rolled onto a rock. "Ow!" She cursed and sat up. "That's it. This is ridiculous. Why am I out here? It's not like Verity has a camera on me."

She climbed out of the sleeping bag and leashed up Nugget. "Come on, buddy. We're going home."

# CHAPTER 13

Morning sunlight streamed through Dee's bedroom windows. She snuggled under her bed's soft blanket, more refreshed than she'd felt in days. Nugget lay splayed out at her feet.

Dee sat up. She swung her legs over the bed's edge and hopped out onto her feet. "It's amazing what a decent night's sleep can do for you, Nugs," she said to the pooch, who was slowly stirring. Dee stretched her arms over her head and released a happy sigh. "I don't think I've ever felt more ready to face a day."

She showered and dressed, then presided over her guests' breakfasts with a genuine smile, instead of the manufactured one she'd been plastering on for almost a week. On the drive to Goldsgone, she hummed along to her favorite playlist. The humming continued as she set up her wares on her table, after which she slathered on sunscreen and popped open the large umbrella she used in lieu of the shade tent afforded to table vendors who were on Verity's good side. She placed the San Francisco Giants bleacher cushion she'd dug out of the motel's Lost and Found on the seat of the rickety folding chair that came with her location, sat down, and waited for customers.

Judging by the next hour's sales, Dee could only assume the universe had picked up on her positive vibe and rewarded her with a steady stream of shoppers. She was completing her biggest sale of the entire crafts fair when Verity sauntered over to her table.

"Here you go." Dee handed a bag full of her merchandise to a visiting family from Nevada. "Have a *beary* nice visit to Goldsgone and a safe trip home."

The family took off with Bud teddy bears clutched in the hands of the children. "They look happy," Verity observed. "As do you. I haven't seen you this well-rested since you joined the fair."

"I guess sleeping in the great outdoors on my Goldsgone property agrees with me," Dee replied. She couldn't resist adding a smug smile.

"Interesting." Verity affected a thoughtful expression. She tapped an index finger, decorated with the image of a gold nugget, to her lips. "Because a little birdie told me you didn't sleep in Goldsgone last night. You slept in your apartment . . . in *Foundgold.*" She dropped the act and ended on a note of triumph.

Dee's jaw dropped. "Wha . . . How . . .You . . ." she stammered.

"Having violated the residency requirement, I'm afraid you can no longer participate in the fair. If you need help packing up, I'll get one of my interns to help you." She gestured to the Trapp twins hovering behind her, dressed as usual in identical gingham dresses and bonnets. They wiggled their fingers in unison at Dee, accompanying the gesture with malevolent smiles.

Dee, infuriated, found her voice. "I can't believe you had your minions spy on me. They better not get credit for it in their internships."

"Learning how to keep silent while tracking in the woods at night is a valuable life skill."

Verity held up a hand to summon the twins. Angel and Addison Rose practically slithered over to Dee's table. Dee defiantly spread her arms over her goods to protect them from the teens. "No! Don't touch anything! I'm not going anywhere."

"I'm sorry, Dee," Verity made a halfhearted stab at faking sympathy, "but like I said, I don't make the rules."

Dee, steaming mad, locked eyes with her. "And like I said, uh, *yeah,* you do."

The twin interns stepped forward as one. Outnumbered, Dee relinquished control. The display she'd spent an hour laying out was rapidly and neatly boxed and stacked up on her luggage cart.

She marched up the street between the two rows of stalls, head held high. "You deserve better," tanner Abraham called as she passed. Other merchants echoed the sentiment, although more discreetly, not wanting to incur Verity's wrath.

"Don't worry, everyone." Dee thrust a defiant fist in the air. "I'll be back! *With a lawyer!*"

She yelled the last sentiment, which earned her applause, even from the more fearful merchants, albeit in their case the applause was muted golf claps. There was no way Dee could afford a lawyer, so they were empty words. But it felt good to yell the threat to the world—and to Verity.

Dee's march turned into a slumped-shouldered trudge. It took a full minute to realize someone was calling her name. She looked up and saw Gillie coming down the road from the opposite direction. He was holding a large box, and giant multicolored lollipops poked through the box's top. He hurried to meet up with her. "You're going in the opposite direction of the crafts fair," he said. "From the look on your face, it's not for a good reason."

Dee gave a mirthless laugh. "Far from it." She detailed her dustup with Verity. His outraged expression gave her some satisfaction.

"Verity. She is the worst," he hissed. "She only gave me a job at the store because she had to. My grandma—her mom—set up her will so that I'll inherit half the mercantile when my dad passes away. She also put in there that I could join the family business when I felt the time was right, which I did. My dad isn't interested in the business, so it's pretty much half-mine already. And boy, is Verity not happy about it."

His eyes narrowed into slits. He leaned in and spoke in a whisper. His breath reeked of coffee and cigarettes. Dee tried not to recoil. "I'll tell you something. Being at the store all the time now, I'm seeing things. Verity's not the rah-rah Goldsgone champ everyone thinks she is. Trust me on this." He straightened up. "I shouldn't say anything else. I'm sorry about what happened. But you're better off not having anything to do with my aunt."

He hurried off before Dee could question him about the possible bomb he'd dropped. Dee filed the exchange away for further exploration and kept walking. She reached the end of the road and was about to pull her cart into the parking lot, but she heard two women arguing. She glanced their way and, to her surprise, saw the women were lingerie shop owner Pamela and techie Gracie. It was an odd pairing, considering the two were strangers—at least to Dee's knowledge. She pulled her cart into an alley and strained to hear the women. She couldn't make out what they were saying, but she could ID their tone. Gracie sounded accusatory; Pamela alternated between defensive and apologetic.

The fight stopped. Dee started to leave her hideout. Gracie marched past, and Dee flattened herself against the old brick wall behind her to stay out of sight. She counted to ten and then casually exited the alley as if it was the most natural thing in the world to be there. Pamela stood stock-still, watching Gracie jump into the techies' luxury vehicle and peel out of the parking lot.

Dee couldn't decipher the expression on Pamela's face, but she couldn't let the mystifying exchange go without further investigation. "Pamela, hi."

The greeting snapped Pamela out of her brooding. "Hi, Dee. It's a bit early to be closing up your fair table. Poor sales today?"

Pamela sounded sympathetic and Dee thanked the universe for delivering the opening she needed. "Good sales, bad circumstances. I was forced to shut down. I've been sleeping in a tent on the bit of our property that's in Goldsgone, to meet the fair's residency requirement—"

"There's a residency requirement?"

*Curse you to hell and back, Verity "Yes-that-Donner" Gillespie!* Dee managed not to say this out loud. She also restrained herself from shaking a fist at the heavens. "To be honest, I think it only applies to me. I don't get along with Verity."

"Who does?" Pamela said with a snort.

Capitalizing on the bond of mutual disdain toward Verity, Dee released a dramatic sigh. She tried to work up a few tears, but they'd never gotten around to teaching that in the one acting class she'd taken in college, so she settled for sniffles. "I don't know why she hates me." This was a lie. She knew exactly why she'd earned Verity's enmity: Verity perceived newcomer Dee, who pushed back against her where others wouldn't, as a threat to her status as *capo di tutti capi* of the region. *But it's better to play innocent victim in this case than share that with Pamela,* Dee decided. "The bottom line is that her animosity is affecting *my* bottom line. If I'm not going to be able to sell at the fair, I need a part-time job. Any chance you could use someone at Miss Mary's?"

Dee didn't pull this out of thin air. She'd overheard Pamela complain to Owen Mudd how hard it was to juggle handing out coupons at the fair with running her shop.

Pamela mulled this over. "It's not a bad idea. I could set up a stall at the fair and not just wander through it trying to hand out my coupons."

"And I could manage the store while you ran the stall. Only for a few hours a day. I can't spend too much time away from the motel."

"I can't afford to hire you for more than a few hours a day. On a commission basis. Twenty percent of whatever you sell."

Even though the job was a front, Dee balked at the cheap terms. "Commission isn't enough. I need an hourly rate."

"Fine. Five dollars an hour and ten percent commission."

"The nineteenth-century miners did better than that," Dee muttered.

"Excuse me?"

"Nothing." Dee ignored the fact that the lingerie shop owner was violating the state's mandated minimum wage. She beamed at Pamela and extended her hand. "You've got yourself a new salesperson."

"Great!" Pamela shook Dee's hand. "You can start tomorrow. Get to the shop early so you can pick out the corset you want to wear."

"Corset?" Dee repeated weakly.

"Anyone who works in the shop has to model the merchandise. It's a valuable sales tool. Although . . ." Pamela cast an eye at Dee's body, currently clad in a tank top with a logo from one of the many canceled shows she'd worked on and shorts Dee had made herself by cutting off a pair of ripped jeans at the knees. "The good Lord wasn't generous with you upstairs, so you'll have to wear cutlets to fill out the corset. And a petticoat that covers your thighs, where the good Lord was too generous. Sidebar, they've made great progress with cellulite creams. Anyway, you can pay off the cost of your outfit up front or out of your salary. Sound good?"

"Absolutely," Dee lied. She had a sinking feeling this was going to be an expensive investigative venture.

The women parted ways. Dee loaded her merchandise into the back of her SUV. She hoped she didn't regret the deal she'd struck with Pamela and prayed no one took photos of her dressed in whatever skimpy outfit she'd have to wear. *The last thing I need is to end up as a meme,* she thought.

She pressed her car fob, hopped into the driver's seat, and was about to drive off when her cell rang with a call from Callan Katz. To Dee's recollection, the agent had never rung her before, which was worrisome. She turned off the car engine and answered the call. "Callan, hi. Is everything okay?"

Callan responded with the amped-up energy Dee recognized when her own agent called with news. The dwindling of those calls to nonexistent was one of the main motivators for her career switch. "It's better than okay," the agent said. Dee could practically feel him vibrating with adrenaline through the phone. "I want to sell your Bud cartoons."

"Oh. Phew, I thought something might have happened to Serena or Emmy or Oscar. Well, thanks, I really appreciate the offer. I'm kind of surprised you need a side hustle, but the timing is perfect because I don't have a table at the fair anymore, which leaves me with a lot of goods to sell. I can drop them off at your place whenever."

"No, no, no. I don't want to sell your merch. At least not the craftsy stuff you made yourself. When the show hits, we'll license the images."

*"The show?"* Dee pinched the bridge of her nose. The ancient clock atop Goldsgone's only three-story building had yet to strike noon and she was already bone-weary. "What show? What are you talking about?"

"I'm talking about a TV deal, Deester. I want to sell Bud the Bear as an animated series. In fact, going by a conversation I had two minutes ago with Penny Kandy Animation Studio, I already have."

# CHAPTER 14

Dee's instant reaction was a combination of excitement and utter panic. This wasn't new to her. Every job offer she'd received had triggered the same combination of conflicting emotions. Writing a TV show could be a wonderful or terrible experience and there was no way of predicting which way it would go. The one constant was that whatever the job, good or bad, it took over Dee's life.

She half-listened as Callan prattled on at agent hyper speed, ending with "You'll be able to check out of the motel business and check back into the entertainment industry. You're welcome, my friend. *And* new client."

Callan signed off. Dee didn't move. She felt paralyzed by the call, which had the potential to upend her life. Then she repeated the word "potential' to herself. *That's all this is at the moment,* she thought. *A potential deal. A possibility. A maybe.* No deal had been struck and even if one was, there was no guarantee it would move beyond a pilot script. Dee relaxed. She restarted her engine and headed for the Golden.

"Bud the Bear a TV star!" Sam exclaimed. "Wouldn't that be something."

Dee and her father were in her living room. She'd filled him in on the details of Callan's phone call and he'd reacted much as she expected.

*Three . . . two . . . one . . .* Dee mentally counted down to when Sam would begin riffing on Bud's voice.

"I'm-a so hungry, I could eat a bear, har, har, har." Sam delivered the joke in a deep, goofy voice.

*And there it is.*

Sam rubbed his chin as he pondered another take on the bear. "Do you think Bud has an accent? Southern, maybe. Or British. You know I love doing Brits." He switched gears to prove this. "I say, old chap, might there be a repast nearby? I'm so hungry I could eat the proverbial bear, dontcha know."

"I don't think I have the strength to create the backstory explaining how a Brit bear made his way to the wilds of California," Dee said.

"I'll work on it." Sam said with a rueful smile. "It's a nice break from worrying about being arrested."

Dee sighed. "Someone reported hearing you say you'd like to push Sylvan down a mine, huh?" Sam gave a woeful nod. "Take comfort from knowing you're not alone," she said. "He inspired the same urge in a lot of people."

Sam rubbed his brow. "It's been a rough week, between that and Elmira."

"She's still icing you out? I know she's doing it to the rest of us, but I thought if anyone had a chance at worming their way back into her affections, it would be you."

"If only. I'm contemplating a couple of charm offensives. In the meantime, would you mind if I black out a tooth today when I play Prospector Pete? We haven't had much action at the sluice since everyone started panning for real gold. But I'm hoping I can drum up interest if I really sell Pete, and the tooth helps me get into character."

"Go for it," Dee said. "But I wouldn't include it in your charm offensive."

Sam left to run the sluice. He almost collided with Raul, who was about to knock on Dee's door. Sam mimed, doffing a cap to the sheriff. "Hello there, I didn't kill Sylvan, goodbye now."

He made a quick escape. Raul watched him go. "I'm hearing that from a lot of people. If someone said, 'Hello there, I *did* kill Sylvan,' it would be a big help."

"For all of us."

Dee stood up from her seat on the room's old sofa. She waved Raul in. The spurs he had to wear as part of his costume-uniform jangled with every step he took. He flicked each side of his full-length duster coat out of the way and sat down on one of the room's two ancient club chairs.

"You want coffee?" Dee asked. "Something stronger? Since your comment tells me you haven't homed in on the killer, I assume you've got a non-update update. That's what I call new information that's interesting but doesn't move the story forward, as we say in the TV biz."

"Nothing to drink, thanks. I'm only here because Jeff texted me he learned something interesting he wants to share with both of us."

"He did? I know he went to the city early this morning, but I haven't heard from him since he left." Dee checked her cell phone. "Oh, wait, there's the text. I missed it because I was talking to my dad."

Raul eyed her. "The instincts developed by my years on the force tell me something's up on your end."

Not ready to share her conversation with Callan about a possible Bud the Bear show deal, Dee dodged this. "Raul, your years on the force aren't even a half-dozen, so not sure how fine-tuned those instincts are."

"I joined up when I was twenty-one and I'm twenty-eight now, which means I have seven years on the force, which is one year more than half a dozen, so ha ha."

Dee wagged a finger at him. "And that made you sound like you're twelve."

To Dee's relief, Jeff blew into the apartment, sparing Dee probing questions courtesy of Raul's vaunted instincts. "I have news," he declared, rubbing his hands together in the anticipation of sharing it.

"Does it start with 'I know who killed Sylvan'?" Raul asked. "Because that would really score you some points today."

"No, but I can deliver something almost as good. A lot more suspects."

Raul groaned. "*No.* That's the opposite of good. We don't need *more suspects*. There's barely time to investigate the ones we already have."

"Trust me, this is valuable intel." Jeff plopped down on the sofa. "I know why Sylvan Burr was trying to buy up Goldsgone and Foundgold. It wasn't about investing in real estate or even an expensive homage to his family's roots in the area. He was competing with another tech bro, Arvi Garner, to see who could buy up a whole town first. The three commas—that's tech slang for billionaires—have helicopters, houses all over the world, and yachts the size of Rhode Island. Owning an entire town is the only thing left to show off with."

"I've read about people buying half-abandoned villages in Italy and Portugal," Dee said.

"Anyone can do that," Jeff scoffed. "But to buy a functioning town in America? That's three-comma-club epic."

"I'm kind of sorry Sylvan died before he could buy

Goldsgone," Dee said. "It would have been worth it to see someone one-up Verity."

"Obviously, this widens the field of suspects," Jeff said. "We already know Sylvan's dealings were causing a lot of friction. If he wanted to buy all of Goldsgone and Foundgold, that's even more people he could have bumped up against. And then there's Arvi Garner's company. He's the self-driving car messiah, the only person who might actually be able to make it work without having the cars go haywire and mow down innocent people. Tech employees can develop intense attachments to their leaders. Attachments that border on cultish. One of them might have gone over the edge and offed his boss's competition."

"This could be something," Raul vaguely acknowledged. "There's also the financial angle. There's a lot of abandoned mines that fall within the property lines of Goldsgone and Foundgold, including the one where we found Burr. If someone buys up every inch of the towns, they could lay claim to the mines. And if the rumors about the rains exposing new veins of gold are proven true in even a single mine, it could generate a fortune. Of course it would take buckets of money to stabilize the mine and do the exploratory work."

"Sylvan had more money than he knew what to do with," Dee pointed out. "Digging up gold would make a nice hobby for him. Plus, there's his familial connection to the area. The gold his ancestor mined is what kicked off the Burr family fortune."

"Someone could have lured him to the mine where he died by telling him the rains exposed a new vein," Raul posited.

"Ice Cream Ida is the most vocal anti-selling-out-to-Sylvan-Burr Goldsgonedian I've run into so far," Dee said.

"She's got a deep and fierce attachment to the land. Uh-oh, that sounded old-timey."

"Afraid it did," Jeff said. "You even added a twang to 'deep and fierce.'" He got up and retrieved the miner talk jar from the kitchen counter. He held it out to Dee. "Quarter in the jar."

"Dang, I'm racking up an even bigger bill. Argh, I said 'dang.'"

"Two quarters."

Dee dug the quarters out of her back pocket and dropped them in the jar. Jeff put it back on the counter. "Ida may be Goldsgone's biggest champion after Verity," she continued. "And she's not someone who could be swayed by a fat check. She's worth taking a look at. Although I'd hate to see anything happen to the creator of those Sweet Licks Homemade Pumpkin Ice Cream Sandwiches. Not gonna lie, I'm kind of addicted to those."

Jeff got a dreamy look in his eyes. "They're awesome, but nothing beats her homemade mint chip ice cream."

"Except her homemade Rocky Road," Raul said with an equally dreamy expression.

"All right, we're agreed that Ida's a suspect, but we're hoping it's not her," Dee said. "I saw Pamela and Gracie arguing, which I found suspicious because I got the sense they somehow know each other, even though this is supposedly the first time Gracie's ever been to Goldsgone. I finagled a part-time job at Miss Mary's Unmentionables. I can use it to poke my nose into their relationship. I'll also see if I can sniff out other members of the anti–Sylvan Burr faction."

"You've got a job on top of the motel and the fair?" Jeff asked, concerned. "That's a lot."

"Verity fired me from the fair. She drafted those creepy

Trapp twins as spies and caught me sneaking home to sleep instead of staying in the Goldsgone tent. I should report her to whatever agency handles intern labor complaints. I ran into Gillie, Verity's nephew, after the debacle. He implied Verity might be harboring secrets that would damage her status as Goldsgone's number one fan. Maybe you can get one of her minions to rat her out. "

"I'll talk to Verity first. I bet there's a fine somewhere on the books for taking advantage of adolescents." The relish with which Raul delivered this on his way out the door indicated that if there wasn't a fine already on the books, there would be soon. Or at the least, the threat of one.

Seconds after Raul left, Dee's phone sounded a text alert. She checked it and her stomach clutched. "It's Callan. He needs to see me immediately. I have news too. Of a different kind." She told Jeff about her conversation with the agent.

"Dee, that's fantastic," he enthused. "I'm happy for you."

Conflicted, Dee began pacing. "I don't know. I mean, the chance to create my own show is exciting. But I have a job—a job that means a lot to me. Running the Golden with you. I can't give that up, but I don't know how I'd do both."

Jeff put his hands on Dee's shoulders, forcing her to stand still. "Stop worrying. We'll find a way to make this work, I promise. *Go*. Take the meeting with Callan. Make Bud a TV star."

Dee texted Callan to meet her at the All-in-One. The choice of location was purposeful. Any visit to the store offered another opportunity to fix things with Elmira. Callan texted back he was already there getting coffee, so she hopped into her car and made the short drive to Elmira's place of business, nabbing the last available parking space.

"I love this store," she loudly announced upon entering, drawing the attention of other customers. "You can't get better deals anywhere else for miles. If I could, I'd take one of everything."

Dee caught the eye of Elmira, who was behind the counter. The shop owner quickly turned away, but not before Dee glimpsed a small smile. Counting it as progress, she made her way to the café, where Callan was waiting for her at a table.

"I got you a coffee drink." He handed her a to-go cup holding a beverage topped with a froth of milk. "It's made from special beans that are personally delivered to me from Central America in unmarked brown bags. One of my clients is a customs agent who's written a screenplay. He won't tell me how he gets the beans, and made it very clear it's in my best interests to stop asking. But I'm telling you, the difference in taste from the swill you usually get here is phenomenal."

Dee took the drink and thanked him, thinking it wise not to mention that first, she hated coffee, and second, the All-in-One had run out of Callan's beans long ago and was making his drinks with the industrial-brand coffee they bought in bulk.

"So"—Callan tapped an anticipatory drumroll on the table and grinned—"it's official. Penny Kandy wants to make a script deal. Congratulations."

"Thank you. Wow." Dee's stomach churned as she processed the development. "I don't know what to say."

"How about, 'Whoo-hoo!'" Callan fist-pumped.

"*Whoo-hoo!*" Dee copied, allowing herself to feel excited. She loved drawing her Bud cartoons and was proud of how they'd become the Golden's brand. An animated series would take this to the next level. The attention would draw new guests to the motel . . . even make it iconic. A series would be a win-win for both Dee and the Golden.

"The studio does have one note."

Dee snapped out of her reverie. "They do?" she asked, wary. "What is it?" A studio note could be as simple as a name change . . .

"Instead of a bear, can you make Bud a squirrel?"

. . . or a complete up-ender.

Instead of letting loose with a loud, frustrated scream, Dee opted for simple and direct: "No."

"I thought that would be your first reaction," Callan said, "but hear me out. The thinking behind this does make sense. Squirrels are small and cute. They can get into places bears can't. Plus, there's precedent with successful squirrel animation. Rocky and Bullwinkle are still in the zeitgeist."

Dee maintained her even tone. "It's Bud the Bear. Not Bud the Squirrel."

"Squirrels are vintage. They're cool."

"It's Bud *the Bear.* Not Bud *the Squirrel,*" Dee repeated.

"You could use your rendering of Bud. All you'd have to do is shrink him and add a bushy tail."

*"It's Bud the Bear. Not Bud the Squirrel."* This time, she delivered it through gritted teeth.

"I'll tell them you'll think about it. Congrats again." Callan drained his cup and smacked his lips. "Man, this is good."

On the drive back to the Golden, Dee relived the conversation. She chided herself for not articulating why the protagonist of the cartoon had to be a bear, specifically Bud. She made a decision. She pulled over to the side of the road and called Callan. The call went to voicemail, so she left a message:

"Hi, it's Dee. I wanted you to know I'm not being stubborn or arbitrary when I insisted the main character had to be a bear. My whole series of drawings is predicated on the humor of a bear doing human actions, while the humans around him react to the fact he's a bear. The humor, at least how I've written it, disappears if the character is a tiny squirrel. Also, squirrels are more generic than bears, in that you can find them anywhere. But bears are specific to the region I'm writing about, which makes a possible series more unique and hopefully more of a draw for viewers. Anyway, I am excited about the deal, but had to explain why I feel so strongly about the studio's note. Thanks."

Dee ended the call and her heartfelt message—happy she'd shared the reasons behind her resistance. Her phone rang. She saw the caller was Callan. *Wow, that was fast. He must have been impressed by my message.* Suffused with confidence, she answered.

"Hey," Callan said. "I saw you called. Whassup?"

*What is the point of voicemail if everyone ignores it?!* "I left you a message," Dee said, trying not to snap at him. "Listen to it."

"'Kay."

He signed off. Dee, feeling irritable, waited for his response. A minute later, Callan texted her a thumbs-up. Optimism replaced irritability and Dee shot back a thumbs-up of her own.

She started her car and was about to drive off. Then she spotted something she'd missed when she pulled off the road. The techies' car was on the opposite side of the road, parked at the trailhead she knew went past a batch of abandoned gold mines. More interesting was the glimpse she caught of another car tucked away in the woods, not far from where the techies had parked. Dee never would have noticed it if she didn't recognize the dented fender of the Froelichs' old sedan.

She stared at the car, puzzling out its presence. The Froelichs' car was purposefully hidden in a thick grove of trees. Could Ed and Trish be following the well-funded techies' hunt for gold, hoping to tap into it for themselves? Dee wondered. She texted the odd sighting to Raul, starting the message with: **I may be overly suspicious and possibly paranoid, but . . .** The road was narrow. For all she knew, the Froelichs had pulled their car far off the road to protect it from being dinged by another car. Still, in a case that had more dead ends than a Goldsgone trail map, anything out of the ordinary was worth further examination.

# CHAPTER 15

The next morning, Dee happily tended to motel business. She checked out guests, then changed over their rooms to prepare for new arrivals. She piled a load of sheets into the industrial washing machine and removed another load from the dryer. The midday temperature hovered in the upper nineties, which amplified the dryer heat, and Dee fought to keep the perspiration on her head from dripping onto the newly clean sheets.

*If my show goes to series, I will pay someone well to do this job,* she thought as she tussled with folding a sheet. *And once Elmira is talking to me again, I have to get her to show me her trick for folding a fitted sheet.*

Motelier tasks in order, Dee prepped for her next venture: her first part-time shift at Miss Mary's Unmentionables. She took a quick shower, her second of the warm day, adding a rare splash of perfume as an afterthought. Next she put on makeup, using navy eyeliner to emphasize her hazel eyes, a trick a makeup artist she'd worked with on a show had recommended. Dee finished with a setting powder she hoped would prevent everything from melting off her face in the day's heat, then set out for the shop.

On the trek to the parking lot, she saw Jeff and Mister removing an ancient canoe that was strapped to the roof of Jeff's SUV. "Look what I found in the county dump," Jeff called to her, gesturing to the canoe with pride.

"A canoe from the dump. That doesn't concern me at all" was Dee's dry response.

"The board games are fine, but we still need outdoor activities for our guests," Jeff said. "It'd be great to offer them a chance to canoe on one of the amazing lakes around here. Tomorrow, Mister and I are going to take it out for a test run on Mirror Lake."

"I gave it a quick once-over," Mister said. "Didn't see any cracks or holes, but I need to give it a closer look. Of course, we won't know for sure until we're on the water."

"Very reassuring," Dee said, continuing her deadpan delivery. "When you do take it out for a paddle, I highly recommend putting your cells in plastic bags so they're functional if you need to SOS for help."

Mister acknowledged the advice with a wink and nod. "We'll be okay. Hey, if you see the missus, tell her what I'm up to." He motioned to the canoe, now listing to the side on the ground next to him. "She went off with the tech bros on another tour of old mines. Their leader may be gone, but that's not stopping them from picking up where he left off searching for a mine to reactivate. I will never understand how rich people always need to get richer."

Dee bid Jeff and Mister goodbye, then headed for Goldsgone and Miss Mary's. The sun blazed down on her during the short walk from the parking lot to the store and Dee welcomed the chance to escape it in the cool confines of Miss Mary's air-conditioning.

Unfortunately, Pamela had other plans for her.

"I don't have time to teach you how to work my computerized sales system," the shop owner said. "So I'll run the store and you can work the crafts fair, modeling outfits and handing out coupons. I took the liberty of selecting the corsets for you to wear. Every hour, change into one of these."

She handed Dee a half-dozen corsets, each skimpier than the next. Panicked by the thought of parading through the fair in any of them, Dee wracked her brain for a way out. "These are so beautiful and delicate," she said, landing on one. "The only thing is, they're so intricate that I think I'd waste a lot of time changing into them."

She held her breath as Pamela evaluated this. "You're right," she said to Dee's relief. "We'll skip the corsets. I have another idea I've been wanting to try."

*There's the walk of shame when you leave a date's house the next morning wearing the same clothes you showed up in the night before*, a mortified Dee thought. *And then there's this . . .*

Clad in the ugliest of brown long johns and the kind of floppy hat worn by vaudeville comedians, she plodded back and forth through the street fair with her head down, carrying a sign: I WANNA TRADE THESE LONG JOHNS FOR AN UNMENTIONABLE! The reactions from vendors and shoppers ranged from avoiding her out of embarrassment to roars of laughter—*at* her, not with her. Her cheeks flamed, adding to the heat that had already destroyed her makeup, and she silently prayed the perfume she'd dabbed on would cover the fact she'd sweated through her deodorant.

*"Dee?"*

She looked up to see Jonas staring at her. His expression broadened into a smile that threatened to turn into a laugh.

"Don't," she warned, brandishing her sign at him.

"Sorry." He choked a little as he swallowed the laugh. "But *whaaaaa*?"

"Pamela's using me as a guinea pig to see if humor helps increase sales."

"And?"

"I don't know," Dee grumbled. "Maybe. People laugh and then are curious, so they go inside the store to check out the unmentionables and shop. I hope. This better be worth it for her. These long johns are miserably uncomfortable. I'm so hot."

"But not at all 'hot.'" Jonas placed air quotes around his pun.

Dee glared at him, then sighed. "It's my own fault. I was trying to get out of parading through the fair in a variety of corsets, which I'd give anything to be wearing now."

"You need a break. I'll buy you a lemonade." He held out his hand. "C'mon, Pappy."

She gave him a baleful look, then took his hand. "Sure. I've earned a break by now."

Jonas led her to a table that was blessedly under an umbrella and went to fetch drinks from a stall in front of the Golden Grub Café. He returned with two large lemonades and handed one to Dee.

"Thank you," she said. Dee took a few large gulps of the cold drink, then leaned back against the brick wall behind her chair.

"You're welcome." Jonas leaned in, eyes twinkling. "And you may not look hot, but you look adorable. Which is even sexier."

Dee blushed and smiled. "It's not, but I love you for saying that." She took another, smaller sip of her drink. "Despite this"—she gestured to her long johns—"I'm glad we ran into each other. Something came up I wanted to run by you. What do you know about Sylvan Burr's plot to buy up Goldsgone?"

The twinkle disappeared from Jonas's eyes. "Wow. That's a one-eighty from long johns and corset talk. I assume you mean the deals Burr was secretly cutting behind a lot of people's backs, including mine. The deals that would have destroyed Goldsgone, on top of depriving me of real estate commissions."

Dee raised an eyebrow. "In that order?"

"Yes," Jonas said, defensive. Her gaze didn't waver and he caved. "Okay, fine. Not in that order. I'm more ticked off that he was cheating me out of commissions. Although I don't think it was intentional. The money's too small to make a difference to a guy like him. His goal was to line up enough sellers to put pressure on the holdouts and eventually make Goldsgone his latest rich-boy toy." He glanced at Dee, suddenly suspicious. "Are you trying to suss out if I belong on your list of suspects? If you are, you owe me for the lemonade."

Dee grinned. "I wasn't sussing you out. I only wondered if you knew anything Raul didn't. I truly appreciate this." She held up the lemonade, then took a sip. "And also, you answering my question so honestly. Can I ask you something else that has nothing to do with nefarious plots or murder?"

*"Please."*

"You're Elmira's cousin. Any advice on how we can win her back as a friend? I miss her. We all do."

Jonas thought for a moment, then said, "I hate to give a pat answer, like 'give her time,' but . . . give her time. She'll come to realize y'all did what you did out of love. In the meantime, the rest of us are grateful that someone cut off her baking pipeline. I know I speak for a lot of people when I say we were tired of buying her baked goods and lying about how good they were. I think I may have sickened a raccoon who dug one of her brownies out of the garbage."

Dee laughed in recognition. "Some of my guests don't take our warning about carefully disposing of their trash seriously, but when Bud or another animal gets into the garbage, the one thing they always leave behind is Elmira's baked goods. Still . . . I worry that the longer it takes for her to come around, the more chance there is that she won't."

"She will. Trust me on this. Frankly, there are so few people in Foundgold, you can't risk holding on to a grudge. You'll run out of friends." Jonas shook his empty lemonade cup. "This was good, but we need something colder. How about one of Ida's homemade ice cream sandwiches?"

"You don't have to ask me twice." An eager Dee rose.

On a mission, the two walked briskly toward Sweet Licks Ice Cream Parlor and Soda Fountain. Dee sniffed the air and slowed down. "Huh. That's weird. I smell fire."

"It's not weird." Jonas, a grim expression on his face, pointed toward the ice cream parlor. Smoke rose from the building.

Dee gasped. "Oh no! A fire could take out half this town."

The two raced to the building housing the parlor, Jonas in the lead. "The fire's in the back," he called to Dee.

She caught up to him and they ran around the building's corner to the back of it . . . and stopped short.

Ice Cream Ida was holding court over a bonfire she and a few friends were feeding with what appeared to be flyers. She saw Dee and Jonas and waved. "Hey there, you two. Wanna feed the fire?" With a cackle, she dropped another flyer on the flames.

"Ida, a bonfire?" Jonas didn't bother to modulate his

anger. "You know you're not supposed to light them. It's summer, the town is dry as dust. You could burn the whole place down."

Ida responded with a dismissive snort. "Gimme a break. I got seventy-nine years in this town. I think I know how to keep a bonfire from getting outta hand." She tossed another flyer on it.

"She does these all the time," Jonas told Dee. "I thought she'd have the sense not to light one on a blistering hot day."

"What are you burning?" Dee asked, now more curious than alarmed.

"Every We Buy Old Buildings flyer that snake Sylvan Burr had his people sneak into Goldsgone and Foundgold mailboxes. He made sure his name wasn't anywhere, but we knew who was behind 'em. They say don't speak ill of the dead, but sometimes the dead deserve it. He was set to destroy our towns for his own selfish needs. And he wasn't above making nasty threats to get his way."

This sparked Dee's interest. "Really? What kind of threats?"

Ida pressed her thin lips together and broke eye contact with Dee, giving off the sense that she regretted her words. "Nothing. Silly stuff. Hey, Zeke, hand me the last bunch."

A grizzled old man, who so resembled a nineteenth-century miner that he might as well have stepped out of a painting, handed Ida a fat stack of flyers. She dropped the pile onto the bonfire. The flames exploded, sending sparks and Ida's pals scurrying.

"Alrighty, we're done here," Ida declared. She limped over to a pail of water, lifted it up, and doused the fire. "Check for hot spots. I'd hate to go back on my promise not to set the town on fire."

Jonas appeared ready to launch into a lecture on fire safety, but Dee pulled him away. "Come on."

He reluctantly went with her. Dee kept going until she was sure Ida couldn't see or hear them. "Jonas, did you notice how Ida suddenly shut up when I asked about the threats?"

"Yes, but I figured it was none of my business. If she was being pressured to sell, she has the right to keep it to herself."

Dee continued, undeterred. "Did you see the Danger, Keep Out signs plastered all over the parlor's back door? And the heavy lock on the door?"

"Yes, and so? She's protecting Sweet Licks."

"*Over*protecting. What's dangerous about ice cream?"

"You have a point," Jonas acknowledged. "But what exactly are you getting at?"

Dee glanced around to make sure they were alone, then dropped her voice to a whisper as an extra precaution. "What if Sylvan made a threat to Ida that led to his murder? If he did, the secret is behind the door with all those Danger, Keep Out signs. We need to get inside the back room of the parlor when no one is around."

Jonas gaped at her. "Dee, honey, I'm a real estate agent. I can't risk breaking and entering into a building, especially one I have nothing to do with. It would ruin me."

"You're right. You can't do it." Dee lifted a corner of her mouth in a half smile. "But I can."

# CHAPTER 16

At two in the morning, Dee and Jeff crept up to the ice cream parlor's back door. Dee had realized she'd need backup, so she'd called on Jeff to assist her. Not to be left out, her dad, Sam acted as a lookout.

"It's so peaceful here at night," she whispered to Jeff. "No evil Verity aura. No competitive shopkeepers. No tourists."

Jeff glanced around nervously. "The quiet makes it extra scary to me."

"You need to calm down."

"Sorry. This is my first time breaking and entering. And my last . . . hopefully." Jeff held up his gloved hands. "I hate wearing these. It's eighty degrees."

"They'll prevent us from leaving fingerprints."

"My hands are sweating so much they'll be able to identify me by DNA from the drops that drip through the gloves."

"We'll go fast, promise."

Dee slid the bolt cutters she'd carried under her arm into her gloved hands. Keeping the cutters at the motel in case a guest lost a lock key or forgot a combination had proven fortuitous. "We'll hurry in, hunt around for anything incriminating, and hurry out. Before we leave, I'll open the cash register, so that in the morning, it'll just look like your average attempted burglary." She held up the bolt cutters. "This'll break the lock in one snap."

She grabbed the padlock on the door. It came off in her hand, along with the rusty, antiquated hardware attached to it.

"Or that," Jeff said.

"Even better." Dee handed the bolt cutters to her father. "Hang back in the shadows. If you see anyone coming, text me. I've got my alerts on vibrate, so I'll feel the message, but there won't be any sound."

Sam snapped to attention and saluted Dee. "Sir, yessir!" He delivered this in the whispered voice of a character.

"I don't know if I'm talking to you or Sergeant Sassafras from the Butternut Squash Brigade," Dee whispered back, annoyed but also amused. "Either way"—she drew in a deep breath and released it—"cover us, we're going in. Wow. I never thought I'd say that in real life. I'd never write it into a script, though. It's a cliché. Like 'Get a room' or—"

*"Dee,"* Jeff said sharply. "Stop talking and let's get this over with."

"Yes, right, sorry. Not gonna lie, I'm nervous too."

Dee slowly pulled the worn old door open slowly in case it creaked. It didn't, so she opened it faster and entered the parlor's storage room, followed by Jeff.

The room was pitch black. Jeff bumped into Dee, almost sending her flying into a metal shelf rack stocked with boxes of ice cream cones and giant jars of sprinkles. She pushed him off and turned on her phone's flashlight, aiming it at the ground to avoid drawing attention to their illicit activity. Jeff did likewise and the two set to work uncovering whatever it was Sylvan Burr might have been holding over Ice Cream Ida's head.

Assuming it would be in the parlor's private confines, they focused the search in the storage room. Ida didn't have an office, just a rickety desk stacked with papers. Dee rifled through them. "I don't see anything but bills here," she whispered to Jeff.

"She's not lying about how many flavors of ice cream she serves." Jeff had opened a door on one of the parlor's giant freezers. He peered inside. "There's gotta be more than twenty flavors here. Ooh, pecan praline. My favorite. You think she'd notice if a container was missing?"

"Yes! We leave the place exactly as we—"

"Hold up. I found something."

"You did?" Dee aborted her search and hurried to him. "What?"

"Check this out." Jeff pointed to the lid on the container of pecan praline ice cream. "Ida's big brag is her ice cream is homemade."

In the light of the freezer, Dee read the label out loud: " 'Newcomb Suppliers and Food Management.' " She typed a search into her phone and held the result up to Jeff. "A national supplier of foodstuffs, including frozen desserts."

"Maybe pecan praline is too complicated for her to make, so it's the one flavor she orders from a supplier?" Jeff guessed.

"We need to check all the lids."

They examined each container, shivering with cold as they made their way through the freezer. Every flavor was from Newcomb Suppliers & Food Management.

The two moved on to the second freezer. "Do you see what I see?" Jeff asked.

"I do." Dee pointed to a large cardboard box stamped: OATMEAL COOKIES. Next to it, another box: CHOCOLATE CHIP COOKIES. "I wondered why there wasn't an oven in here to bake her 'signature cookies.' Because Ida doesn't bake them."

"Newcomb Suppliers does."

"Exactly." Dee shut the freezer door and rubbed her arms for warmth. "We've found Ida's secret. Her homemade ice cream and cookies are made by . . ." She read from her phone, "'The number one food supplier in the Western United States.'" Dee had a revelation. "I bet that's why Ida's always lighting bonfires, even in the summer. She's burning the lids and boxes to get rid of the evidence. It's false advertising. All Ida does is put a scoop of Newcomb's ice cream between two of their cookies."

"Maybe she thinks that classifies them as homemade? Because she's doing the sandwich part herself?"

"That's a reach."

"I know. But she—or Newcomb—does make a good ice cream sandwich, and I'd hate to see the parlor close because she got in trouble for selling a fake product."

"Forget getting in trouble for selling faked goods," Dee delivered in an urgent whisper. "It might have led to *murder.* If Sylvan uncovered this and threatened to reveal it if she didn't sell him her building, it could have driven her to kill him. We need to let Raul know what we discovered, but without incriminating ourselves."

"How exactly do we do that?" Jeff asked.

"I'm thinking while I do a little messing up to fake a robbery."

Dee tossed around some papers from the desk and opened the parlor's cash register; then she and Jeff hurried outside.

Dee closed the door behind them, which barely stayed closed, due to its decaying hinges.

Sam scurried over. "You find anything?"

"We did." Dee motioned toward Jeff's EV, and the three headed to it, being careful to mind what was underfoot and might create unwelcome noise. "And because Raul will recognize our voices, when we get home, you're going to leave an anonymous message in a character voice on the sheriff's station's voicemail telling them exactly what we found."

Hours later, Dee was back once more in long johns pimping for Miss Mary's. After an hour of baking under the sun's relentless glare, she retreated inside the shop, ready to use the excuse she almost fainted from the heat if Pamela gave her any grief for the unscheduled break. But Pamela wasn't in the shop—at least not in the sales area. Dee heard her voice coming from the stockroom, along with another voice she recognized: Gracie's. Dee pretended to be examining a display of panties hanging toward the back of the shop, which positioned her closer to the other women.

"Gracie, sweetie, I can't begin to tell you how sorry I am. I never would have . . ."

Dee couldn't make out what Pamela, who sounded like she was in tears, said next. The shop owner blew her noise.

"I'm over it," Gracie responded.

"Oh, thank goodness. I'm so relieved. You know I love you. I always have."

Dee's eyes widened. This was news. *Huge* news.

There was a pause where Dee assumed they were hugging . . . or more.

"So we're good with the plan?" Pam asked.

"A hundred percent. I'm really glad I found you. You were always my favorite stepmom."

Dee's eyes grew even wider. *Stepmom! Wow. That is not where I thought this was going. But plan? What plan? Does it have anything to do with Sylvan's death?*

Dee heard footsteps, then the shop's back door open and close. Pamela, now alone, drew back the curtain separating the stockroom from the showroom. Dee grabbed a pair of underpants from the rack and held them up to her. "I like these," she said, lamely trying to cover her proximity to the showroom.

"They're granny panties," Pamela said, casting a suspicious eye on her. "Extra, extra large."

"I know," Dee fibbed. "I like large underwear. Much more comfortable."

"You'd have to belt those," Pamela said, clearly not buying what Dee was trying to sell.

"They still beat thongs. I'm not a fan of butt floss." Dee rehung the underwear. "I came in for a minute because I was dying out there. I need to hydrate."

"You can take a bottle," Pamela said, gesturing to the small fridge from which she sold bottled water to parched tourists for a nice markup from their big-box bulk price. "Then consider your shift over. I'll pay you for the day, but I won't be needing you anymore."

"But the humor angle is working," Dee protested. The startling revelation of the relationship between Gracie and Pamela strengthened Dee's drive to keep the job. She had to uncover the plan the two were plotting.

"It is," Pamela said. "But I think the long-johns bit would work even better with a man wearing them."

"But—"

"Thank you. And goodbye."

"I need to get my tote bag with my change of clothes. It's in the back." Dee grabbed at one last straw to visit the stockroom and sniff around for a possible clue.

"I'll get it for you." Pamela disappeared, then quickly reappeared with Dee's tote bag. "You can keep the long johns. I'll need a larger size for a man."

"Can I at least change?"

"The dressing room is for customers, not nosy ex-employees."

Pamela's tone brooked no pushback. Smarting from the double whammy of losing a priceless chance to snoop and being fired for a sexist reason, even if it was a cover on Pamela's part, Dee hefted her tote bag over her shoulder and slunk out of Miss Mary's.

Dee took the dusty old back streets to avoid the crafts fair. She wasn't in the mood for the good-natured teasing of the vendors and the last thing she wanted to do was run into Verity, who had probably already heard via the Goldsgone warp-speed gossip pipeline that Pamela had fired her. She knew Verity would relish an opportunity to rub this in Dee's face, especially since it came on the heels of her ouster from the fair.

Disheartened, Dee trudged up Callahan Way, named after a successful prospector whose charming nineteenth-century cottage had recently been turned into a tearoom. She saw Raul, dressed in full old-time sheriff mufti, ticketing an illegally parked Porsche SUV, and her spirits picked up. She called out his name and waved to him, evaluating the best way to subtly find out if he'd received Sam's anonymous message and investigated the goings-on at Ice Cream Ida's.

Raul slapped a ticket on the Porsche and strode over to Dee, spurs jangling. "I was looking for you."

His tone indicated it wasn't for a cheery reason. "Glad you nailed that Porsche," Dee said, aiming for a jocular tone. "I hate when people think the parking rules don't apply to them, especially when they're driving cars that cost more than any of us would make in a year. Good job, Sheriff."

She gave him two thumbs-up, but her flat-footed attempt at flattery failed. Raul glared at her. "I got an 'anonymous' call from Barry Balloony Baloney telling me I needed to investigate Ice Cream Ida, who's selling homemade ice cream under false pretenses. Then I got a call from the kid who's working a summer job with Ida saying someone broke into her storeroom. Didn't take my detective credentials to ID the perp in this case."

"You recognized the voice of Barry Balloony Baloney?" Dee asked, genuinely surprised. "That cartoon was barely on a year."

"I watched it as a kid when I stayed overnight at my *abuela*'s. She couldn't afford cable. I took what I could get."

"That show was a mess. What do balloons and baloney have to do with each other? And with a Barry? Nothing made sense. You can't build a show on alliteration. There has to be connective tissue."

"I'll remember that if I'm ever building a show—which I never will be, because I'm in law enforcement and should be arresting *you* and your pals for breaking and entering."

"But we didn't break and enter," Dee said, calling up her minimal acting skills to project a naïve innocence. "The lock came off in my hands. We were worried someone might have tried to break in and only went inside Ida's to make sure everything was okay."

"Did you, now?" Raul's sarcastic tone indicated he wasn't buying this for a second.

"Yes, we did." Dee stubbornly stuck to her story. "Luckily for Ida, we didn't find an evidence of a burglary. But we did find evidence of illegal activity. Activity that could incriminate Ida in Sylvan's murder. Raul, she's selling her product under false pretenses. It's not homemade at all. She uses products from a food services company. Sylvan Burr was trying to buy up the town, and Ida was one of his most outspoken opponents. What if he found out about what she was doing and tried to blackmail Ida into selling her property to him?"

The look on Raul's handsome young face transitioned from anger to reluctant resignation. "It's possible," he said. "But no more making up stories like you just 'happened on' Ida's broken lock. You got it? You may write fiction, but I'm not one of your TV bosses you're trying to sell a script to."

"The lock did come off in my hand, but you're right about everything else," Dee admitted, chastised. "I'm sorry."

"I need to get back to the station." Raul began walking toward Main Street. Dee kept pace with him. "Just so you know," he said, "when I checked out Ida's storeroom, I saw what you saw and confronted her about it. She confessed, but explained she's only been using the Newcomb supplier for about the last year when she began feeling her age in a big way. She's got bad arthritis in her hands and a lot of other places and didn't have the strength and stamina to make her own product anymore. She sold her industrial oven to pay for the increased cost of ingredients from Newcomb."

"Oh." Dee felt for the elderly woman. Still . . . "There is the chance Sylvan found out about this and threatened to expose Ida. And she lured him to the mine, then killed him."

"There would be," Raul acknowledged. "Except Ida

has an iron-clad alibi for the time of Sylvan's death. She slipped on a puddle of melted ice cream in her shop from a cone a kid dropped and banged up her hip pretty bad. She spent the night at Gold County Medical Center."

"I did notice she was limping at the bonfire where she burned up Sylvan's files," Dee said, feeling morose as another suspect in Sylvan's death went up in metaphorical flames.

"If it makes you feel better, I called her out on false advertising. She has to stop pitching her ice cream and cookies as homemade or face the consequences." Raul noticed Dee's gloomy expression. "We'll get Sylvan's killer, Dee. Trust me on this."

"I only hope Murder Motel survives the notoriety."

The stagecoach clip-clopped by, filled with families laughing and chattering with each other. It followed the trail into the woods behind Goldsgone, and the sound of the horse's hooves faded.

For all Dee's issues with Verity and jokes about the kitschy aspects of the historic town, she realized she'd come to be quite fond of it. And she truly loved Foundgold and the little rustic paradise in the woods that was the Golden.

Jobless and fair-less, and still stuck in long johns, a dispirited Dee walked to her car, got into it, and drove home.

# CHAPTER 17

Dee reached the Golden's small lot. As she parked, she realized she and Raul had been so caught up in discussing Ida, she'd forgotten to share the news that Pamela was Grace's stepmother. She texted him this new development, then exited the car.

She saw Jeff and Mister crossing the parking area from where they'd stowed the canoe next to the pool area. Both were sopping wet. Neither looked happy. "I'm guessing the canoe lesson at Mirror Lake didn't go well."

"It's way harder than it looks," Jeff said. "I had trouble getting the hang of it."

"He was a disaster," Mister said, not bothering to mince words. "No matter what I told him, we wound up going in circles and then tipped over. My recommendation is he stick to dry land."

"Which I plan to do," Jeff said. "I'm going to towel off, then go to the outdoor supply company and see if I can trade in the canoe for a mountain bike."

Recalling how poorly he'd fared on an electric bike, Dee shot a concerned look at Mister, who raised an eyebrow in return.

"Enough about me," Jeff said. "Why in tarnation are you still in those ugly long johns?"

"Quarter in the miner jar for 'tarnation,' and the short answer is that I'm no longer an employee of Miss Mary's Unmentionables. I'll fill you in later."

Mister studied her unsightly outfit thoughtfully. "You plan on keeping those?"

"God no. They'll be a bunch of rags as soon as I can take a scissor to them."

"I'm sure Missus could make use of them as undergarments, especially when there's a chill to the night air."

"They're hers. I'll wash them and leave them under the big bell."

Mister gave her a happy smile. "Thanks muchly. I'll tell her the good news." He headed off into the woods to his and Missus's encampment.

"I never thought I'd be in a universe where a pair of hideous old long johns are someone's good news," Dee said, watching him go. "Yet here I am."

Jeff left to change into dry clothes and Dee went to her apartment to shed the loathed long johns. Her path crossed with Ed Froelich's. He was hurrying out of the lobby carrying a full grocery bag.

Ed started at the sight of Dee. "Oh, hey there." He spoke in a casual tone, but his guilty expression sent a different message. "I picked up a few snack bags and left money for them on the lobby counter."

"Hi, Ed." The bag's heft belied his claim he'd only picked up a few snack bags. Knowing the strain the Froelichs were under, Dee chose not to call him on this, but she wasn't going to pass up a chance to play detective. "How was your hike the day before yesterday?"

"Hike? What hike?" he asked.

Dee picked up on his effort to sound puzzled and pressed on. "I saw your car parked in the woods between here and the All-in-One. Since it wasn't anywhere near the stream you usually go to pan, I figured you were taking a break for a hike."

Ed flushed so red, Dee feared he might have a stroke. He took a minute to swallow and calm himself. He nervously shifted the bag from one hand to another. She waited patiently for the excuse the accountant was obviously trying to come up with.

"Oh, that," Ed said, adding a dismissive chuckle for effect. "The 'check engine' light came on. I was afraid we were going to overheat, so I pulled over to rest the engine. But everything seemed fine. Must be an electrical short circuit." He let out a sigh of what sounded like relief. "Gotta go. Trish is gonna think I got lost in the woods." He scurried off, taking his snacks and lies with him.

Dee stepped inside her apartment, where Nugget yawned a hello, then went back to sleep. In the way one yawn triggers another, Dee also yawned. It occurred to her she'd only caught a few hours of sleep after sneaking into Ida's. She checked the time on her phone. *How can it be only eleven a.m.?* she wondered. It felt like she'd endured an entire day. Deciding she'd earned a nap, Dee texted Jeff to hand off all her motel duties that arose in the next couple of hours, then ditched the long johns for an oversized T-shirt and cotton drawstring pants. Nugget was sprawled over half the couch, so she fit herself around the dog, claiming his large tummy for her pillow.

Dee closed her eyes. Questions surrounding Sylvan's murder instantly began swirling around in her mind: *Why are the surviving Core Four, Gracie excepted, so unaffected by Sylvan's death? In terms of Gracie, Pamela was her stepmother? What was the deal with that? And does their mysterious plan have anything to do with Sylvan's death? Ida might be in the clear as a suspect, but what about the other Goldsgonedians who hated Sylvan for bullying them and their friends into selling their property? And the Froelichs are up to something—but what?*

*All good questions,* Dee thought. *And I'm way too tired to answer any of them right now.*

She woke up two hours later with no answers, but feeling better. She leashed up Nugget and the two left the apartment for a walk. She saw techies Gavin and Austin emerge from the Rivian and decided to pull the same passive-aggressive, catch-'em-by-surprise move on them that she'd pulled on Ed.

"Hi!" she called, waving.

The techies returned the wave without much enthusiasm. Dee ignored this and beelined to them, helped by Nugget, who'd spotted a squirrel picking an acorn out of the graveled lot near their car. The squirrel saw the big dog coming and skittered away. Nugget gave a disappointed grunt and plopped down on the ground. He lay prostrate, conveniently blocking the path from the car to the cabins.

Austin bent down to pet him. "Don't worry, plenty more squirrels where he came from."

Aiming for the element of surprise, Dee went for it. "Hi there, you two. How was your hike in the woods to the abandoned gold mines . . . must have been the day before yesterday?"

The techies, much more savvy than Ed, were unfazed by her blunt approach. They didn't bother to dissemble. "Fine," Gavin said. He added with a knowing glance at her, "Nothing nefarious about it. I'm a businessman and Austin's a tech whiz. If there's a mine that can be reactivated and no one has a claim on it, we're the guys who can get it going again."

Austin stopped petting Nugget and stood up. "I know you're trolling for clues that would ID one of us as Sylvan's killer. For the record, murder is for low-tech Luddites. I'd go more high-tech. You know, like starting a nasty rumor on the internet and then amplifying it until the rumor goes viral and destroys someone's reputation and life. Murder is so mid." He punctuated the slang term for mediocrity with a scornful expression.

Gavin and Austin carefully stepped over Nugget and headed to their cabins. Dee waited until they were out of earshot, then muttered to the dog, "You know what neither of them said? We'd never kill Sylvan because he was our friend. And we cared about him." She thought about Jeff's comment that relationships with someone on the level of Sylvan eventually devolved into purely transactional. That appeared to be the case here. Although if Sylvan did replace Austin in Gracie's affections, that would certainly prompt a relationship pivot. And a motivation for murder, despite Austin's scoffing.

With some effort, Dee coaxed Nugget to standing. He was loping toward the motel with Dee in tow when an idea occurred to her. Nugget stopped to relieve himself against a pine tree and Dee used the break to text Jeff and her father: **Meet me in lobby in 30. Wear hiking gear.**

Late afternoon found the three trekking through the woods along the path trod by Gavin and Austin, and mostly likely the Froelichs. "We're pretty deep into the woods here," Jeff said. Apprehensive, he peered in an opening between two giant pine trees. "I heard a sound. You don't think it's Bud, do you?"

"I'm sure it isn't, and even if it is, he'd probably be more scared of us," Dee replied.

Jeff shot her a look. "A few nights in a tent and you're Mother Earth. 'Probably' is the operative word in that sentence. Bud might be all cute and cuddly in your cartoons, but in real life, he's a scary SOB."

Dee emitted an annoyed grunt. "You sound like Callan and the studio. I don't care what they say, squirrels aren't funny."

"Huh?"

Dee realized she hadn't shared the latest from Callan with Jeff and her father. She relayed their conversation. "So for now, my protagonist Bud stays as is."

"I'm glad for you," Jeff said. "But for the record, squirrels can be funny. Look at Rocky and Bullwinkle."

"Rocky was the straight guy in that relationship," Dee rebutted. "He set up Bullwinkle for the funny stuff."

"It's all in the voices," Sam weighed in. "Bullwinkle had a funnier voice. Whoa!"

"He sounded a little dumber than that, Dad."

"I'm not imitating Bullwinkle. Look." Sam pointed to a giant hole haphazardly covered with chicken wire held down by rocks. "There's your first abandoned mine."

"And here's the second."

Jeff pointed to an entry that was similar to the one marking the mine where Sylvan's body had been found in the far reaches of the woods behind the Golden.

"This one is Deep Hole Mine," Sam said, pointing to his find, "and that one's Muddy Mine. Miners tended to be literal when they named things.."

"The names Foundgold and Goldsgone are proof positive of that," Dee said as she examined the entrance to the second mine.

"Muddy got the name because it suffered a cave-in from a series of bad storms back in the 1870s," Sam said. "This means that as opposed to mines deemed inactive after being stripped of gold during the rush, there's a chance Muddy still has active veins, which were buried during the cave-in. Modern techniques of excavation might be able to access them. Same could be true of Deep Hole. There's no definitive report on its status."

"Intriguing." Dee peeked into the opening to Muddy Mine. All she saw was ominous and forbidding darkness. "If the techies and Froelichs have done their research, like you've done, it would explain their interest in these two mines."

"My 'research' mostly involved yakking about local history with Ma'am and Mister over a campfire with a couple of beers," Sam admitted. "Ma'am's the one who knows the history of the mines around here. But the background of some of them is even a mystery to her. Unfortunately, the one where Sylvan died is one of those. I'm still working on researching it. No luck so far."

"Shush." Jeff held up a hand to quiet the others. They heard a loud and rhythmic crunching of underbrush.

"Now *that* could be Bud," Dee said. "Or a friend of his."

"Time to go."

Jeff and Sam began the reverse trek to the car. Dee began to follow, but a glint of sunshine bouncing off an object partially buried under a leaf caught her eye. She bent down and pushed the leaf aside to reveal a key. But not just any key. It was a key to room 1 at the Golden Motel . . . which happened to be the Froelichs' room.

"Dee, come on." Jeff cast an anxious glance into the woods. "Those footsteps are getting louder, which means they're getting closer."

"Sorry." She held up the key. "Just picking up proof that the Froelichs were here."

She rose and hurried after the others.

The three returned to the Golden, where motel tasks took precedence over amateur sleuthing. Dee replaced the snacks Ed snitched. She used a half-empty bookcase to set up a display of Bud the Bear merchandise she could no longer sell at the crafts fair. The day was warm, and even with the motel's new air-conditioning doing a fine job of cooling the lobby, Dee broke a sweat. She turned on the table fan sitting atop the reservations counter and stood in front of it, enjoying the cool breeze on her face.

While the fan whirred, Dee glanced out the window and saw Ed Froelich making his way between the cabins, clutching his placer mining pan. He gave a furtive look around, then took a path in the opposite direction of the one motel guests usually took to the panning sites of Golden Brook.

Concerned the senior aspiring miner was heading to the less forgiving sites on Dry Creek, Dee turned off the fan. She grabbed her phone, shoved it inside the front pocket of her jeans, and darted out the door to track Ed.

The path to Dry Creek was less traveled than the one to the brook, and Dee stumbled over rocks a few times as she tried to catch up with Ed. The sound of rushing waters from the swollen creek grew in intensity. At long last, the creek came into view. Dee slipped on a mossy rock and grabbed a tree branch to steady herself, which put her in the position to see Ed reach the bottom of a row of low waterfalls. It was a good location for placer mining. Thanks to the spring rains, the usually dormant waterfalls were strong enough to loosen flakes lodged in the rocks. But as Mister had lectured Dee and Jeff, and they had subsequently lectured their guests, the rain also made the creek home to unexpectedly deep pools.

Ed positioned himself by the lowest waterfall. Pan in hand, he took a tentative step toward it. He took another step and then a third. He let out a cry as he tumbled into a pocket of water deeper than he expected. His arms flailed and the pan went flying as he desperately tried to pull himself back. It was no use. He tumbled into the water and disappeared from sight.

# CHAPTER 18

"Ed!" Dee screamed.

She raced to him, slipping and falling on the stony wet surfaces until she reached the waterfall's edge. Ed's head bobbed up. She'd never seen a more terrified expression in her life.

"Help," he gasped. He managed to make his way to her, but couldn't raise himself out of the water. "I can't get my footing. The rocks are too slippery."

"Hold on." Dee pulled out her phone and sent an SOS. She screamed a voice text to Jeff, ending: **BRING YOUR PADDLEBOARD PADDLE!!!!** Then she tossed her phone behind her to a dry section of ground and reached for Ed.

"The water's f-f-freezing." The man's teeth chattered as he said this.

"Grab my hands! I'll pull you out."

Ed reached for Dee. She grabbed his hands and pulled him toward her, but his foot slipped on the rocks and he fell backward. "I can't. The rocks."

"You can do it!"

Despite her desperate attempt to motivate him, Dee saw Ed was fading. She tried to reach him again and failed. Fueled by the fear of watching the man die before her eyes, she combat-crawled closer to the edge of the waterfall and managed to grab his wrist, but he slipped from her grasp. Panicked, she screamed, "Help!"—knowing it was against all odds anyone would hear their location deep in the woods and over the sound of the waterfall.

"I'm coming!" someone yelled back, to her shock.

Seconds later, Jeff broke through the brush on a mountain bike, paddleboard paddle under one arm. "I'm here!" he shouted. "Man, this thing can move!" The bike hit a rock and Jeff tumbled off of it. He scrambled to his feet and ran to the waterfall's edge. He held out the paddle to Ed. "Grab it, I'll pull you in!"

Ed grabbed the paddle and Jeff pulled the older man toward him. Ed tried to get his footing, but slipped again. "No use," he said, exhausted. The accountant let go of the paddle and sank into the water until he was submerged.

"No!" Dee cried out.

Jeff jumped into the pool. He slid his arms under Ed's armpits and yanked him up. Dee waved him toward her. "Come this way! I'll help pull you both out."

Jeff dragged Ed to the water's edge. "I found a rock that's not slippery," he gasped. "Ed, I need you to work with me."

Ed gave a weak nod. He gave his hands to Dee. She pulled, while Jeff pushed. Jeff lost his balance, but fought to regain it. With a last burst of strength, Jeff gave Ed a shove. The older man fell onto Dee, toppling them both to the ground. "Jeffrey Milo Cornetta," Dee said as Jeff climbed out of the water and collapsed next to her, "you're an effing hero."

Jeff spit out a mouthful of water in response. He lay prone on the ground, spent.

Dee sat up, then helped Ed do likewise. "Let's get you back to your room before you freeze to death."

"*Agh.*" Ed grimaced in pain and clutched his chest. His wet face went sheet white.

"Oh no!" Dee stared at him, horrified. "I think he's having a heart attack."

Jeff and Dee sat in the Gold County Medical Center ER waiting room, an all-too-familiar location for Dee, who'd been there multiple times a few months earlier, thanks to run-ins with a murderer. The two were wrapped in silver emergency medical blankets provided by the EMTs who'd arrived in time to stabilize Ed and rush him to the hospital.

The glass door separating the waiting room from the ER slid open and Trish Froelich came into view. Dee and Jeff stood up and went to her. She looked terrible. Her eyes were shadowed and her full face gaunt. "Eddie has three badly blocked arteries," she said in a weary voice. "They're doing triple bypass surgery on him. It was touch and go when he got here, but the doctors think he'll be okay once the surgery is over."

She let out a sob and dropped her face in her hands. Dee and Jeff led her to a chair. "I'll get you a bottle of water," Jeff said.

He went to the room's vending machine. Dee took a seat next to the distraught woman. Trish lifted her tear-stained face and grabbed Dee's hands. "You two saved my husband's life. We'll owe you forever for this."

"You don't owe us anything, Trish," Dee said. "We were in the right place at the right time and did what anyone would have done in the same circumstances. And more clichés like that."

Trish managed a weak smile. She released Dee's hands. "Deny it all you want, but it's true."

Jeff returned with water bottles for the three of them and sat in the chair on the other side of Trish. Dee furrowed her brow. "I have to wonder how Ed wound up in a location he was warned against visiting. Do you know?"

Trish's face darkened with anger. "He was lured there."

Dee and Jeff traded puzzled looks over Trish's shoulders. "*Lured?*" Dee asked. "How? By who?"

"I don't know. But whoever it was knew exactly what they were doing."

Dee took this in. She removed her phone from her pocket, brushing off dirt from where she'd thrown it on the ground by the stream. "I think Sheriff Aguilar needs to give the whole situation a look-see," she said, texting him as she spoke. "Does 'look-see' count for the miner jar?" She directed the question to Jeff.

He shook his head. "Old-timey, but still in use. Besides, considering the current circumstances, I think we can say whatever we gol-dern want."

The three fell silent as they waited for Raul. With distances between the tri-villages of Foundgold, Goldsgone, and the county seat of West Camp minimal, he showed up at the waiting room barely ten minutes after Dee texted him.

"I know a private place where we can talk," Dee told the others. She led them to the hospital's interfaith chapel, a lovely room with muted seafoam-green carpet and stained-glass windows, one showcasing the rolling hills of Gold Rush Country, the other featuring the pines and granite outcroppings of Majestic National Park.

Dee closed the door behind them, while Jeff arranged two pews to face each other. He and Raul sat down across from Dee and Trish. "Trish, why don't you tell the sheriff your suspicions about how Ed ended up at the waterfall?" Dee kept her tone gentle and sympathetic. She had a feeling Ed's almost-demise could be tied to Sylvan's death and wanted to be sure Trish didn't second-guess herself or change her mind about talking to Raul.

Trish cast an unsure glance at Dee, who responded with an encouraging nod. "Ed and I haven't had much luck panning. No luck, to be honest. This morning, he told me he got a lead on a panning site guaranteed to deliver gold. He said the site was so top secret he couldn't even tell me the location or how he heard about it. That's all I know. But it was obviously a setup. Why Eddie? He was a good man. A good accountant. He doesn't deserve any of this. I blame Tax Hax. For *everything*." She spewed this with venom. "That horrible app ruined our lives. It destroyed Eddie's business and drove him to risk his life for a flake of gold."

"You're right," Raul said. "Your husband didn't deserve what happened. Can you remember anything else that would help me identify the person who set Ed up? Did he specify a gender? You know, say something like 'he told me' or 'she told me'?"

Trish shook her head, a pained expression on her face. "No. I'm so sorry."

Raul gave her a comforting smile. "No apology necessary. I'd like to take a look at his electronics. Phone, computer. That might provide clues."

Trish turned to Dee. "I want to stay at the hospital and be here when he wakes up from sedation. Would you give the items to the sheriff? His phone is on the desk in our room, next to his laptop."

"Of course," Dee said. "Do you need us to do anything else for you?"

"No. But thank you." Trish stood. "I'm going to Eddie. If anything else comes to me, I'll let you know, Sheriff."

Trish left. Dee closed her eyes and leaned back. The day's dire events had caught up with her. Her entire body ached. Her bruises throbbed and her scratches stung. She opened her eyes. One glance at Jeff told her he felt exactly the same way. "Let us know when you can come by the motel to get Ed's electronics," she said to Raul. "In the meantime, I think Jeff and I need to recuperate from the morning's heroics."

Jeff shivered under his medical blanket. "Gotta say, I'm still effing freezing. And I thought the Pacific was cold. It's like bathwater compared to the creek."

"It's not just water from the rains—it's also runoff from the snowpack melt," Raul said. "Pretty much a hypothermia cocktail."

The three rose. "Mister says the water's so deep in spots, it could be a year before they're accessible to placer mining," Dee said as they left the chapel. "Whoever sent Ed on this fake gold hunt made sure no one knew where he was going and sent him to a spot where the odds were pretty good that he'd drown. Which brings us back to Trish's point: why would someone do this to Ed, a struggling accountant?"

# CHAPTER 19

A call for Raul's services from the sheriff's station's dispatcher preempted a deeper dive into the question of who would target Ed. "I gotta go," the young sheriff said. "A couple of wannabe miners tried to lay claim to the same patch of stream and it's gone from an argument to a fight and a full-on brawl, thanks to their friends piling on." Raul rolled his eyes. "I can't wait until Gold Rush 2.0 is over."

Raul took off to rein in the greedy gold panners. The moteliers exited the hospital and got into Dee's Forester for the drive back to the Golden. Neither spoke, each preoccupied with their own thoughts.

Jeff's phone pinged a text. He read it and chuckled.

Dee shot a quick look his way. "What?"

"Verity wants to write about my 'heroics rescuing Ed' for the *Goldsgone Gazette.*"

Dee reacted with disgust. "Ugh, are you serious?"

Jeff faked a self-effacing shrug. "She obviously sees something in me other women have missed."

"Before the two of you ride off into the sunset on the town stagecoach, tell her you don't live in Goldsgone, so how can she possibly write about you for the Goldsgone rag?" Dee, still smarting from her crafts fair rejection, couldn't resist a dose of sarcasm.

"As the saying goes, heroics know no boundaries."

"That's not a saying anywhere in the universe."

Jeff's phone pinged another text as Dee pulled into the motel's parking area. "Verity wants to do a photo shoot at the stream." He gave his stomach a pat. "You think I can develop a six-pack in an hour?"

"How many hours are in infinity?"

Jeff ignored Dee's wisecrack. He hopped out of her car and sauntered off to prep for his fifteen minutes of fame.

Dee got out of the Subaru. She heard the sound of a conversation and traced it to the pool area. Gavin and Austin were camped out under the umbrella shading the round glass table Dee had snagged at yet another garage sale. She'd managed to convince herself that the table's four mismatched chairs she'd picked up at other sales were "a look."

She moved closer to the tech bros. She couldn't hear their conversation, but their body language telegraphed Gavin was trying to talk a skeptical Austin into something. Gracie emerged from the woods with her placer mining pan tucked under an arm. She set the pan down on the table and held up a vial of gold flakes. The men congratulated her, but even from her parking-lot location, Dee picked up a patronizing edge to it, at least on Gavin's part, which ticked her off. She marched over to the trio.

"Hi. I wanted to give you an update on Ed's condition." She was met with three blank stares. *These are the most self-involved yutzes I will ever meet in my lifetime,* Dee thought balefully. "You haven't heard about Ed Froelich, have you?" They shook their heads. "Missed the breaking news? The police sirens? The ambulance?" They nodded.

Dee swallowed an exasperated grunt that was dying to get out of her system and filled them in on Ed's near-death experience. "He's in a coma and not expected to make it," she said, exaggerating for effect. "Someone lured him into panning in an extremely dangerous location." Her eyes narrowed. "And I bet it was one of you."

The three gaped at her. Each opened a mouth to protest, but Dee barreled on. "Was it a prank? Did you think it was funny? Or did you actually want to kill him? Why? What did he ever do to you except take a swing at your friend Sylvan, who none of you seem to like that much, if at all, anyway?"

There was a brief pause; then the techies all protested their innocence simultaneously. Dee held up a hand. "One at a time, please."

"Not that it's any of your business, but I didn't hear about Ed because I was panning myself, at the other stream," Gracie said, fuming.

Austin looked at Dee like she'd lost her mind. "In what universe do you think I would do something so horrible to that poor old guy? If anything, I feel bad for him."

"A reminder of the human cost that sometimes comes with the progress we create," Gavin said, adding a sage nod to his pontification. "Not pleasant. Trust me, after his dustup with Sylvan, the three of us would have gone out of our way to avoid Mr. Froelich, not engage with him."

"Besides," Austin said, "where's our motive? I didn't even know the guy's last name until you just mentioned it."

"And you have zero right to say I didn't like Sylvan," Gracie shot at Dee. "I *loved* him. We were talking about getting married."

This instantly pushed a button for Austin. "A conversation you and I would be having if Sylvan hadn't stolen you from me," he said, scowling.

Gracie slammed a fist on the glass table, startling the others. Dee said a silent prayer the table, a good forty years old, didn't break under the surprising force from the delicate young woman. "Don't you dare talk about me like I'm the last pair of leggings at a yoga store sale," Gracie snapped at Austin. "Nobody *steals* me. I was in a relationship with Sylvan because *I* wanted to be." Gracie pounded her chest. *"I. Me."*

Gavin raised his hands up and down in a gesture to calm the other two. "Now, kids, let's not—"

*"Kids?"* Austin whipped around to face him. "I am so sick of your patronizing attitude. The only reason you glommed on to Sylvan was for the money. Sylvan knew it, but he liked how you sucked up to him. Well, I'm not him. No one's gonna flatter me into a deal that makes zero financial sense. When I look at that mine you're so eager to have me invest in, I don't see a gold pit, I see a money pit. If you want to dig it up, you'll have to kiss some other techie's keester." He stopped, hearing himself. "'Keester'? Where did that come from?"

"Goldsgone," Dee said with a knowing expression. "It gets to you."

Gavin's face burned with anger. "You'll be sorry, especially when some of your buddies *do* get involved with the Muddy and make a fortune."

"I already have a fortune," Austin shot back.

In Dee's mind, Sylvan and his entire crew already had too much money. *They are the poster people for income distribution,* she thought as the argument continued.

After directing a stream of profanity at Austin, Gavin stormed off. Gracie picked up her mining pan. "I'm going back to the stream."

Austin stood up. "I'm going for a walk. In the opposite direction."

"Go for it," Gracie said. "There's probably a trail around here that'd take you all the way back to Palo Alto."

Austin barked a laugh. "Ha. And give you the satisfaction of me leaving? Yeah, don't think so."

Grace shot him a look of loathing. Then she went one way, and Austin, true to his word, went the other.

Dee's instincts ratcheted up to high alert. She'd sensed a heat emanating from beneath Gracie and Austin's antagonism. She wondered if Raul had tracked down anything indicating who, if anyone, inherited Sylvan's estate. She'd read more than one mystery novel where a couple faked a breakup so the man could marry an heiress, kill her off, and inherit her wealth. Could Gracie and Austin be following the same plotline?

No, Dee decided. As Austin threw in Gavin's face, he had his own fortune. She assumed Gracie did too. Still, Dee's gut told her the two were still very much attracted to each other . . . and if Sylvan had survived, his relationship with Gracie might not have.

*Splash!*

"Huh?" muttered a groggy Dee, sitting up in bed. Nugget, asleep at her side, grunted and rolled over. Dee yawned. "Must be Bud," she said to the snoozing mutt, then lay back down and closed her eyes.

*Splash!*

She opened her eyes and sat up again. Bud wasn't in the habit of doing cannonballs, which is what the splash sounded like.

*Splash!*

*Splash!*

Dee threw off the covers and slipped into her sneakers. She checked her phone. It was one a.m. Feeling grumpy and sleep-deprived, she zipped up a fleece jacket—nights in Foundgold leaned chilly even in summer—and stuffed a can of bear spray into a jacket pocket. To Dee's ear, the splashing sounded more like it came from guests breaking the midnight pool curfew, but she wanted to be prepared in case the troublemaker *was* of the furry persuasion. She grabbed her heavy-duty flashlight and headed outside.

The flashlight's bright beam guided Dee from the apartment to the pool. When she reached it, she stared at the sight in front of her, mystified. All four of the chairs usually surrounding the glass table were now floating in the pool.

Fearing Bud had been feeling mischievous, she scanned the woods with the flashlight for signs of the bear, but saw nothing. Dee's spine tingled with a feeling of foreboding. Jeff's cabin was too far from the pool for the splashes to wake him. Dee's apartment wasn't. Her churning gut sent the message that somebody had done this on purpose. To attract her attention.

She turned to run. A paddleboard paddle loomed in front of her, blocking the view and route. It suddenly flipped up and came crashing down on her head.

All Dee saw was blackness.

# CHAPTER 20

"Well, hello again." The cheery greeting came from nurse-practitioner Tuva Abadie, one of the Gold County Medical Center ER nurses who'd tended to Dee on her prior visits to the hospital.

According to Jeff, Dee had cried out loud enough for him to hear when the paddleboard paddle connected with her head. In a fortuitous bit of timing, he'd awakened to relieve himself. Upon completing his business, he'd rushed out to find a dazed Dee struggling to her feet. The end result was Dee's current reunion with Tuva in an antiseptic hospital room.

The nurse-practitioner studied the screen of a laptop parked on top of a rolling medical stand. "A mild concussion. Not your first, is it?"

"No," Dee said, abashed.

Tuva wagged a finger at her. "If you're not careful, you're gonna end up like one of those football players who takes too many hits to the head."

Before Dee could respond, Raul and Jeff poked their heads into the room. "How are you feeling?" the sheriff asked, concerned. "Good enough for visitors?"

"I have a migraine-level headache, but aside from that, okay. I'm so sorry you had to be dragged from your bed in the middle of the night to deal with this."

"I'm more sorry you took another blow to the head," Raul said. "If you're not careful—"

"I know, I know. I'll end up like a football player." Dee lifted her head to fluff the flat pillow behind it. The movement made her grimace in pain.

Tuva closed the laptop. "I'll check in with you before I finish my shift in the morning. Don't stay too long, boys. Our girl needs her rest."

She wheeled off. Raul pulled the room's single chair up to Dee's bedside, while Jeff plopped down at the foot of the bed. "Thanks for rescuing me," Dee said to him. "More heroics for your biggest fan, Verity, to write about."

Her bestie gave her leg an affectionate pat. "We'll keep this one between us."

"By order of the sheriff." Raul reinforced that order with a stern expression. "I don't want people tromping around your pool until we investigate. Tejada's already out there," he continued, referencing Gerald Tejada, another sheriff from the station, "but he's got nothing to report so far, except whoever did this threw the paddle in the pool and probably wiped it clean for extra insurance, so bye-bye fingerprints."

"I wish I remembered something." Dee closed her eyes to replay the moments leading up to her attack. Even simple thinking hurt her head. "After the splashes of the chairs being thrown into the pool, I didn't hear anything. Whoever did this kept quiet, waiting for me."

"They took a chance," Raul said. "There was no guarantee you'd be the one to check out the noise."

"I think it was a pretty safe bet. We do a good job of

warning our guests to be extremely careful at night. If anything, people would have assumed the splashing came from Bud the Bear paying a visit and stayed away from the pool. Jeff's cabin is set too far back for the splashes to wake him up. Plus, he's a sound sleeper and snores like a freight train."

"Aw, you remember," Jeff said, touched.

Dee resisted rolling her eyes. "Considering it's been almost twenty years since we were a couple, I'd label it a recovered memory." She turned toward Raul. "I'm guessing my attacker was one of the techies. The guys say they're still staying with us for business reasons involving the mines. Gracie says she's not ready to go home and close up the life she and Sylvan had together, and she also doesn't want to leave until Sylvan's killer is caught. Personally, I think these are all excuses and they're only sticking around to tick me off."

This inspired a slight smile from Raul. "Don't worry, they'll be waking up to interviews with me. In the meantime, get some rest. Sheriff's *and* doctor's orders."

The men left and Dee pulled the thin hospital blanket up to her chin. She was too stubborn to admit it to Jeff and Raul, but the attack frightened her. Someone was determined to prevent her from nosing around Sylvan's murder and Ed's near-death dunk in the creek. She hated the thought of caving to a killer, but had to admit that spending a bit of downtime in the relative comforts of the hospital was not unappealing. She closed her eyes and quickly fell asleep.

When Dee's eyes fluttered open several hours later, she saw an apparition that made her wonder if she was still asleep. Estranged friend Elmira stood at the side of the bed, and she held a small bakery box. "Elmira?" she whispered. "Am I dreaming?"

"You are not," Elmira responded. Her warm smile brought tears to Dee's eyes.

Elmira opened the bakery box to show Dee, revealing an assortment of baked goods. Hewing to the baker-shopkeeper's demand for honesty from her friends, Dee said, "I'm sure the brookies and brownies are as heavy as doorstops, the sugar cookies could sub for hockey pucks, and the blondies taste like a tree branch would taste, if we could eat it. But thank you so much."

Elmira laughed. "These are all edible. I made them with my new baking assistant: Sam."

"Did someone say my name?"

Dee's father came into the room. "I was parking the car. Boy, is it terrific to have free parking lots where you don't have to validate. Nice break from L.A." He reached down to hug his daughter, then hesitated. "Is it okay? I don't want to accidentally hug you in the wrong place. I'm sure you're in pain enough, as is."

"I feel much better. Amazing what a box of treats and a smile from a friend can do." Dee held out her arms and she and Sam hugged. "Now, Dad, tell me about your new role as Elmira's assistant."

Sam looked at the All-in-One proprietor with a fond expression. "Less a role and more an excuse to spend time with this marvelous woman."

Elmira blushed under her deep cocoa skin. "Oh, you. *Stop.*" She affectionately batted his arm.

"I won't ever stop wondering how a lovely young woman like you wants to keep company with an old geezer like me." Sam spoke in the reedy tones of Pappy Abner, an elderly character he'd voiced for an adult-diaper commercial. While he did have about twenty-five years on the mid-forties Elmira, the Pappy Abner voice made him sound like a centenarian.

Sam switched to his normal voice. "I came up with a way to convince Elmira to forgive me. I'm her assistant and tester. We're going through her recipes together to make sure they're as delicious as she intended. I also recalibrated her oven, which was cooking everything five degrees hotter than the temperature it displayed. This is why a lot of the baked goods were dry as dust."

"Everything is safe to eat now," Elmira said with only a tiny hint of asperity.

She offered the box to Dee, who removed a blondie. She took a bite and relished it. "Fantastic. And that's no lie." Elmira put the box on the table next to the hospital bed. Dee laid a hand on Elmira's arm. "Please be my friend again. I miss you."

"We're good," Elmira said. She leaned over the bed to give Dee a hug.

"Just so you know, on my way in, I ran into your doctor," Sam said. "She's going to hold you over tonight, to be on the safe side."

Dee, in no rush to return to the scene of the crime, nodded. "Could you do me a favor? I bought a book on the original Gold Rush, but haven't had time to read it. It's on my coffee table. Could you bring it here for me?"

"Course we will, Deedle-dee." Sam kissed his daughter on the forehead. "I'm gonna keep a much better eye on you when you get back home."

"I'll be fine." Dee patted the bakery box. "Spend your time making sure I have a steady supply of these blondies."

Once Dee was alone in her room, she fell back asleep. She woke up to find a colorful floral arrangement on her bedside table. She was proud of herself for being able to identify several as local native wildflowers. A card protruded from the middle of the arrangement. Dee extracted it. She smiled as she read the message from Jonas: *Help, I'm a prisoner in Fresno at the world's most boring conference on fluctuating mortgage rates! Kidding . . . not. Seriously, get better ASAP and try to stay out of trouble. Unless you wanna get in trouble with me, wink wink.*

"Do I ever, wink wink," Dee said to the card in a sultry voice.

She placed the card on the table and saw Sam had dropped off her copy of *There's Gold in Them Thar Hills: A History* on the bedside table. She picked up the book and was about to start reading, but there was a tentative knock on the half-open door. Trish Froelich peeked around the edge of it. "Dee?"

Dee sat up in bed. "Hi, Trish. Come on in."

Trish did so. "I heard you were here. What happened?"

"My head connected with a paddleboard paddle. Not my choice."

Dee shared the details of her assault. Trish's forehead creased with concern. "That's horrible. I'm so sorry."

"I'll be okay. But how's Ed?"

Trish's face lit up with a relieved smile. "Resting for a day in the ICU before they move him to a regular bed. He should be out of the hospital in a few days, but we won't be able to go home right away. He needs to get his strength back before we make such a long drive, so I'm afraid you'll be stuck with us a little longer."

"Happy to have you. And we'll help in any way we can."

"Thank you so much."

"Have the police been able to interview Ed about what happened?"

"Not yet. The doctors won't let anyone but me see him

until he's out of the ICU, which should be tomorrow. Right now, my poor hubby's too woozy to form a sentence."

"Ah. Well, I'm really glad he's going to be okay."

Considering the conversation over, Dee made a motion to pick up her book. Trish didn't take the hint. She stood planted to the floor. Her expression indicated an internal struggle. Intrigued despite herself, Dee put the book down. "Trish, is something bothering you?"

Trish nodded. Her eyes welled with tears.

"Shut the door and pull up a chair," Dee said.

Trish did as instructed. "Ed told me you saw our car hidden in the woods and asked about it. The thing is . . . I was the one who followed those young tech men, Gavin and Austin, not Ed. He lied to you to cover up for me. I overheard them talking about a mine that might still be active, and I snuck along behind them to find it. I hoped there might be a way for us to tap into it, but once I saw what they were talking about, I knew simply exploring the mine would entail an expensive operation, and you could spend all that money without ever finding gold. It was a complete waste of time."

Dee pondered Trish's confession. "You overheard Gavin and Austin. But someone must have overheard Ed lie to me. He did sound like he was covering something up, which must have made the eavesdropper suspicious. And paranoid."

"Exactly. But do you see why I'm upset? They tried to kill Eddie for no reason. And it's my fault."

"Trish, no. You can't blame yourself for someone luring Ed to his death. That's the actions of a psychopath."

"I know. But still . . ." Trish didn't finish the sentence. She wiped her eyes and stood up. "Thank you for listening. And not judging me. I blame the gold. It literally drives people to madness."

"Truth," Dee said with a rueful nod.

Once Trish was gone, Dee picked up her book again. But she couldn't concentrate. She closed her eyes and replayed her exchange with Ed, picking through it for any hints of someone lurking nearby. All she got for her efforts was a throbbing sensation from the goose egg–sized bump on her head. She decided she'd try again—once she was back at the motel, that is. Reliving the conversation where it took place might jog her memory.

She picked up her book for the third time. There was a rat-a-tat-tat of a knock on the door and Callan Katz poked his head in. "Hey. You decent under that sheet? I've got something to show you."

"It's not a sheet, it's the hospital's version of a blanket, and yes." Dee found the agent's lack of interest in her condition, or what landed her in the hospital, both expected and amusing. "Come on in," she said, once again putting aside *There's Gold in Them Thar Hills*.

Callan strode in, his usual confidence on full display. He wore a bespoke gray suit tailored to perfectly complement a body made fit by Hollywood's best trainers. "I'm on my way back to L.A., but I've got the concept art for Bud and I'm pretty excited about it."

Callan pulled a tablet from his Italian leather briefcase and powered it up. He handed the tablet to Dee. The image on the screen prompted a double take from Dee. "I think my concussion is worse than they thought. This isn't a bear."

"The studio respected your wishes. Bud isn't a squirrel. Instead"—Callan mimed a drumroll, which Dee now viewed as his go-to move to deflect from what she considered bad news—"Bud is a bird. A big, goofy, wacky bird. Ta da!"

Dee scrunched her eyes closed and silently counted to ten. She opened her eyes and said, as calmly as she could, "It's Bud the Bear, not Bud the Bird."

"They thought this would be a great compromise. Birds fly."

"Yes, I believe this has been a known fact since the dawn of time." Dee somehow managed not to scream this rejoinder at Callan.

"It makes them more active. In contrast to bears. They fly. Bears lumber." Callan mimed a lumbering bear. "Birds are a more motion-oriented choice. Animation is all about activity. It's go, go, go. You know . . ." Callan flapped his arms and mimed flying.

"I grew up around animation," Dee said, priding herself on maintaining an even tone. "With a father who's the industry-famous Man of a Million Voices. I also wrote for two animated series, so I'm pretty familiar with the format. I repeat for the bazillionth time, the character I created is Bud *the Bear,* not Bud *the Anything Else.*"

Callan gave a nod meant to give the illusion of understanding. Dee took it for the empty gesture it was and patiently waited for Callan to tell her the real reason she faced resistance from the studio to her original pitch. He pulled a chair up to the side of the bed. "Dee, here's the problem. According to the studio, market research shows bears are scarier than squirrels or birds."

"Smokey Bear isn't. Yogi isn't. Boo-Boo isn't. The toilet paper bears aren't. And I'll point out that a tiger's been promoting a popular cereal since . . . Well, let me check." Dee entered a quick search on her phone. "Since 1952! And tigers are way scarier than bears."

"Yeah, but no one in America is going to run into a tiger on a camping trip. The studio is worried that promoting a cute bear could inspire some kid and his family to get too close to a real one and blame the consequences on the studio. They could get sued."

"Unbelievable." Dee ground her teeth in frustration. She'd moved hundreds of miles from Hollywood, only to be thrust into the same endless development loop she'd found herself in multiple times while pursuing a writing career in La-La Land. "For the final, bazillionth and one, time, it's Bud the Bear. Not Bud the Bird. Not Bud the Squirrel. Not Bud the Fuzz-Wuzzy Lawsuit-Safe Whatever. If they want to move forward with this project, it's Bud. The. *Bear.*"

"Dee, here's the deal." For once, Callan sounded like something akin to a genuine person rather than a super agent. "Things are different than in 1952. People are so into taking selfies they don't care if they risk their lives doing it. These days, someone would pose with a tiger, get eaten, and their loved ones would post the photo on all the social-media platforms to milk it for likes. The studio isn't being paranoid. It's being practical."

Dee's head pounded—not from her injury, but from deliberating her response to Callan.

"When you put it that way, I do get it," she finally said. "But here's *my* deal. I'm trying to keep the business venture I've sunk everything into from going bankrupt. I'm also trying to keep people I love safe from the threat of going to jail. There's also the undisputed fact that murder is a heinous crime—and no one should ever get away with it. I know there are ways to make a bird or squirrel or any living creature funny. But I just don't have the bandwidth to figure out how right now. If the studio doesn't want to make a cartoon with Bud as the lead, I understand and respect their decision. Hopefully, though, they will. And even more hopefully, for the sake of humanity, there are still people out there who have the good sense to know that approaching a real bear under any circumstances is incredibly stupid."

Callan nodded. "Okay. I hear you. I'll go back to the studio."

"Thanks. Do me a favor and close the door on your way out."

Callan headed off to work his agent magic, pulling the door shut behind him. Eager to escape everything weighing down on her—the fallout from Trish's confession, the paddleboard paddle attack, Bud-the-Anything-but-a-Bear—Dee picked up her book for the fourth time. She glanced at the table of contents. Her eyes widened when she read the title of the fifth chapter: "Brute Burr: Silas Burr, Gold County's Meanest Miner."

"I am *so* skipping to that!" Dee said out loud, thumbing through the pages until she reached her destination. She began to read.

Dee was only on the second page when she concluded Brute was an understatement. She had described Ed's would-be killer to Trish as a psychopath. Silas "Brute" Burr put whoever that was to shame. Claim jumping was the least of the nasty means he used to draw the last gasp of gold out of nearby mines and streams. Dee recognized names of the state's founding families in the long list of people he'd wronged: Sutter, Verdugo, Hanford, Huntington, Marshall, Hunt—even, yes, a Donner. Dee wondered if Verity knew. She wouldn't put it above the woman to off someone whose ancestor had messed with her treasured ancestors.

Fascinated and appalled, Dee couldn't stop reading.

Threats, bullying, the seduction of wives and daughters leading to blackmail—these were just a few of the tools in Silas "Brute" Burr's evil and often illegal arsenal. Two confrontations with other miners left the men dead of gunshot wounds. Burr got off by claiming self-defense in both cases. Dee didn't consider it a leap to assume he'd bribed his way out of a guilty verdict—not once, but twice.

A nurse delivered the day's lunch of chicken soup, turkey sandwich, and apple sauce. As she ate, Dee thought about what she'd read and how it applied to late motel guest Sylvan Burr. His underhanded transactions with local residents whose homes and businesses he was determined to buy proved he'd inherited at least a few of his ancestor's ruthless genes. Somehow Silas Burr managed to dodge any consequences for his actions and lived to the ripe old age of ninety-eight.

Sylvan Burr, Silas Burr's descendant, hadn't been so lucky.

# CHAPTER 21

Dee was cleared for release in the morning. "By the time your insurance is done paying for your hospital visits, you're gonna have a wing named after you," orderly Elliott joked as he pushed her in the requisite wheelchair to the exit.

To avoid family and friends fussing over her, Dee took a Gold County cab home. The cab deposited her under the Golden's retro neon sign, its 1940s letters and blinking gold nugget brought back to blinding life by Dee and Jeff's generous friends.

Dee started for her apartment, but was flagged down by Gavin. She waited while the financier sauntered down the slope fronting his cabin. "I heard about your accident," he said, concern lacing his voice. "How are you feeling?"

"More of an assault than an accident, but I'm feeling all right. Thank you for asking."

Gavin gave a slight nod, acknowledging her thanks. "Here's hoping the police figure out who's responsible for all this. If I didn't have business in Gold County that requires me to stick around, I'd be gone. No offense."

"None taken."

Gavin glanced at the watch Dee knew he wore as a status symbol, since she'd only seen him check the time on his phone, like pretty much everyone else in the world. "I've got to put in a call to our office in China. If you see that guy Ed's wife, give her my condolences. It's gotta be rough having her husband in a coma."

"Good news on that score," Dee said. "Ed is doing well. He came through bypass surgery and will probably be in better shape, post-op, than he was before."

An expression of dismay passed so quickly Dee second-guessed whether she actually saw it. "Awesome news," Gavin said brightly. He adopted a more serious tone. "I know that nearly drowning can cause brain damage. Any worries for him on that score?"

"Nope. At least not that Trish mentioned. He was woozy post surgery, but that's to be expected."

"Uh-huh. It could also be a sign of neurological problems."

"Possibly," Dee acknowledged, wary. She found Gavin's obsession with Ed's mental state suspicious. "But for Trish's sake, let's hope not, right?"

"Right."

Gavin headed back up the slope to his cabin, walking at a much faster clip. In case he glanced back at her, Dee strolled off at a purposely leisurely pace. The minute she heard his cabin door shut, she took off running. She hurried into her apartment, slamming and locking the door behind her. Nugget roused himself from where he lay splayed out on the couch and barked a hello. "Hi, love you, gotta call Raul," she said, yanking her phone from her jeans front pocket.

Heart pounding, she sat on the couch, squeezing into the few feet Nugget didn't occupy. She took a couple of deep breaths to calm herself, then hit Raul's number, which had earned a place of honor on her Favorites list. "Answer, answer, answer," she muttered. The call went to voicemail and she cursed. "Raul, it's me. I have an incredibly strong feeling that Gavin Walsh, Sylvan's finance guy, is the one who lured Ed to the creek and beaned me with the paddleboard paddle, and it all could tie into Sylvan's murder. Call me."

The lobby bell trilled notice of an arrival. Dee opened the security app Jeff had installed on her phone to provide a view of the lobby. A couple, with a little boy, about five, in tow and an infant strapped to the woman's chest, stood at the reservations desk. Dee brushed the dog hair from her pants and crossed into the lobby through the door connecting it to her apartment.

"Hello there," she said, favoring them with her best motelier smile. "Welcome to the Golden."

"We're the Bricklins," the father said. "We booked a room in the main motel."

"I remember. From Sherman Oaks. Right next to my hometown, Studio City." She made small talk with the Bricklins about common points of San Fernando Valley interest, while calling up their reservation. "You're in room 10. It's an end room, so you get more light than with an interior room."

"Daddy, look, it's Bud." The little boy pointed to a Bud the Bear kids T-shirt, part of the display Dee had created after being exiled from the Goldsgone Crafts Fair. "Can I get it?"

"Sure," his father said with an indulgent smile.

"I'll put it on your room bill." Having decided to drive into Goldsgone and see if she could track down Raul herself, Dee was eager to see the family to their room. "Here's your key. If you'd like to pan for gold in our sluice, I'll call up Prospector Pete, who mans it."

This was met with a chorus of excited yeses from the parents, as well as their son. Dee texted Sam while she briskly walked the Bricklins to their room. He texted back confirmation, along with a promise to show up with a plate of homemade cookies for their guests, the product of his successful baking hookup with Elmira.

After piling on more smiles and exhortations for the family to have a good time, Dee ran to her car. She jumped in and buckled her seat belt. She ignited the engine and was about to put the gear in reverse, when she spotted Gavin between the tall evergreens separating the motel from the road. He checked his phone and tapped a foot impatiently. A Gold County cab pulled up in front of him and Gavin jumped inside. The cab shot off. Dee's SUV created a cloud of gravel and dust as she drove out of the motel lot in pursuit.

Once on the road, she found herself behind a pickup truck, which allowed her to follow the cab unobserved. The pickup turned down a dirt road and Dee dropped back. A rickety delivery truck pulled out of a lumberyard in front of Dee. It moseyed along at a slow pace, putting more distance than Dee was comfortable with between her and Gavin's cab. While she had a strong hunch where the financier was headed, she feared if her hunch was wrong, and she allowed him too much of a head start, she'd lose him. Dee hadn't put much thought into what she'd do if she actually caught up with him; all she knew was that she couldn't let him get away.

She glanced down at the passenger seat and saw her trusty can of bear spray had rolled onto the floor below it.

Feeling more confident knowing she had an ersatz weapon if she needed one, Dee pressed on the gas and passed the delivery truck, heart in her mouth as she crossed a double yellow line on a curve, which earned an angry honk from the delivery truck driver.

The cab passed the road leading to Dee's favorite hike and the meadow where Sylvan's chopper had originally landed. Dee's confidence wavered. She was sure the financier was on his way to a private chopper out of town. She shrugged off her hesitancy. *In it to win it,* she thought. Gavin's presumed flight from Foundgold had her more convinced than ever that he was the culprit behind the recent crimes. And she couldn't imagine any criminal who was more of a flight risk than Tax Hax's shady moneyman. Plus, *Solved*-Murder Motel had a way better ring to it than Murder Motel. Dee clutched the steering wheel with renewed determination.

The cab sped along, passing through hamlets even smaller than Foundgold, merely a couple of houses and maybe a general store, which dotted the path to the county seat of West Camp. The cab shot through the town, and for a moment, Dee wondered if Gavin had commandeered the vehicle as his means of escape. Then she heard the sound of a helicopter. She peered at the sky through her windshield and saw a chopper on a flight path to the edge of town.

The cab reached the outskirts of West Camp, where the county fairgrounds lay. The helicopter hovered overhead. A gate blocked entry to the field. The cab stopped at the gate and Gavin jumped out. Dee parked behind a massive oak tree and leaped out of her car, bear spray in hand.

Gavin ran toward the chopper. Dee ran after him. The chopper slowly set down on the large, empty field. Its roar prevented Gavin from hearing anything that would indicate Dee was closing in on him. She reached spraying distance. "Gavin!" she yelled. He didn't respond. "Hey, *Gavin*!"

He turned and saw her. Shock turned to an ugly fury. Dee pressed the button and a stream of bear spray hit Gavin in the eyes. "Agh!" he screamed, clawing at the air with one hand and covering his eyes with the other. He choked and coughed as he groped for the helicopter. Then he suddenly lunged for Dee. Caught by surprise, Dee jumped backward. She lost her balance, dropping the bear spray as she fell to the ground. Gavin noticed the can through the slits of his teary red eyes and grabbed it. He aimed it at Dee and sneered, "Your turn."

Dee turned her head, but the spray still found its way into her eyes. Dee struggled to her feet in time to see Gavin climb into the helicopter. Through stinging eyes blurred with tears, she caught a last image of him dousing his own eyes with a bottle of water as the chopper rose and flew away.

# CHAPTER 22

Officers who responded to Dee's 911 call found her hunched over a water fountain shooting a plume of cold water into her burning eyes. She continued this as she filled them in on Gavin's probable criminal actions and escape by air. Within a half hour, a variety of law enforcement officials representing every agency, from local to the FBI and the U.S. Marshals Service, filled the field, which crackled with the sound of competing walkie-talkies. Raul was there representing the jurisdiction where the financier's alleged crimes took place. Even Tom O'Bryant showed up on behalf of the national park rangers.

"We've got skin in the game," the park ranger told Dee. Clearly outranked, he sounded defensive. "Weather could turn bad over the Sierras. Chopper goes down in Majestic, it's ours." He rubbed his hands together with gusto at the thought.

By the time the men and women in blue, or the colors of their particular division, finished scouring the field for clues, Dee's eyes burned less and had almost completely cleared. She confirmed her contact information with an agent, who had the generic looks of an actor whose credit read U.S. Marshal #2 at the end of an action movie. "Don't worry, we'll get the guy," he assured Dee before loping off. Dee felt less sure. The internet was filled with stories, many actually true, of one-percenters like Gavin Walsh using their buckets of bucks to avoid capture.

She blinked a few times. Noting her vision was still too blurry to drive, she sat down on a bench next to a closed stall that sold fried pickles, fried Oreos, fried sticks of butter, and other nausea-inducing fried foodstuffs when the county fair was in season. A YOU BUY IT, WE FRY IT! banner flapped above her.

Raul and Ranger Tom approached her. Adversaries in the past, the two competitive lawmen seemed to have formed at least a temporary truce. "Eyes still bugging you from the spray, huh?" Ranger Tom said. Dee nodded.

"Neither of us likes the idea of you waiting here alone for someone to come get you," Raul said. "I need to stick around, but since the chopper hasn't bailed over Majestic, Tom's partner is going to drive their park jeep so that Tom can drive you back to the motel in your car."

"Thank you." Dee's eyes welled up, but not with bear spray tears. The traumatic recent events chose this moment to catch up with her. She swallowed, then said quietly, "I'd appreciate it."

On the drive home to the Golden, Dee took advantage of being a passenger to gaze out the car window at the scenery, finding comfort in its beauty. Golden hills alternated with stands of forest. A pastoral creek ran alongside the two-lane road for a mile or two. Rainbows danced in the mists formed by the creek's water splashing over rocks.

Dee felt a growing sense of optimism. Gavin's hurried departure took the threat of danger with him. She leaned back against her seat and breathed a sigh of relief.

Tom noticed. "Somebody's doing a mite better," he said in a jovial tone.

"'Mite.'" Dee chuckled. "That's a miner jar word."

"Huh?"

"Never mind. Thanks again for the lift home." She flashed a mischievous grin. "Keep up with these good deeds and I might grow to like you."

"Uh-oh. I'm goin' soft. Not a good look for a guy in my position." Unsure if he was teasing or serious, Dee didn't respond. "So," O'Bryant said, "this Walsh character had his eye on the Muddy Mine."

"He was trying to get the funding to reactivate it."

"I assume he did his homework on its status. Believe it or not, there's a lot of old mines that are still entailed to the original claimants. And the descendants still fight over them. My family and Verity 'Yes-*that*-Donner'—"

"You call her that too?" Dee asked, amused.

"We didn't before, but since word got around you and your friend Jeff gave her the nickname, it caught on."

"No wonder she hates me," Dee murmured, feeling a hint of remorse.

"Anyway, me and Verity were at it for years, because both our families claimed the rights to By the Crick Mine. Our grudge went back to the original Gold Rush. I only got off her you-know-what list when I generously gave up our claim to the mine."

"And then you got back on her you-know-what list by dating her."

Tom guffawed. "Yup. Live and don't learn." The ranger dropped his voice to a stage whisper. "Between us, before I gave up my family's claim, I had a couple of prospector pals take metal detectors to the mine and all the land around it. They came up empty. Doesn't mean there still couldn't be some gold deep down. But it does mean it'd be way outta my means to tap into it."

"When did your families start fighting over the claim?"

"I can tell you the exact date. April 23, 1851. We both have the paperwork to show it. Ours wasn't a case of claim jumping. The guy filing claims got money from both our families. He had a nice scam going. Old Ice Cream Ida's still fighting with three families. Their descendants all got taken the same way. Other descendants got taken other ways." Tom glanced out the window. "What's above ground is pretty. The problem is what's below ground."

They reached the motel. Tom parked Dee's car and then took off with his ranger partner, who was waiting to retrieve him in the park jeep. Dee's arrival at the Golden attracted the attention of Austin, Gracie, and Jeff, who appeared to be watching a video on Austin's phone. They hurried to her. "We saw you on a breaking news report from the Fresno station," Jeff said.

"Look." Austin held up his phone. A news report showed law enforcement swarming the county fair field. Dee could make herself out pouring a bottle of water into her eyes, while a reporter droned on about a helicopter with fugitive Gavin Walsh aboard disappearing into the ether.

Dee started toward her apartment. "I'll tell you everything, but I haven't eaten since my breakfast at the hospital. At this point, I could eat a stick of fried butter."

They trooped into Dee's kitchen. The others waited impatiently as she heated up a reduced-calorie frozen mac and cheese, which she quickly devoured. "Short version of a long story, I picked up a vibe from Gavin that indicated he wasn't too happy about Ed's recovery, which marked him as a logical suspect in the attempt on Ed's life. This also made him the most likely candidate to have bonked me on the head with a paddleboard, since I accused all three of you of being the possible culprits." Dee stopped for a sip of water, then continued. "Anyway, Gavin must have noticed my reaction to *his* reaction, because the next thing I knew, he hopped into a cab and zoomed off." Dee relayed how she'd left a message for Raul, but fearful he wouldn't get it in time, she followed Gavin.

"I'm still in shock," Gracie said when Dee finished.

Austin nodded agreement. "Gavin lost a ton of money investing in start-ups that flamed out. He tried to downplay his losses, but I knew the dude was hard up. Still, to kill over it . . . I mean, he must have killed Sylvan, right?"

"I can't confirm it," Dee said, "but it seems likely. Gavin was on a mission to find an active mine. He must have gotten into a fight with Sylvan about excavating Rich Diggins. When Sylvan died, Gavin switched his focus to Muddy Mine to distance himself from the scene of the crime. Which sounds very dramatic when you say it out loud."

Gracie shivered. Austin laid a hand on her shoulder. She didn't push it away. "I knew a big part of the reason Gavin hung around with us was because of the perks," she said in a low voice. "But I wanted to think that we were also friends." She turned to Austin. "I was wrong. You were right."

"I wish I wasn't," the coder said. He sounded forlorn.

"My dad used to call guys like Gavin Walsh gladhanders," Jeff said. "They come across warm and friendly, but beneath the façade, they have an agenda."

Jeff's comment made Dee think of how Tom described the scenery they'd driven past. It was true: Everything was pretty on the surface, but not so much below it.

"Glad-handing served Gavin Walsh well," she said. "Until it didn't."

* * *

The rest of the day proved blessedly uneventful. Raul let Dee know he had been able to interview Ed, who confirmed Gavin was the one who lured him to the deepest waters of the creek. In the evening, Dee and Jeff gathered the families lodged at the Golden for a cookout and campfire, which proved to be a huge hit. Through online videos, Jeff had learned the basics of playing a banjo and he strummed out a few simple tunes. Sam followed this by getting guests and moteliers on their feet to do the prospector song and dance he'd made up. "'La di dah, la dee dee, it's a prospector's life for me!'" they all sang as they copied his jig–Sailor's Hornpipe moves. The song ended to roars of laughter and high fives. It was the kind of evening Dee had dreamed of when she envisioned owning the Golden Motel.

Dee got a restful night's sleep. Upon waking up, she walked Nugget and prepared breakfast for both of them. She took a long, hot shower, then made her way into the lobby to check the website for new reservations. Suddenly the screen went dark. "What the . . . ?! Oh no. Oh no!"

Technology was Jeff's forte. Panicking about it was Dee's. Heart racing, she called Jeff. "Hey," he said, his voice hoarse from his lusty singing of the previous night.

"Something's wrong with the computer, it's—" A face slowly appeared on the screen. Gavin's face. "Wha . . ." Dee stared at the screen, dumbfounded.

"Delilah, what's going on?" The fact Jeff used her full name telegraphed his annoyance. "This was my morning to sleep in."

"Not anymore. Gavin is on my screen."

"What the—I'll be right there." He ended the call.

Austin and Gracie suddenly burst into the room. "Gavin texted he'd hacked into your computer," Gracie said, out of breath.

"Knowing him, I'm sure he probably paid someone else to do it," Austin said, glaring at his estranged coworker on the screen.

Gavin smirked from the motel monitor. "You know me so well, Nyugen."

Jeff stumbled into the lobby, still wearing sleep shorts. "What's going on? What's that criminal doing on our computer?"

"I'll tell you in a minute," Gavin said. "First I want to make sure Sheriff Aguilar's joined us."

Dee's phone pinged a text. She checked and saw a string of cusswords, along with angry emojis. "Raul's logged in from his end."

"So he has. Excellent." Gavin gestured to the blank white wall behind him. "As you can see, I'm in an unmarked location. That's basically for dramatic effect. My tech genius friends can easily track me down. Not that it matters if they do. I'm calling from a country without a U.S. extradition treaty, my home now, and will be protected by the apparatchiks I now call my pals. But before I disappear from all of your lives forever, I wanted to clarify a few things."

The others huddled around the computer monitor. "He said 'apparatchik,'" Jeff whispered. "He must be in Russia." Dee shushed him.

"Good guess, but wrong," Gavin said, "So . . . about the Ed thing."

"I wouldn't call attempted murder a thing," Dee said, "but go on."

"I was on my own gold hunt when I ran into Ed panning a spot way up on Little Stream. Trish wasn't around and the poor old guy had run out of steam after filling only a quarter of a vial with flakes."

"A sign of heart trouble he ignored," Dee said to Jeff, who affirmed this with a nod.

"I could tell by looking in the water, Ed had found a rare rich site. I wanted to pan it, but I had to get Ed out of the way, so I downplayed his find. I told him he'd gotten as much out of the site as he could. The homeless couple had warned me about the deep spot in Dry Creek—"

"Ma'am and Mister Ma'am, and they're not homeless, they're off the grid," Dee said, insulted on the Ma'ams' behalf.

"I told Ed the deep spot they told me about was a secret site loaded with gold," Gavin continued, ignoring Dee. "I made a 'deal' to split whatever either of us extracted and made him swear not to tell anyone about it, which he, of course, was perfectly willing to do. I didn't count on the meddling moteliers coming to his rescue."

"Our bad for being the good guys," Jeff retorted.

Gavin gave Dee and Jeff an amused look, then returned to his story. "Between the gold I panned from Ed's original site, and selling the Tax Hax stock I had left, I managed to finance my escape. I plan on doing very well here. My skills as an American financier will be much appreciated in the country I won't name."

"I want to confirm you're the one who took a paddleboard to my head," Dee said, "so that when the techies or Interpol or whoever tracks you down does find you, I know where to send the bill for my insurance deductible."

"Consider it confirmed."

Gracie leaned into the screen. "You're a monster," she spat at him. "Trying to kill Ed. Full-on killing Sylvan."

"And clobbering me," Dee interjected. She placed a hand on her head. "Ow. It still hurts."

"You always said Sylvan was one of your closest friends,

if not *the* closest," Gracie said, ignoring Dee. "How could you do something so evil to the person who gave you your biggest break?"

The smirk on Gavin's face disappeared, replaced by what appeared to be genuine emotion. "That's why I wanted to hold this call," he said. "I wanted to be completely honest with you about what I did do, so you'd all believe me when I say I absolutely, one hundred percent, *did not kill Sylvan.* I had nothing but respect for him and will always be grateful that he took a chance on me. My reputation wasn't great, but he didn't care. He had my back and I had his."

The financier bit his lower lip in an attempt to control his feelings. Then he looked straight into the camera. "I know you two thought I was a mooch, only in the relationship to get whatever I could out of it. But you're wrong. Sylvan's friendship meant a ton to me. I never would have harmed him. *Never.* To repeat . . . *I absolutely did not kill Sylvan Burr.*"

The screen went black. Dee and the others stared at it in silence. Austin got a text alert. He read it, then held up his phone. "Turkmenistan. That's where he is. Not that it matters. No extradition treaty."

# CHAPTER 23

Gracie and Austin left, taking Gavin's news with them back to their tech inner circle. With glum expressions, Dee and Jeff pondered Gavin's adamant denial that he'd killed Sylvan. "I wish I wasn't so sure he was telling the truth," Dee said.

"I know," Jeff said. "Because it means . . ."

He didn't have to finish the sentence. Dee knew what he meant. Sylvan's killer was still out there. Law enforcement was back to square one. And the Golden was back to being Murder Motel.

She sighed. "I hate that it's too early to drink."

"Are you up for a trip into Goldsgone? I'm hungry, but too depressed to make my own breakfast. I was thinking about hitting the Golden Grub. I could go for their Hungry Panners Pancake Breakfast."

"I already ate, but I could use a break. I'll keep you company."

Jeff went back to his cabin to change. Dee occupied herself by turning over a room where a couple had checked out. She stuffed the sheets and towels into the motel's washing machine and gave the bathroom a thorough wash.

She never thought she'd find comfort in cleaning, but focusing on physical labor cleared her mind to wander. The wandering had proven productive in the past, even leading to breakthroughs on crimes. At the moment, however, her brain felt foggier than her vision had been after the bear spray dousing. When Jeff texted he was ready to go, it came as a relief.

Sunshine warmed the dusty streets of Goldsgone, its bright glow a contrast to the moteliers' dark moods. Craftspeople and vendors were setting up for the day's fair. A couple greeted Dee with sympathy and anger about her disbarment from the event, which made her feel a little better. She kept her head down when they walked past Miss Mary's Unmentionables. She didn't have the bandwidth to deal with Pamela. A day earlier, Dee would have jumped at the chance to pepper the shop owner with questions about her relationship with Gracie. Now the thought of it exhausted her.

Rather than sit outside and put themselves on view to the Goldsgone world, Dee and Jeff opted for an inside table toward the back of the restaurant. Jeff ordered the pancake breakfast, while Dee treated herself to a cappuccino. Restaurant owner Liza came to their table, clad in her much more stylish version of the Goldsgone pioneer costume, a solid navy maxi dress and pale blue apron, as opposed to the cutesy calico that was de rigueur for the rest of the town's female residents. "Your guest Austin placed a delivery order and told me you'd heard from Gavin Walsh," she said. "He said it means his friend Sylvan's killer hasn't been caught yet."

"I'm afraid so," Dee said. "I hope the news hasn't spread fast enough to have people start calling us Murder Motel again." Liza, looking uncomfortable, played with the edge of her apron. Dee's stomach sank. "Oh no. They have."

"I only heard it from one person." Liza let go of her apron and forced a smile. "You know what, breakfast is on me."

She hurried away. "Argh." Dee let out a groan. "You know that *one person* is Verity." She folded her arms on the table and dropped her head down on them, then lifted her head and shook a fist in the direction of Verity's lair, the Goldsgone Mercantile and Emporium. "Curse you and the horse you road in on, Verity 'Yes-*that*-Donner' Gillespie!" The occupants of the next table shot her a nervous glance.

"Liza is so nice," said Jeff, who hadn't taken his eyes off her since she'd walked away. "And so pretty."

Dee held up a warning finger. "*No*. Do not go there, Jeffrey. You know Raul is hopelessly in love with her."

"But she's much closer to my age than his," Jeff argued. "He's, what, twenty-eight? She's gotta be in her mid-thirties."

"Look at me."

Jeff toyed, instead, with the cactus decorating the table.

"*Look at me,*" Dee repeated.

He reluctantly made eye contact.

"Given what we've gone through in only the few months we've lived here—and I mean *murders* and *assaults*—do you really want to make an enemy of the one law enforcement official we can count on for support?"

"No," Jeff muttered. "It's just that when it comes to dating, there's slim pickin's in these parts. And yes, I know that was very miner-y. I'll put two quarters in the jar when we get home."

Dee placed an affectionate hand on his. "You get a pass today. Jeff, you're a catch. Especially in *these* parts. Kidding! You'd be a catch anywhere. You'll find someone wonderful who deserves you. I know it."

"Easy for you to say," he groused. "You've got Jonas."

"I don't *have* anyone. My relationship with Jonas is so casual, you can barely call it a relationship." Dee grew wistful. "I do like him. A lot. I'm not sure he feels the same way about me, though."

"If he doesn't, it's his loss," Jeff declared. He brightened. "Hey. We just spent almost five minutes talking about something besides murder."

Dee laughed. "Yay, us." She held up a hand and the two high-fived.

Jeff's pancakes arrived and he dug into them. Per the old friends' usual routine of sharing when dining together, Dee traded cappuccino sips for bites of pancake. Satiated, they bid goodbye to Liza and left for the return trip to the Golden.

Dee noticed Raul in his sheriff costume-uniform posing somewhat reluctantly for a photo under the metal awning hanging over the brick-fronted sheriff's station. He caught Dee's eye and motioned for her and Jeff to wait. The blonde who'd cornered him was clad in tiny shorts and a tank top, her entire look screaming "influencer." She mugged for a series of selfies, then released him.

Raul loped their way. "You're Goldsgone's rock star," Dee joked.

He made a face. "Sometimes I think I might as well be a cardboard cutout." He used the back of his hand to wipe sweat gleaming from his brow. "It's heating up today. I wanna ditch the duster." He motioned to his full-length lawman's jacket. "But I need to talk to you. In private."

He tilted his head toward the station, then started in its direction. Dee and Jeff followed.

Inside, the front half of the station was pure historic restoration. The room was sparsely decorated, with an old wooden desk, a potbelly stove, a coatrack, and a washbasin on top of a rickety stand. The building's original jail cell sat across from the desk, the better for the nineteenth-century sheriff to keep his eye on whatever miscreant he'd locked up.

Raul led Dee and Jeff through the room to a door that served as a portal between the fictional and real world of sheriff-ing. Not that the modern headquarters was particularly modern; the décor hadn't been touched since the 1950s, including a faded portrait of President Eisenhower no one had ever bothered to take down. Fortunately for the people of Goldsgone, the computers and crime equipment were up-to-date.

Raul led them into his office, closing the door behind him. He sat behind his desk; they took the two cold metal chairs opposite him. "I wanted to let you know that the higher-ups in the county sheriff's office have brought in the FBI to help hunt for Sylvan's killers. With all the craziness generated by this stupid second Gold Rush, none of us locals can devote the time that the investigation calls for."

"It makes sense," Dee said. "And I assume part two of this conversation is telling us to ixnay the amateur investigating."

"Exactly. If you think O'Bryant and the park rangers aren't fans of amateur sleuths, you have no idea how much the FBI hates them."

"I can guess," Jeff said.

Raul leaned back in his chair. "I'm disappointed to be

taken off the case, but I'm also kind of relieved. Sylvan's death is a big deal. It's big news everywhere. Honestly, it would suck to have the department tagged as local yokels who couldn't solve the case."

"We get it." Dee assumed a crafty expression. She double-checked that the door was closed and spoke in a low voice. "I was thinking maybe we'd go over a list of suspects before we completely sign off. You know—sort of like one last hurrah."

"I still have my suspicions about Gracie and Austin," Jeff jumped in, not giving Raul a chance to respond. "I don't care if she was dating Sylvan, those two are definitely hot for each other."

"Agreed," Dee said.

"We also can't forget Ed went after Sylvan when they first met," Jeff said.

"You guys—" Raul tried interrupting, but the others were on a roll.

"We definitely can't forget Ed going for Sylvan," Dee seconded. "And Trish is a real mama bear. I think she'd do anything to protect her Eddie."

Raul tried again. "Come on—"

"I know Ice Cream Ida has physical issues, but she's the kind of person who would want to get revenge on someone who messed with her. Then there's Pamela Pryor. She was Gracie's stepmother."

"*What?*" Jeff reacted with astonishment. "You never told me that."

"I texted Raul, but forgot to tell you. Other things kept happening that pushed it down my list." Dee grew excited as a memory sparked. "And I just remembered, you know who else had a major issue? Abraham Tanner. The man selling leather goods at the crafts fair. He hated that Sylvan was trying to buy up the whole town. What if he decided the only way to stop Sylvan was to kill him? Either alone or with other townspeople who wanted to keep Goldsgone *Goldsgone*?"

"I like it," Jeff enthused.

"HEY!"

Raul's stern bark startled Dee and Jeff. They slunk down in their chairs. He glared at them, his professionalism belying his youth. "What did I say about no amateur sleuthing?"

"Sorry," Dee said meekly.

"Go run your motel. Get hobbies. Ones that don't include snooping." He focused on Dee. "Make some more Bud the Bear swag." He switched to Jeff. "Learn how to canoe. Do anything but try and figure out who offed Burr." His phone lit up with an alert. "Great, a miner broke another miner's nose with his placer pan. I have to go deal with this."

He stood up. Dee and Jeff followed suit. "Message received, Sheriff," Jeff said. "We'll be good."

"Thank you." Raul rounded his desk for the door.

"But I am curious," Dee said. "Did you write down anything we said about possible suspects?"

"*No,*" Raul said, adamant. Then he held up his phone and winked at her. "I recorded it."

# CHAPTER 24

Dee and Jeff respected Raul's wishes and curtailed their amateur sleuthing. Jeff returned to experimenting with activities the Golden could offer their guests, while Dee put her latest brainstorm in motion.

"Our very own Foundgold crafts fair," she told Serena and Elmira. Hoping to rope them in on creating the fair, she'd invited her friends over for lunch, which included a cheeseboard, thoughtfully provided by Serena.

Elmira reacted with disbelief. "Are you looking for more murders around here? Because Verity would take us all out."

Dee clapped a hand to her forehead in a gesture of frustration. "I swear, that woman has more power than a mafia don. But do you know why she has that power? Because you and everyone else in the county give it to her."

She fixed a hard stare on the two women. Serena was the first to falter. "A Foundgold fair *is* a good idea. We'd certainly make it more inclusive than Verity's."

Elmira mulled the idea over. "Drivers coming from Los Angeles pass through Foundgold on their way to Goldsgone, which means they'd see our fair first."

"And drivers coming from San Francisco go through Goldsgone before they reach us, so it's not like we'd cancel out their fair," Dee said. "We're offering a second option."

"Yes," Serena said, warming to the idea. "I like it. And you're right. Why do we let Verity intimidate us? It's time to take back our power."

"Preach, Serena!" Elmira, now fully on board, hooted and clapped her hands above her head. "We can host it in the town rectangle." The narrow streets making up tiny Foundgold ran like ribbons carved into its rocky hillsides and parallel to the main road, hence the village had a town rectangle and not a square. "The rectangle's pretty, got plenty of shade, and the ponderosas don't shed their pinecones until November, so we don't have to worry about anyone getting conked on the head by one."

"And we won't limit participants to Foundgold residents only, right?" Serena asked.

"Correct," Dee said. "Our fair will be inclusive, not exclusive. I think we should give residents first dibs on entry, but all are welcome. In fact, let's set up a meeting here for any craftspeople interested in participating. We'll get the word out that the meeting is happening tonight, which will give less time for blowback from Verity. People can come over right after her fair shuts down for the day."

It occurred to Dee the meeting could serve a double purpose. Despite her promise to curtail sleuthing, the prospect of corralling anti-Sylvan citizens who might be murder suspects in one room was tantalizing. The unsolved murder of a guest, even one as unpleasant as Sylvan, upset Dee. Aside from the ramifications for the motel, she hated to think someone might get away with the most serious of crimes.

"I'm not worried about the short notice, since there's not much of a nightlife around here," Elmira said. "As in none. So in terms of activities, I don't think we have competition. But the threat of retribution will for sure scare some people off."

"Serena, are you up for doing a couple of boards for the meeting?" Dee asked. "One charcuterie, one dessert?"

"Sure. And"—Serena leaned in, a conspiratorial expression on her lovely face—"nothing goes better with my boards than a few bottles of expensive wine from Callan's collection."

"Free food, free vino, and the prospect of making more money from their crafts." Dee grinned with satisfaction. "I call that a recipe for a strong turnout."

Once Dee added a keg of a local craft beer to the meeting menu, her prediction came true. Elmira, Serena, and Dee emailed everyone they knew who'd be interested in the event. Even on such short notice, craftspeople packed the Golden lobby. Dee's former employer Pamela didn't show up, but otherwise the lure of Serena's famed food boards and pricey potables proved irresistible. The atmosphere was surprisingly jovial, considering the Goldsgone contingent pretty much all greeted Dee by nervously saying, "Don't let Verity know I was here." Even Ice Cream Ida put aside her grudge against Dee for exposing her "homemade ice cream" operation and came to the meeting.

Dee was particularly glad to see Tom O'Bryant in the crowd. He'd parked himself at the charcuterie station, where he was busy piling cheeses and cured meats onto a plate. Dee went to him. "Thanks so much for coming."

Tom held up his plate. "You won't find me turning down designer cold cuts. Plus, I got a new batch of sculptures I'm looking to unload on unsuspecting tourists, so the fair works for me."

Dee dropped her voice. "When you finish eating, you might want to strike up conversations with a couple of people who weren't too disappointed by what happened to Sylvan. Abe Tanner and Ice Cream Ida despised him. And I heard a rumor that blacksmith Steve was furious when he found out that instead of preserving his shop, Sylvan planned to tear it down and replace it with electric vehicle charging stations designed to look like hitching posts."

The ranger popped a piece of prosciutto into his mouth and eyed Dee with amusement. "You can't help yourself, can you?"

"What do you mean?"

"This." He gestured with his plate to the attendees. "It's not a meeting about a fair. It's an excuse to get suspects in Burr's murder together in one room."

"Why can't it be both?" Dee responded, feeling defensive. "A Foundgold fair is a good idea. And if a few of the people here happen to hate Sylvan, well . . ." She dropped her defenses and sighed. "Aside from the fact no one should ever get away with murder, it's hard to live with the threat of our new business going under because someone slapped a nasty nickname on it that isn't without a basis in truth."

"Murder Motel," Tom said.

Dee nodded. She pressed her lips together to keep from bursting into tears.

The ranger lifted a hunk of cheese from the board and wrapped his last slice of prosciutto around it. "Tell you what. After I do some damage to the dessert board, I'll sniff around and see if I can pick up any leads."

"Thank you. I'll put off starting the talking portion of the meeting for another half hour."

Dee used the time to do her own eavesdropping, but heard nothing useful. The half hour passed. Sensing people were getting restless, Dee launched into her pitch for a second crafts festival. "We see it as augmenting the Goldsgone fair rather than competing with it," she explained.

"Good luck convincing Verity of that," Abe Tanner said, earning a few chuckles and nods of agreement.

"Summer is high season," Dee said, determined to forge on. "On top of that, we've got an increase in visitors, thanks to the second Gold Rush. My friends and I stand by our belief there's room for more than one festival in our corner of the county."

Elmira waved a tablet in the air. "If you're interested in signing up for a spot, see me."

The meeting broke up. A handful of people left, but Dee was pleased to see a respectable line form for Elmira. She began to clean up. Tom walked up to her. "I got my spot at the fair," he said. "But no leads."

"Oh, well," Dee said, disappointed, but not completely surprised. She had to admit it was hard to imagine one of the mostly senior crafters as a killer.

She thanked the ranger for trying and gifted him with a box of leftover cookies from the dessert board. The room gradually emptied, until only Dee, Elmira, and Serena were left.

"Between Foundgold and Goldsgonedians, I got twenty signups," Elmira said, showing off the list on her tablet. "We're gonna get even more, once word starts spreading."

"People were so enthusiastic they dropped everything to be here tonight." Serena hugged Dee. "Your idea is a hit. Congratulations."

* * *

Dee continued to straighten up the lobby after Elmira and Serena left. Her cell rang and she chided herself for the bump in her heart rate when she saw the caller was Jonas. "Simmer down, Stern," she muttered to herself as she took the call. She answered brightly, "Hi there!"

"Hi, yourself," Jonas responded. "I'm calling from the car on my way home from dinner with a real estate colleague in West Camp. He brought up something I had to share with you."

"Ooh, hit me with it."

"He wanted to know whether any of the people rumored to be interested in selling their property to Sylvan Burr were still up for it. He went down a list of names he'd put together and one was a shocker: Verity Donner Gillespie."

Dee gasped. "*What?! No . . .*"

"Yup."

"*Verity?* Miss Goldsgone of every year since she was born? The person I assume has it in her will that when she dies, her ashes are to be spread like sawdust on the streets and barroom floors of the town?"

"Only V. D. Gillespie in the county I know of."

"Jonas, you rock. This is awesome. It totally tracks to what her nephew Gillie implied when he said she wasn't the rah-rah Goldsgonedian everyone thinks she is." Dee practically vibrated with excitement. "I can add Verity to the list of suspects. Also, I hadn't put together her initials spelled 'V.D.,' which is a huge bonus."

"Her name showing up on the list is a surprising development, but I'm not sure it makes her a murder suspect," Jonas cautioned. "Remember, anyone who wanted to sell would have a vested interest in Sylvan living, not dying."

"Unless," Dee posited, "Verity had a change of heart, but Sylvan threatened her by saying if she backed out, he'd tell everyone she was negotiating to sell. It would ruin her in town. I can't see how she could even go on living in Goldsgone."

"True. But one more thing. My colleague's list was based on word of mouth. Names he's heard mentioned around the county. He doesn't have proof of any actual deals Sylvan made."

"He may not," Dee said, "but I bet I know who does."

Gracie typed on the keyboard of her late boyfriend's laptop, which the police had returned to her, along with his other electronics. She'd been awake when Dee texted to say she had a lead on another suspect, but needed Gracie's help.

"I found a folder marked as Goldsgone," Gracie said. She opened it. "What exactly am I looking for?"

"Anything having something to do with real estate."

Gracie scrolled down. "Here's a spreadsheet named Acquisitions."

"Open it."

Gracie did so, revealing a document set up in columns. The first listed names, the second property addresses, the third property values. Two final columns were labeled as Yes and No. "It looks like a list of every parcel in Goldsgone."

"It is," Dee said. "The last columns must indicate who was a yes or no in terms of selling to Sylvan."

Dee bent over Gracie to get a closer look at the screen. She ran her eyes down the list until she found the name she was looking for. She followed the line across the spreadsheet to the last two columns. "A checkmark in the Yes column." Exultant, she straightened up. "Proof Verity Donner Gillespie was sneaking around, making real estate deals for her property behind Goldsgone's back."

Gracie contemplated this. "If she wanted to sell, why would she kill Sylvan?" she asked, bringing up the same point Jonas had made. Dee explained her theory about the threat to Verity if her perfidy was exposed, but Gracie didn't seem convinced. "I don't know. It's kind of a reach. And if she's the lady I'm thinking of, I can't see her attacking someone. She'd break a nail."

Dee thought of Verity's long, bejeweled fingernails, so beloved by the Goldsgone doyenne that she was willing to part with her historical pioneer look to sport them. "If she was desperate enough, she'd risk it," Dee insisted with more certainty than she felt.

Dee instructed Gracie to email her a copy of the spreadsheet to share with Raul. But as she trod the path back to her apartment, she knew in her heart Gracie was right. Pegging Verity as a suspect in Sylvan's murder was a reach. *But a gal can dream,* Dee thought. She spent the rest of her hike home indulging in a fantasy of Verity behind bars, locked up hopefully forever in Goldsgone's rudimentary jail cell.

*"Ahhhhhh!"*

A woman's scream woke Dee up at dawn. She bolted out of bed and dashed out of the apartment, running toward the sound of a second scream, which came from the motel parking area.

Sleepy-eyed guests stuck their heads out of their room doors. "What's going on?" the Bricklin dad called to her as she ran.

"I don't know, but it's probably nothing," Dee called back, hoping she was right.

She reached the parking lot. Jeff was already there. He had an arm around a distraught Trish. "What happened?" Dee asked, out of breath.

"You're not gonna believe this."

Jeff pointed to the Froelichs' sedan. The door handle on the left passenger side dangled from a wire. Inside the back seat, all Dee saw was brown fur. "Oh. My. *God*. Is that . . . ?"

"Bud the Bear," Jeff confirmed. "He got into the Froelichs' car. And he's stuck."

# CHAPTER 25

Dee calmed a hysterical Trish while Jeff called 911. "I brought a box of those homemade fiber bars they're selling at the All-in-One for Ed, but the hospital won't let him eat food brought in from the outside," Trish said, anguished. "I had so much on my mind when I got back to the motel, I accidentally left the bars in the car. The bear must have smelled them."

"It's okay," Dee said, offering comfort. "You're not the first person to leave food in their car. There's probably a whole series streaming online called 'Bears and Food in Cars.' "

Jeff tapped on his phone. "There is. Here." He held up his phone to show a photo of a furry tush sticking out a car window as a bear went to town on a bag of groceries left in a minivan.

Trish wrung her hands. "How are they going to get him out of my car? Will they have to take it apart?"

"Probably not," Dee said.

"*Probably?!* It's a *probably*?!" Trish shrieked. She began hyperventilating.

Fearing Trish was going to end up in the cardio ward

with her husband, Dee gave her a soothing pat on the back. "Why don't you go lie down in my place? Nugget is there. He'll keep you company." Dee took the Honda car fob from Trish and steered the panicked woman in the direction of her apartment.

Bud shifted inside the car, knocking into the rearview mirror. He released an annoyed grunt and gave the mirror a swat. It dangled from a wire like the car door handle. "Any word on the rangers?" Dee asked Jeff, watching as Bud shifted position again, his claws leaving long scratches on the windows.

"They're on their way. Poor guys. They were *barely* awake."

Dee groaned. "No bear puns, please. I can't *bear* them." She couldn't resist.

The rangers showed up minutes later. Curious motel guests had gathered and Tom O'Bryant, who was leading the bear extraction team, ordered everyone to retreat to a safe distance. "We don't know what kinda mood Bud will be in when he gets out."

"If he ate a box of fiber bars, we definitely want to stay clear of him," Jeff commented, to snickers from one of the rangers.

"Although Bud wanting to eat them is a testament to how much Elmira's baked goods have improved," Dee said. "I've seen garbage he's gotten into where he left her old stuff untouched. I think he once tossed an entire box of brownies back into the garbage can."

Tom addressed Dee. "You got the owner's fob?"

Dee nodded.

"Unlock the doors."

Dee pressed a button. The sound of doors unlocking followed. Tom attached a rope to the door handle. "Line up," he instructed his fellow rangers, who lined up behind him. "Dee, Jeff, we could use some extra heft here."

The moteliers hurried to the rangers and joined them for a round of tug-of-war, rangers versus car door. They stood with their feet apart for balance, gripping the rope tightly with both hands. "On the count of three," Tom yelled in the voice of a drill sergeant. "One . . . two . . . *three*!"

The group gave the rope a hard yank, tumbling backward as the door flew fully open. The observers applauded as the rangers, along with Dee and Jeff, scrambled out of the way. Bud stuck his head out the door. Everyone waited in silence for his next move. He grunted and turned his behind toward the transfixed onlookers. He wiggled his butt as he maneuvered his way backward out of the car, until he eventually extricated himself. He landed on the gravel with a thud. He looked at the car with disdain, then waddled off to more applause from the amused guests.

"I think we should charge for entertainment like that," Jeff said as their guests dispersed, followed by the rangers.

"Yikes. What a disaster." Dee examined the inside of the car, which Bud had trashed. The seats were ripped up. Pieces of the car's interior were strewn throughout it. "The poor Froelichs. This has to be a total loss."

"I'll let Trish know Bud's gone," Jeff said.

"Thanks. After that, why don't you man the motel while I help Trish clean up this mess?"

"Sounds like a plan." Jeff's phone grunted. "I recorded Bud to use as a notification alert for bear-in-car videos," he said, checking. He chuckled. "Ha. Good one here. This guy got into a cooler of ice cream. He's covered in mint chip."

Jeff retrieved Trish, who had transitioned from hysteria

to a state of shock. Dee handed her back the car fob and Trish turned on the engine. "It drives, thank goodness," Trish said. She turned off the engine, placed a hand on her heart, and let out a sigh of relief.

"Which means the damage is cosmetic," Dee said. "Which is as close to good news as you can get, considering the circumstances. Now, let's see what we can do with the interior."

For the next hour, she and Trish did their best to clean up the Civic, tossing out anything that couldn't be salvaged. Dee used a portable vacuum to suck up the last of the bear hair coating the back seat, then aimed it under the driver's seat. She bumped up against books and reached down to move them. "You have *The Sierra Hiker's Guide* and *There's Gold in Them Thar Hills*. So do I."

"*There's Gold* is a signed edition," Trish said with pride. "Eddie used it as source material for where to pan. The bear didn't damage the books, did he?" she asked, worried.

"They were under the seat, so they're untouched." Dee handed them to Trish.

"They're about the only thing in this car that is," Trish said with a sigh, taking the book. "I better go call the insurance company. I'll bring the car to the repair shop in West Camp for an estimate. I hope we're covered for bear damage."

"It's California, so I'm sure you're not the first person making that call. But if you need a witness, let me know."

The women went their separate ways: Trish to tangle with her insurance company, Dee to take care of some motel business and see if she could mine cartoon gold from Bud getting stuck in the car. After hours of setting up and clearing breakfast options, overseeing checkouts, smiling at arriving guests, and envisioning cartoon panels, she realized she needed some fresh air. Dee headed outside to clear her mind and stretch her legs.

Preoccupied, she almost collided with Gracie. Dressed in brown leggings and an oversized T-shirt patterned in shades of green, the young techie looked like she was wearing camouflage. The girl's face was drawn. Gracie had aged since she'd shown up at the Golden.

"Hi," Dee said. "You missed the excitement. I didn't see you with the other guests watching Bud the Bear get freed from the inside of the Froelichs' car."

"I had to make a bunch of calls," Gracie said. "I'm glad I found you. I wanted to let you know I'm checking out tomorrow."

"Oh." Dee was oddly surprised to hear this. She'd begun to feel like the techies were permanent residents. "We'll be sorry to see you go."

Gracie fiddled with the edge of her T-shirt. "I know I said I wanted to stay here until the police caught Sylvan's killer, but that was partially an excuse," she confessed. "I've been procrastinating. I couldn't face dealing with everything after Sylvan died. The business stuff. The personal stuff . . ." She trailed off. Grief etched her face. "I know he was horrible to some people. He wasn't to me. I hate how Austin always says Sylvan stole me. Aside from being incredibly insulting, it's not true. We were all at a party and Austin was flirting with someone else. I got mad at him and came on to Sylvan. I knew he liked me, but wouldn't do anything about it because of Austin. I was the one who pushed Syl to date me. At first, I did it to get back at Austin. But it grew into more than that."

It suddenly struck Dee how much in common the young

tech entrepreneurs had with the child stars she'd worked with in television. Success came before their brains fully developed and they could handle it. They were emotionally immature. Dee would go as far as to consider a lot of them emotionally stunted. From what she'd learned about Gracie and Sylvan, they came from dysfunctional families, like a lot of young TV actors.

Sylvan and his ilk had the advantage of endless streams of income, which allowed them to think they could solve any problem by throwing money at it, while most of the child actors flamed out before they earned a big payday. But the techies and actors both seesawed between insecurity and inflated egos, while a coterie of people fawned over them—until they didn't.

"I'm sorry," Dee said, feeling sympathy for Gracie. "My mother died not even a year ago. Losing someone you love is traumatic. I know I've offered before, but if I can do anything to help, I'm here for you."

Gracie teared up. "Thank you. I have a lot of business associates, but not many friends. *If any* anymore. I became one of those girls who's only about her relationship. I'm not proud of it. Then again, being in a relationship with a high-octane person like Sylvan, it's easy to fall into that."

"I bet."

Gracie wiped her eyes. "There is one thing I need to do before I go." She took in a deep breath. "I want to go back to our mine—the one Sylvan took me to on our hike. For closure. I know you're busy running the motel and everything, but could you maybe go with me?"

"Of course. I need to change first. I'm covered in bear hair."

"I'll wait."

Dee went inside. She yanked off her clothes, wrinkling

her nose. *I'm not just covered with bear hair, I smell like one,* she thought, tossing her clothes into the bathroom hamper. She slipped on a fresh T-shirt and jeans, then laced up her hiking boots. She stuffed her phone and a small bottle of water into her capacious fanny pack, then added bear spray as an afterthought. She doubted Bud the Bear would make a return visit so soon after his dramatic exit, but it wouldn't hurt to carry protection. Especially since she still had at least a modicum of suspicion regarding Gracie. *I'm ninety-nine percent sure she didn't kill Sylvan,* Dee thought, zipping up the fanny pack. *But I don't want to take a chance on that one percent.*

She joined Gracie outside and they began the trek into the woods behind the motel. They climbed through scrubby new trees and majestic old growth. Pine needles crunched under their feet, emitting a rich, soothing scent. Violet petals of Jacob's ladder carpeted their path. Stalks of butterweed, topped with scraggly yellow flowers, clung to the moist slope under a canopy of white alder trees.

"It's so beautiful," Gracie said. "This hike is special to me. The mine Sylvan took me to was one of the ones his family mined. He was sure he could still get enough gold from it to make us wedding rings someday."

"That's actually really sweet. And romantic." Gracie's insight into unexpected facets of Sylvan's character made Dee feel guilty for not mourning him. She made a note to share what Gracie had told her with Raul. If Sylvan was convinced he could mine more gold from one of his family's old mines, maybe he bragged about it to the wrong person: his killer.

They reached a summit. The trees parted, giving way to a spectacular view of Majestic National Park's granite wonders. "We stopped at this view," Gracie said. "Our mine isn't too far."

Gracie led the way, over rocks and along the edge of Little Stream. They reached a patch of earth fitted with a corroded metal cover. Rocks piled high along its edges kept it in place. Gracie dropped to her knees. "This is it. Our mine. Burr Mine. The first one his ancestors laid claim to." Gracie placed a hand on the metal. She closed her eyes and murmured a prayer, then crossed herself. She opened her eyes. "I haven't been to church since I was a little girl. But at a time like this, I feel like I need to make the sign of the cross."

"I get it," Dee said. "I was raised Jewish, but my mother was Catholic. I'd probably do the same thing." The setting sun cast a shadow on the old mine. Leaves rustled on a nearby tree, making Dee jumpy. She knew the sound probably came from a bird, but she still hadn't lost her city girl's fear of the woods at night. "We need to get back before it gets dark."

Gracie stood up. "I'm ready. Thank you." The women began retracing their steps. "I'll never understand what Sylvan was doing at the other mine. The mine where he died. It doesn't make any sense to me."

Dee paused. Gracie's statement exposed how off course the investigation into Sylvan's murder had gone. Everyone had been distracted by his status as a global force in the tech world. Gavin's attack on Ed and flight from Gold County and America had exacerbated this focus. But Gracie's comment pivoted Dee's thinking back to the most obvious question in the investigation.

It all came back to the original, simple question: Why was Sylvan at the other mine?

# CHAPTER 26

The women reached the Golden just as any trace of the sun disappeared. Gracie went to her cabin to pack. Dee returned to her apartment with the goal of doing what she could to research the specific mine where Sylvan died. She first texted Sam to see if he'd come up with anything new on it. He wrote back apologizing. He'd been preoccupied with getting Elmira's baking back on track and promised to research the mine first thing in the morning.

Too antsy to wait for him, Dee turned on her computer and entered a search that led her to a site for aspiring and active gold prospectors. As she created a log-in and was about to open a topographical map showing defunct mines in the region, her cell rang. She saw the caller was Callan and answered.

"Great news!" His enthusiasm matched the statement. "I convinced the studio that a bear was the way to go with your project."

"Wow, that is great." As opposed to Callan, Dee found herself faking enthusiasm. She felt a sinking feeling in the pit of her stomach.

"I need a couple of new cartoons. It'll help amp up the excitement."

"Sure. Give me a day or two."

"Make it a day. You know the business. Some shiny new development toy could come along tomorrow."

Callan signed off. Dee sat for a moment, distressed by the fact that instead of feeling celebratory, she felt dread. Bud the Bear offered her a chance to create and run her own show, an opportunity she'd dreamed of her entire career. But creating any kind of TV series, animated or live action, was an enormous undertaking. There was no way she could run a show *and* the Golden.

"Stop it, you can make this work!" she declared out loud, startling Nugget. He responded with a grumpy bark, then went back to sleep. Dee knew Jeff would be happy for her and provide whatever support he could. He could take over most of the motel managerial duties, with an assist from the Ma'ams. Dee was sure she could convince her father to stick around, especially given Sam's burgeoning relationship with Elmira. In exchange, she'd stay at his house in Studio City when she wasn't working remotely at the Golden.

*I'm getting ahead of myself,* she thought with a laugh. *First I have to write the pilot. We'll see if it gets picked up.* But having formulated a game plan should this happen, Dee felt genuine enthusiasm. She'd create a show for children, but she'd never write down to them. Bud the Bear's show would be one that parents enjoyed watching too.

She tabled her research. For the next few hours, she doodled cartoons featuring Bud. None felt right. Once again, she was stuck on the image of Bud trapped in Trish's car. *There* has *to be something to mine from that,* she thought. *I'll check out the car in the morning and see what it inspires.*

Dee yawned. She glanced down at her phone and saw it was only nine-thirty. *But I'll need plenty of rest if I'm going to juggle two careers*. Dee put her computer to sleep, then followed suit herself.

The insistent ringing of her cell roused Dee in the a.m.

"I wanted to give you an update on the Verity angle," Raul said.

"Great," Dee said eagerly.

"I called her in and dropped the bomb that we knew she was negotiating with Burr to sell her place. I'm not exaggerating when I say I've never seen someone look so shocked. She had no idea what I was talking about."

"Maybe she was acting?" Dee asked, ever hopeful.

"Not for a minute. She yelled, 'I've been set up!' and stormed out. Talk about angry. She may not have killed Sylvan, but whoever messed with her might be my next case."

The conversation ended with Dee disappointed, but resigned. She decided to view the latest dead end as a sign from the universe to focus her energies elsewhere. After a bracing shower and hearty breakfast of scrambled eggs, which she shared with Nugget, Dee picked up her sketchbook and headed outside.

She marched down to the site of the Froelichs' Bear-versus-Car debacle. But the Civic wasn't there. Disappointed, she shook it off. *Not a problem! I can do this!*

She dropped onto a large rock on the edge of the parking area. Dee closed her eyes and replayed the scene from the day before. She jotted down a couple of possible cartoons, then crossed them all out. Dee rested her chin on her fist and thought for a moment. Then she made a quick sketch showing Bud's ample backside sticking out of the car's back door. Under the drawing, she added a caption: *Where's a weight loss drug when you need it?*

Dissatisfied with her work, she put a big X through the

cartoon. *No weight loss drug jokes,* she thought. *I can do better.*

A fruitless hour later, the disheartened artist was doubting she could. Stiff from her perch on the rock, Dee stood up and stretched. Her left leg had fallen asleep, which she discovered when she took a step and the leg buckled beneath her. Dee tumbled into the bushes.

She sat up and extended the leg to shake it awake. The bush she leaned against shook with her. A piece of paper stuck to a branch detached and floated onto her lap. Dee picked it up. The paper was a torn copy of the Froelichs' car registration, collateral damage from Bud's foraging in their vehicle for Ed's fiber bars. Dee noted the car was registered in Trish's name. She was about to pocket the registration form to return to Trish when she noticed something else. The name on the registration: *Trish Hanford Froelich.*

"Hanford," which Dee assumed was Trish's maiden name, struck a familiar note. She wracked her brain to figure out why, and then it came to her. The name had been referred to in *There's Gold in Them Thar Hills.*

Dee closed her sketchbook and raced up the hill to her apartment. She hurried into her bedroom and grabbed the history book from where she'd left it on her nightstand. Too amped up to sit down, she stood as she flipped to the book's index. She located the name Hanford and turned to the first page listing it. There, among the names of miners Sylvan Burr's ancestor Silas had stolen from and forced into ruin, was the name Ephraim Hanford, along with details about the case that Hanford brought against Burr.

Dee recalled the story Tom O'Bryant had told her about his family's centuries-old feud with Verity Gillespie's family over an old mine. If Trish could call Ephraim Hanford an ancestor, an old family grudge against the Burrs might have been reignited by the sight of Sylvan, Silas Burr's descendant.

Dee stopped reading. She yanked her cell phone out of her jeans pocket to share the discovery with Raul. Then she stopped. While it seemed a likely bet Trish was a descendant of Ephraim Hanford, Dee had no proof.

But she had an idea on how to get some.

Dee returned the phone to her pocket and left the apartment for the motel housekeeping storage room. She wheeled out the janitor cart and pushed it toward a motel room. "Housekeeping," she called, knocking on the Bricklins' door.

"We're okay," a Bricklin called back.

Dee did the same with the next room, purposely choosing ones that were occupied. They'd be less likely to take her up on the offer, but if anyone saw her, they'd assume she was merely making the rounds.

She reached the Froelichs' room and knocked. "Housekeeping." As expected, no one answered. Dee put the motel master key into the lock and turned it. She opened the door and entered the room.

She gave the Froelichs credit for keeping the room neat. A hazmat suit would have come in handy for cleaning up after some of the Golden's messier guests. Dee positioned the cleaning cart by the window to lend truth to the lie she was there to tidy up the room. Then she began her search for anything that might link Trish to Ephraim Hanford.

Dee was beginning to wonder if the room's spotless state was a purposeful way of hiding clues, and then she noticed a corner of a book sticking out from under one side of the bed. She reached down and picked up Trish's copy of *There's Gold in Them Thar Hills*. Opening it, she saw the copyright page, which was autographed by the author: *Trish, thanks for sharing so much about Ephraim and your family—especially the documents regarding the lawsuit. You were a "gold mine" of information!*

Dee's phone rang with a call from Sam. She replaced the book where she'd found it and answered.

"Prospector Pete here with an important update." He sounded excited. "I'm at the All-in-One. Elmira and I just put a pan of peanut butter cookies into the oven. But I wanted to let you know that I looped Ma'am into our quest to uncover the history of the mine where Sylvan died. She took me to a hermit living in the backcountry. I'm pretty sure we hiked through a cartel marijuana field to get there."

"And?" Dee prompted. Nervous about being caught by Trish, Dee opened the room's door with her free hand and awkwardly tried to maneuver the janitorial cart out of the room's tight quarters. A wheel caught on something and she yanked it outside with her.

"This old geezer—and I say this as a geezer myself, although this fella could be old enough to date back to the original Gold Rush—"

"Dad, tell me what you found out."

"Before it got the name Rich Diggins, the mine was called Fight Mine, because two miners got into a fight over it. It's on land originally claimed by a prospector named Ephraim Hanford. But someone claim-jumped, insisting they had the site first, without any proof. Ephraim sued, but didn't live to see the results. He got into a gunfight with the other claimant and wound up on the wrong end of a bullet, as they'd say in Goldsgone. And you'd never guess the name of his killer."

"Silas Burr," Dee said. "He's the one who claim-jumped

Ephraim Hanford. Ephraim brought a lawsuit. The Burrs ruined the Hanfords."

"Yes," Sam said, surprised and a little miffed he didn't get to reveal this himself. "How'd you know?"

"It's all in the book," she said.

"What's all in the book?"

Dee froze at the sound of Trish Froelich's voice. She hadn't heard the woman approach. Instinct told her that was intentional. "I've got to go, Dad." She forced herself to sound casual. "Trish Froelich just got back." She ended the call and faced Trish. She couldn't decipher the expression on the woman's face. "Hi, I was thinking about you. I just cleaned your room."

"What's all in the book?" Trish repeated.

"Nothing." She had no idea how much of her conversation Trish had overheard, but feared it might be the name of her ancestor. "Dad and I were saying how that *There's Gold* book reads like fiction. I mean, come on." She gave a derisive snort. "The author has to be making half of it up, am I right?"

"I see you found my copy."

Trish pointed to the ground. Dee looked down and saw what was blocking the wheel of the janitorial cart: Trish's copy of the book.

She bent down and picked it up. "I'm so sorry," she said, handing the book to Trish. "It must have gotten stuck when I was doing the daily cleaning of your room."

"I thought you only cleaned rooms when guests requested it, as a way of observing an environmentally positive policy." Trish spoke in an even tone, but the icy glint to her eyes made Dee's heart thump.

"Wow, that's a direct quote from our website. Nice." Dee gave a nervous laugh. "Sometimes we break our own rules for special guests. Like you and Ed. We want to make sure he comes back to a spotless, germ-free room. And don't worry, if the book is damaged, I'll pay for it. I know it's worth a lot to you, being autographed and a first edition. Oh, I just remembered, I found your car registration. You'll need that for your insurance claim."

"I never told you it's a first edition. You'd only know that if you looked inside. And saw the inscription next to it."

"The book fell open to that page." Dee's face flushed red. She cursed her tendency to blush when lying. "So cool. Anyway, let me get you your registration. It's in my apartment."

Dee gave the cart a push, but Trish blocked her path. "You know what's even *cooler* than the book? This." Trish spoke in a whisper.

She pulled an antique pistol from her purse.

*Somebody, anybody, come out of your room,* Dee prayed. *Please!* But her guests stayed put. She debated making a run for it, but she didn't put it past Trish to shoot her in the back and claim she was stopping the theft of a rare book.

"I started packing this yesterday, after the bear got into my car. Isn't it a beauty?" Trish caressed the barrel. The mother-of-pearl inlay decorating glittered in the sunlight. "Since you found my registration, you know my birth name is Hanford. This gun belonged to my three-times great-grandfather Ephraim Hanford. It was a family tradition that we all learned how to shoot with it. The book got Ephraim's story right, you know. Thanks to me. I shared all the papers handed down in my family, everything chronicling how Silas Burr jumped Ephraim's claim. And then when it looked like Ephraim would win his lawsuit, Burr shot him and paid off the judge to acquit him on a verdict of self-defense."

"He was one of the two miners Silas killed," Dee said, recalling the chapter on Silas Burr in the book.

"And got away with."

"But that was a long time ago," Dee said, growing desperate. "So, *sooooo* long ago." She stuck a hand in her pants pocket, framing it like a nervous gesture. She subtly fished for her phone to trigger the emergency alert, but couldn't touch both necessary buttons at the same time.

"You've learned so much about my family's mine." Trish pointed the gun at Dee, low enough to keep it out of sight, but angled to aim at her. "I'd like to take you on a tour of it myself."

# CHAPTER 27

Trish led Dee on a forced march through the woods behind the Golden. For the second day in a row, Dee scrambled over rocks and crunched pine needles underfoot. They reached the view she'd admired with Gracie. Now she noticed how close it was to the edge of a ledge and a vertiginous, deadly drop. She took small comfort from Trish urging her on and not pushing her off the ledge.

"If only you hadn't bought that book," Trish grumbled. "Why did you have to be so interested in the history of the Gold Rush? Didn't you get enough of all that in fourth grade, like everyone else in California?"

"Long story, but no," Dee said, ducking under a low-hanging branch she hoped Trish would walk into. "I needed to brush up on it for our guests. Who knew two of them, you and Sylvan, would be descendants of the original Forty-Niners?"

Trish ducked under the branch, to Dee's disappointment. They continued in the opposite direction of the previous day's trek, toward the mine where Sylvan Burr met his fate. "Silas Burr tricked and bullied a lot of people out of their claims." Trish said this through huffs and puffs of breath. She carried at least twenty pounds of extra weight and the exertion of the climb was getting to her. Unfortunately for Dee, the Hanford descendant kept trudging along, her gun pointed at the motelier. "But before Fight Mine was Rich Diggins, my ancestors called it the Hanford Mine. It's the one that really kicked off the Burr family's road to riches. It gave up more gold than any of the others."

"That's why you chose to stay with us," Dee said. "The Golden is the closest lodging to it."

"Exactly."

"Ugh, mosquitoes." Dee swatted at an imaginary insect. "It's from all the water from the rains. They're breeding like mofos." Dee faked scratching an itch, then slipped her hand into her pockets. She felt around for her phone one last, desperate time.

"Hands where I can see them, please."

Dee reluctantly pulled her hands out of her pockets.

They came to Golden Brook. The first time Dee and Jeff had crossed it on their way to the mine where Sylvan died, Jeff had slipped and nearly fallen in. Dee willed the universe to make Trish lose her balance on the slippery rocks and topple into the brook's rushing waters, but the universe didn't deliver. Trish negotiated the stones with surprising agility.

"I almost fainted when I saw Sylvan Burr at the motel," she said, taking a small jump from the last rock to the brook's edge, right behind Dee. "I've been keeping track of his career ever since I first read a profile of him in the *L.A. Times*. I assumed he was staying at the Golden for the same reason I was, proximity to Rich Diggins. After Ed took the swing at him, I was terrified Sylvan would follow up on his threat to sue us. I found him after he and his friends returned from the crafts fair and begged him not to follow through on the threat. All he'd say was he'd think about it. I tried to suck up by saying we had so much in common as descendants of the original miners. It turned out he knew about the Burr mines, but didn't know Rich Diggins was where it all began for his family."

"I'm surprised. The only interest he seemed to have in his family was how it got so rich." Dee did her best to sound conversational. She remembered reading about a woman who was taken hostage during a bank robbery and established a bond with the robber that kept him from killing her. She couldn't remember if the story was fiction or nonfiction, but given the dire situation she was in, Dee figured the approach was worth a try. "Sylvan and his friends think gold can still be extracted from a lot of the local mines if modern techniques are used. Do you think that's the case with the Hanford Mine?" She purposely used Trish's family name, hoping to sound sympatico.

"Sylvan sure did. When I mentioned it delivered the mother lode of Burr gold, he started salivating, I swear. The location of the mine has been a family secret handed down through generations of Hanfords. Not many of us are left at this point and I'm the only one who's still got any interest in it. I told Sylvan I'd take him to the mine if he swore to secrecy and promised to split any profit from it with me fifty-fifty. I got a 'sure, whatever' from him, and I knew he was lying."

"But you still took him to the mine? Why?" Despite the circumstances, Dee was genuinely curious.

"Revenge, my friend." The note of triumph in Trish's voice gave Dee goose bumps. "It was a test and he failed. His family destroyed my family. His business destroyed my husband's. If we'd come to a deal for the mine, everything would have been okay. But he was so obviously going to cut me out. So it was his turn to suffer."

"Or . . . and I'm just spitballing here"—*And stalling for time!* Dee thought as she blathered on—"you could have gone to the media to share how Sylvan Burr was continuing his family's tradition of ripping off your family. The court of public opinion would have been on your side. Billionaire versus nice office manager lady? No contest."

"Maybe. But being a nice, middle-aged, middle-class lady also helps make you the least likely murder suspect. Although I never intended to kill him." Trish sounded wistful. "I wanted him to *think* I was going to push him into the mine. The knife was only supposed to make him do what I told him to do: stand at the edge of the mine, look down, and get the scare of his life. But, as I figured, he told me to forget about getting a share of whatever gold was left in the mine. Any claims the Hanfords had would never stand up to the years it was in the Burrs' possession, and if I sued, he had the money to drag the case out until I died. Oh, good, we're here."

In front of them lay the trunk of the giant pine tree Dee had climbed over to reach the law enforcement officials who'd tracked Sylvan to where he died. Behind the tree trunk was the small clearing in front of the Hanford-Fight-Rich Diggins Mine, the entrance carved out of the largest rock of the outcropping. Dee noticed that more chunks of the rotting wood framing the entrance had splintered off and fallen to the ground since her last trip to the site.

"Here's a thought." Dee knew what she was about to say was a reach, but she gave it a go anyway. "With Sylvan gone, you could reclaim this mine for your family. I'm sure there's a wannabe prospector with money who would fund reopening it."

Trish shook her head sadly. "The irony is, no matter what Sylvan thought, of all the mines that might still contain gold, this one is the least likely. Really, any mine Silas Burr got his hands on—you can bet he stripped them all clean." She gestured with her gun toward the derelict entrance. "Move, please."

Dee took tiny, terrified steps. "I have to be honest." Her voice quavered. "I really, really don't want to die. The motel is taking off. I may get to create a TV series. I may or may not be in a relationship. There's a lot going on in my life and I'd like to stick around for it."

"I don't want to kill you," Trish said. "I only want you in the bottom of the mine long enough for Eddie and me to get to Mexico."

"Not much of an escape plan." Dee had reached the point where she didn't care if she ticked off her captor. "Mexico is very been-there, done-that by a lot of criminals. Plus, you and Ed scream American citizens. I don't think you'd last long."

"The ad agency I work for specializes in bilingual advertising, so I happen to be fluent in Spanish. Plus, Eddie's mother's family is from Oaxaca. They'll take us in. We'll change our appearances and become *tía y tío* Name-I'll-Never-Tell-You. Now I'm running out of time. Please get in there."

Dee peered over her shoulder into the mine's entrance. All she saw was blackness. "I remember the ranger said it's a twenty-foot drop. You say you don't want to kill me, but I'm not seeing a way around it right now."

"Just get in!"

Trish yelled this, startling Dee, who almost lost her balance. She screamed as she instinctively jumped away from the entrance. The move startled Trish, which triggered one last-ditch effort from Dee. She began hopping back and forth, from one foot to another, imitating her father's ridiculous Prospector Pete dance. "'La di dah, la dee dee,'" she sang as she hopped, "'it's a prospector's life for me!'"

"What are you doing?" Trish, thrown by the bizarre dance, moved her gun back and forth, trying to train it on the moving target that was Dee. "Stop. Stop it right now!"

"Dancy dee dancy do," Dee improvised, "I'll dig up gold and share it with you!"

"I said stop—*ow!*"

Trish jerked her head as something beaned her. She shook it off and aimed at Dee, who continued her herky-jerky dancing.

"I love gold and it loves me, fol-de-rol and fiddle dee dee!"

Trish mimicked Dee's moves in an attempt to get the motelier in her crosshairs. She was about to pull the trigger when a volley of small but hard silver balls flew out of the woods, some striking her, others ricocheting off trees. Dee fell to the ground to avoid being hit. A ball hit Trish in the head, this one with more force. She screamed and reached for her wounded head, dropping the gun.

Before Dee could grab it, Jeff and Sam burst out of the woods holding slingshots. Jeff tackled Trish, while Sam rushed to pull his daughter away from the entrance. There was the sound of people crashing through the woods. Seconds later, Raul, FBI agents, and park rangers swarmed the clearing. They took over containing Trish from Jeff.

Sam helped Dee to her feet. He gave her a fierce hug. "I don't know what was scarier, seeing that woman try to get you in her eyeline, or watching you dance."

"We'll call it a draw," Dee said, hugging her father back. "How did you find me?" Dee asked. "I kept trying to trigger a 911 alert on my phone, but I didn't think I got it to work."

"You didn't. Jeff happened to be practicing with one of the slingshots when he saw Trish march off with you. He sounded the alarm with Raul, but was afraid the police wouldn't get here in time. I was cleaning out the sluice, so he grabbed the second slingshot, grabbed me, and we took off after you. We kept enough distance not to alert Trish. It wasn't easy keeping quiet, but we hoped if she heard anything, she'd think it was an animal. Like her pal Bud."

"You both did an amazing job of tracking," Dee said, overwhelmed with gratitude. "Prospector Pete might have a new skill to add to his résumé."

Jeff walked over to them. He held a hand over his left eye. "Trish is officially under arrest."

"Oh no!" Dee exclaimed. "Your eye." She gently lifted his hand, revealing an angry red welt and swelling lid.

"One of the balls ricocheted and hit me," he said. "You were right, slingshots are not a good Golden guest activity."

"We need to get you to a doctor. But first"—she threw her arms around her best friend and hugged him—"thank you for saving my life."

She gave him another squeeze, then let him go. Jeff grinned and did his own version of the Prospector Pete. "Yippity dee and yippity do," he sang off-key, "you're welcome from me for rescuing you!"

# CHAPTER 28

Dee met up with Raul and the FBI agents at the Goldsgone sheriff's station to make a report detailing every step of her run-in with Trish, and subsequent kidnapping. When she was done, she drove to the Gold County Medical Center, where Jeff had gone to have his eye treated. Dee was glad she wasn't the one checking into the ER for a change, but nurse-practitioner Tuva expressed disappointment. "I was looking for you to break a record on visits here," she said as she applied salve to Jeff's eye.

"Still could happen," Dee responded with a grin.

"Ha. I don't doubt it." Tuva handed Jeff an eye patch. "Apply the ointment as needed. Cold compresses every few hours. Wear the eye patch until the morning. And take a break from being a hero. I read about your last adventure in the *Gazette*. If you're not careful, you're gonna break *her* record in the ER." She gestured to Dee with her thumb.

"It's outta my hands." Jeff lifted his shoulders in a what-can-you-do shrug. "Heroes gonna hero."

"Oh, *groan*!" Dee punctuated this by miming sticking her finger down her throat.

Jeff ignored her. He put on the black eye patch and gave the rubber band holding it in place a cocky snap. Then he hopped off the edge of the examination bed, where he'd been sitting, took a step, and immediately bumped into a chair. "Ouch. My vision's distorted with this thing."

"Ha, like you wouldn't bump into things without it," Dee affectionately teased her oft-clumsy friend. She crooked her arm. "I'll be your eyes."

Jeff slid his arm through hers. They bid Tuva goodbye and headed out of the hospital.

"I know I'm supposed to rest," Jeff said, "but I'm too wired."

"Me too," Dee agreed. She lifted the corner of her mouth in a mischievous smile. "Can I talk you into one of Ida's non-homemade pumpkin ice cream sandwiches?"

"You betcha." He wrinkled his brow. "'Betcha.' Miner's jar?"

"Not today, my friend. After what you did, you can talk like a miner all you gol-dern want." Her phone pinged. She let go of Jeff's arm to remove her cell from her pocket. "We'll have to put a pin in the ice cream sandwiches. Gracie wanted to check out today. She saw all the police action and wondered what was going on." Dee grew serious. "We need to let her know Sylvan's killer has been caught."

"Am I weird for feeling a little sorry for Trish?" Gracie asked.

She sat across from Dee at one of the lobby breakfast tables, clutching a coffee cup. Jeff had stayed behind in Goldsgone, commandeered by Verity, who wanted to hear the whole story of how he rescued Dee. This was accompanied by flirty comments about how sexy men looked with eye patches, which, to Jeff's amusement, earned a massive amount of eye rolls from Dee behind Verity's back.

"It's not weird, it's empathetic," Dee said, answering Gracie's question. She noticed Gracie had changed out her diamond nose piercing for one of black onyx, reflecting her somber mood. "Murder is a heinous act. I'd never condone it. But I think Trish suffered from a form of generational trauma that eventually poisoned her. The Hanfords blamed the Burrs for their troubles. They watched the Burr family fortune grow while they struggled to even attain middle class status. The family passed their anger and resentment down to their descendants for over one hundred fifty years. And then it turned out a *Burr* descendant—Sylvan—was responsible for destroying Trish's husband's business. I think that's what set Trish off and made her determined to avenge the injustice she'd had drummed into her all her life."

Gracie took this in. "Has Ed been arrested too?"

Dee shook her head. "The authorities interviewed him. He was clueless about what she did. All he was focused on was finding enough gold to dig him and Trish out of their financial hole. Plus, Ed wasn't feeling well. He was having symptoms of a heart problem, but trying to ignore them."

"I feel sorry for him too, then."

Dee saw Gracie's coffee cup was empty. "Do you want a refill before you hit the road? I know you wanted to check out today."

"No thanks. And if you don't have someone checking into my cabin, I'd like to stay a few more days, if it's okay with you."

"Absolutely. I think Gold Rush 2.0 is winding down. Your cabin is available. Stay as long as you want." Dee debated bringing up what she'd heard at Miss Mary's Unmentionables, then went for it. "Is this about your plan with Pamela?"

Gracie gaped at Dee. "How do you know about that?"

"I don't know what exactly it is," Dee backtracked. "I only know you have one. When I was working at Miss Mary's, I overheard you and Pamela talking. I heard you mention she used to be your stepmother."

The young techie gazed at her almost in wonder. "How do you have time to run a motel with all the snooping you do?"

"Good question," Dee said with an embarrassed chuckle. "I'm sure you're not the first to think it, but you're the first to ask. The thing is, I never set out to snoop. But I've sunk my life and savings into the Golden, and dragged my best friend along with me. I can't risk anything threatening its success, like being known as Murder Motel."

"That's actually kind of a cool nickname."

"Not sure the kind of guests we want to attract would agree." Dee gave Gracie's question more thought. "Also, I think as a writer, there's a part of me that can't deal with an unfinished story. And until they're solved, every murder is unfinished."

"Truth," Gracie said, nodding. "Just so you know, my plan with Pamela isn't nefarious. And you snoopily heard right, she was one of my five stepmoms. Yup, *five*. My dad was a popular NorCal DJ, who was also an alcoholic and burned through five wives. Pamela was number three and the nicest to me, but we lost touch after they divorced. My own mom moved to Amsterdam when I was in college and I hardly saw her. She was always into her own life. Dad died last year from liver disease. I felt lonely for a parent, so I tracked down Pamela. That's the real reason I wanted to come here. But the first time I saw her, she was dressed like an old-time prostitute and flirting with Sylvan and the others, and . . . I thought I made a big mistake."

"But from what I 'snoopily' overheard, you and Pamela worked it out."

"Yes." Gracie smiled, but Dee couldn't help noticing it was tinged with sadness. She'd been through a lot in a short amount of time. It would take Gracie a while to completely recover. "I'm going to put my marketing muscle behind expanding Miss Mary's Unmentionables into a global presence. I've got the money for it, thanks to Sylvan's will."

"So he did have one. Raul was never able to track it down."

"That's because Sylvan's estate lawyer was heli-skiing in the New Zealand Remarkable Mountains and was unreachable. He only heard about Sylvan's death yesterday when he was dropped back into Queenstown."

"You rich people sure spend a lot of time in helicopters."

This earned a true smile from Gracie. "The one-percenters' favorite toy," the young woman said.

"That and owning towns," Dee said with meaning. She cast a reproachful look at Gracie. "I don't know what Sylvan would have done with Goldsgone and Foundgold if he did manage to buy them up, but these little towns are a piece of our state's history. In a way, we're custodians of them for future generations."

"I agree a hundred percent," Gracie said. "Sylvan had deals going all over the place that I knew nothing about. Believe me, if I'd known what he was up to here, I would have done everything to talk him out of it. It might have been the thing that broke us up." She pressed her lips together to contain her emotions. Then she continued. "Anyway, I'm going to fund the expansion of Pamela's business with the money Sylvan left me. He left the rest to his high school and college for brand-new buildings."

"Named after him, I'm sure," Dee wryly noted. "Yet another one-percent toy."

"It's probably a reason he was so into cryonics." There was a glimmer of mischievousness in Gracie's eyes. "So he could be brought back to life to admire them."

Dee burst out laughing. Gracie hesitated, then joined her.

The apartment door opened. Jeff, still wearing his eye patch, burst into the room, followed by Austin. "We ran into each other in the parking lot," Jeff said. "Boy, does he have breaking news."

Austin pointed to his phone. "I got a notification. Gavin's been arrested."

Dee and Gracie responded with disbelief. "No!" Gracie exclaimed. "You're making it up."

Jeff went to the motel computer, managing not to injure himself bumping into tables or chairs on the way. The others clustered around him. He typed in Gavin's name and a long list of results populated the screen, all referencing the arrest of the fugitive tech mogul.

Jeff clicked on a link and a video opened to a live update from a reporter standing on the tarmac in front of a large airplane at the Frankfurt, Germany, airport. "Tech exec Gavin Walsh earned a spot on the FBI's Most Wanted list when he escaped an attempted murder charge by fleeing to a country without a U.S. extradition treaty," the reporter intoned. "But when Walsh decided on a little R and R in the Maldives, another country that doesn't share a treaty with the U.S., he didn't count on his plane being forced to make an emergency stop in Germany—a country that's been shipping criminals back to the United States for almost forty years. You could say that thanks to the malfunctioning lavatory system on the Boeing 777 carrying Walsh to the Maldives, the wanted fugitive was 'flushed' out of hiding."

The reporter chuckled at his own joke, then continued. He shared that Interpol had been tracking Walsh ever since the private plane he'd transferred to after choppering out of Gold County entered international airspace. Devoid of a functioning bathroom on the airplane to the Maldives, Walsh was forced to step off the plane to relieve himself. Interpol agents nabbed him the minute his feet touched friendly soil.

"It's perfect Walsh got nailed because of a faulty bathroom," Austin commented, "since he turned out to be a piece of excrement himself."

The report ended and Jeff closed the link. He noticed the time on the computer. "It's five o'clock somewhere, and that somewhere is here. Could anyone else besides me use a drink?"

"Me, me!" Dee waved both hands in the air.

"Thanks for the invitation, but I'm gonna pass," Gracie said. "I feel like I need some alone time to process everything that's happened."

"I'll walk you back to the cabins," Austin said.

"Before we go," Gracie said, hugging Dee, "thank you for being so snoopy. You helped find Sylvan's killer. I'll always owe you."

"You don't owe me anything," Dee said. "Just do me a favor. When you write a review of the Golden, promise not to call it Murder Motel."

# CHAPTER 29

The next few days were good ones for the Golden. Having saved the lives of two people in a short time span, Jeff cemented his status as a local hero. His eye healed, but the eye patch stayed on, adding to the allure of his exploits. Dee listened with amusement as the details of his rescues grew more dramatic with each retelling.

"At least we're getting a few free meals out of your theatrics, I mean *heroics,*" she teased, digging into her complimentary slice of Aunt Aggie's Mile-High Apple Pie, courtesy of Liza and the Golden Grub Café. The moteliers were sitting outside on the restaurant's patio, enjoying the lovely summer day.

Jeff puffed out his chest. "All in a day's work, my friend." He speared a forkful of his own free slice of pie. "My eyes have adjusted to this patch. I think I might keep it and—"

Commotion from across the street interrupted him. Raul burst out of the Goldsgone Mercantile and Emporium pushing a handcuffed Gillie Gillespie in front of him. Verity came out of the store behind them. She leaned against a lamppost and watched as Raul led Gillie down the street to the sheriff's station.

"You can't do this, Aunt Verity!" Gillie yelled at her. "We're family! Verity! Auntie! Come on!"

Verity ignored him and sauntered across the street. Dying to learn what was going on, Dee didn't object when Jeff invited her nemesis to join them.

Verity waved down a waitress. "A glass of Chardonnay. I've earned a round or two of day drinking."

"We saw Raul take Gillie away," Jeff said. "What happened?"

"Apparently, Vernon Donner Gillespie, my brother's sorry excuse for a son, was trying to sell me out to Sylvan Burr."

"V.D.," Dee murmured, recalling Sylvan's spreadsheet.

"He knew if he made arrangements to sell his share of the store, even though he doesn't have ownership of it yet because my brother is still alive and kicking, I'd be forced to sell my share," Verity continued. "He's always been a conniver. And as I recently learned, a thief. He's been dipping into the store's petty cash." The waitress delivered Verity's wine. "So I had him arrested. I'll drop the charges, of course." She took a sip of wine and smiled smugly. "Right after he signs over the rights to his half of the mercantile." She raised her glass. "To Goldsgone!"

Tables around her raised their glasses and echoed the cheer. "To Goldsgone!"

"They'll have to carry me out of here in a pine box!" Verity declared, glass still aloft.

"You and Ice Cream Ida," Dee said, defeated.

Dee and Jeff got a message that Ed was being released from the hospital. Knowing a return to the room he'd shared with Trish would be difficult, they prepared one of the cabins for him. To Dee's surprise, Austin and Gracie offered to pick up the accountant at the hospital and bring him back to the motel. She was more surprised by what followed.

She waited as Austin parked the car. Gracie got out of the back seat first and helped Ed out of the front seat. Dee went to him. "Ed. We've all been thinking about you. How are you feeling?" She knew it was a fatuous question considering he'd just had major surgery and his wife had been arrested for murder, but she wasn't sure what else to say.

"Been better," the accountant said with a weak smile, looking every year of his age and then some.

"Jeff and I will do whatever we can to help you. Stay here for free as long as you want. Our motel is your motel."

"Thanks. That's very generous of you. I have been worried about Trish's legal bills on top of everything else."

"I'm sure," Dee said, filled with pity for him.

"I swear, I had no idea what she did to Sylvan." He couldn't bring himself to use the word "kill."

Dee recalled the moment Ed attacked Sylvan Burr. "When you went for Sylvan, you yelled, 'You ruined me! You ruined my family!' The last part . . . was about Trish, wasn't it?"

Ed nodded. "I knew she'd inherited her family's grudge against the Burrs. But I didn't know how much it poisoned her mind." He turned to Gracie, who was holding his arm to offer support. "Again, I'm so sorry." He sounded plaintive, almost on the verge of tears.

"You don't have to say that anymore," Gracie responded, her tone gentle. "I don't blame you."

"It's the gold," Ed said. "It pushes people to the boundary of their senses. They don't remember the end of the Midas story. King Midas wound up getting his wish and everything he touched turned to gold. But that included his food, so he wound up starving to death."

"Talk about a cautionary tale," Austin said, somber.

"Austin and I have agreed not to touch the old mines," Gracie said. "This may sound crazy or woo-woo, but re-opening any of them felt like it would stir up some really nasty ghosts."

"It doesn't sound crazy to me at all," Dee said. "In fact, reopening a mine reminds me of another cautionary tale: the one about Pandora's box and the evil that flew out of it. But Ed, there has to be a way Jeff and I can help you out financially. Maybe we can do a fundraiser. Or a raffle where the prize is a week's stay at the Golden with a bunch of activities—minus the ones that might injure Jeff."

"You won't have to do anything," Austin said. "I'm bored out of my mind being retired. I mean, I'm not even thirty. It's insane. So I'm going back to Tax Hax as CEO and hiring Ed as a consultant. We've been talking a lot about the company and I have to own the downside of what we created. I've heard my own parents scream '*Human*!' into the phone a million times trying to get through a chatbot to an actual person. Ed is going to help us add a human touch to the app and make it more user-friendly." He put a hand on the older man's shoulder. "And we're going to pay him well to do it."

"That's fantastic," Dee said. The thought that something good would come from the tragedy of Sylvan's murder made her choke up. "If you promise me a human being at the other end of my call, I may use Tax Hax myself."

Two nights later, Dee and Jeff bid goodbye to Gracie, Austin, and Ed as one final helicopter took off from the Gold County Fairgrounds. "Do you think Austin and Gracie will get back together?" Jeff asked as they waved the chopper off.

"Maybe," Dee said. "Austin has got a lot of growing up to do, but he's definitely taking steps in that direction. I find him a modicum less annoying than I did when they all first showed up."

She and Jeff watched the helicopter disappear into the horizon, then started the walk to Dee's car. "Well, that's done," she said. "Now it's back to the Golden and a good night's sleep before the crafts fair."

Jeff eyed her with affection. "Ha. You're kidding yourself. You know you're barely gonna sleep at all tonight with the first Foundgold fair looming in front of you."

Dee released a theatrical sigh. "You couldn't let me live in a delusional state, could you?"

Jeff proved right. Nervous about how the fair would go, Dee barely slept a wink.

To her relief, despite the threat of rain, day one of the first annual Foundgold Food and Crafts Fair dawned sunny and temperate. She pulled a luggage cart of Bud the Bear swag past tables holding the creations of her fellow Foundgoldians on the way to laying out her own merchandise. Serena and Elmira had taken the lead on organizing the event. They'd done such a fantastic job, all Dee needed to do was show up.

She took in the wide array of offerings as she walked by the tables. Serena was surrounded by shoppers interested in purchasing the charcuterie boards showcased at her stand. A shopper walked by, with one of Tom O'Bryant's found-objects sculptures tucked under his arm. Ma'am and Mister had set up a table to sell Ma'am's mysterious yet incredibly effective ointments and balms. The ingredients were top secret, but Dee guessed at least one of the illegal marijuana grows in the Sierra's backcountry was short a few plants, harvested by the Ma'ams for their potions.

Sam waved at his daughter as she made her way past the All-in-One baked-goods stand. Dressed as Prospector Pete, he was performing double duty, promoting the Golden and its sluice by handing out a motel postcard with each sweets purchase. He held up a treat cosseted in plastic wrap. "Want the last Nutty Almond Date Bar?" he asked Dee. "We're already sold out of them, and it's not even ten a.m."

"Sure, thanks." Dee took the bar from Sam. "And congrats on the awesome sales."

"Elmira's Elegant Edibles are a hit," he said, beaming.

Dee did a double take. "Edibles? Really? That's a new take on Elmira's goodies, but okay."

"Huh?" Sam appeared confused by Dee's reaction, then it dawned on him. "*Oh.* No, not that kind of edible. There's no CBD in anything we bake." Sam wrinkled his brow. "Hmm. I was going for alliteration, but I think I better come up with a new name."

"Probably a good idea," Dee said, guessing the current name was responsible for the stall's instant success.

Dee continued on until she reached her own table. She removed her wares from storage containers and carefully arranged everything, making sure the teddy bears clad in T-shirts with the Golden Motel logo were front and center.

Callan Katz strolled over, daughter Emmy tucked into the baby carrier on his chest. "Looks good."

"Thanks. Can I give Emmy a bear? I want to make sure it's age appropriate."

"Sure."

Dee handed the baby a bear. Emmy cooed in delight and began nibbling on one of its ears.

"As long as we're on the subject of Bud," Callan said, "I've got an update on your project."

Dee could tell by the tone in his voice it wasn't good news. "Hit me."

"The executive I was dealing with got fired this week. The studio brought in a new head of the animation department and his mandate is edgier shows. I can take the project back to him if you make a few adjustments. What do you think about making Bud sexy? Or a rapper?"

"I can't say no fast enough."

Callan accepted with equanimity. "Yeah, I figured that would be your answer."

Instead of disappointment, Dee felt relief. Despite what she'd told herself about being able to balance a TV series with the motel business, she knew it was wishful thinking. "I'm sorry the project's dead. I know you put a lot into it."

"A show deal may be dead—for now—but Bud isn't. I looked into syndicating your cartoons for online publications and I got a positive response from several outlets. Interested?"

"Very," Dee said, thrilled. "It's perfect. I can totally make that work."

"Excellent. I'll get on it ASAP."

"You're a great agent, Callan," Dee said.

"That's the first thing I tell myself every morning," he said with a wide grin.

Baby Emmy let out a grunt. She scrunched up her face, turning bright red. Seconds later, an unpleasant odor wafted Dee's way. Dee wrinkled her nose and waved it away. "Grateful as I am to you for the syndication idea, I'm not going to change Emmy's diaper."

"You don't have to, I learned how," Callan said, proud of himself. "Did you know there's a woman in L.A. called the Diaper Whisperer?"

"I didn't, but of course there is."

"For only four hundred dollars, you get an hour-long one-on-one lesson in all the top diapering techniques. Great idea for a sitcom, right? I signed her and we're working up a pilot pitch."

"Best of luck to you both," Dee said, amused and not remotely surprised.

Callan left, on a mission to change his daughter's diaper. Dee saw Jonas walk toward her, and her pulse rose a few points. She willed it back down and greeted him with a casual hello.

"Congratulations on a fantastic event," Jonas said. He gave her two thumbs-up. "Ten outta ten."

"Serena and Elmira get all the credit."

"For implementation. But the idea was yours. Elmira told me so. Um . . ." Jonas hesitated. "I don't know if you're still up for . . . you know . . . going out. But if you are, any chance you're free for dinner tonight?"

"I am, and I am." She and Jonas exchanged a warm smile. But dread replaced Dee's happiness about her burgeoning relationship with the real estate agent as she eyed nemesis Verity in the fair crowd. "But we better not go to Goldsgone. Thanks to the success of this fair, I think I'm number one with a bullet on Verity's enemies list."

Verity noticed Dee and strode her way. The Trapp twins followed a few paces behind, like matchy-matchy teen bodyguards. "So," she said, lips pursed, "a crafts fair. Hmm, I wonder where you got the idea?"

"Hey, I see an old friend." Jonas made a move to escape.

"Leave and we're over," Dee growled. He stayed put. She addressed Verity. "I got the idea from the Goldsgone fair, which you deserve all the credit for. It was a fantastic idea. We only started one in Foundgold because you banned us from your fair. If we worked together, Verity, we could create a mega fair, holding them on different days so they didn't compete with each other. A Solid Gold Food and Crafts Festival, presented by the twin towns of Goldsgone and Foundgold."

To Dee's amazement, Verity's expression relaxed an infinitesimal amount. "Your business partner had the same idea. Jeff, yoo-hoo!"

"I've never heard anyone actually say 'yoo-hoo' before," Dee said to Jonas under her breath.

"If anyone would, it's Verity," he whispered back.

Jeff, still wearing the now-unnecessary eye patch, sauntered over to Verity's side. "What up, Vee?"

"I told Dee you had the marvelous idea of combining our crafts fairs and she loves it."

"Sounds good. Let's talk details over an Ice Cream Ida ice cream sandwich."

Jeff put an arm around Verity's waist. She giggled. As he led her off, he turned back and mouthed, "You're welcome."

Dee and Jonas stared after the couple. "Wow," Jonas said. "That's a relationship I did not see coming. What do you think?"

Dee watched as Jeff bought an ice cream sandwich for Verity . . . and then fed it to her. "I think," Dee said, "I liked it better when she called us Murder Motel."

# EPILOGUE

Bud the Bear stood on the edge of the deepest section of Dry Creek—the spot where Ed Froelich almost lost his life. Bud contemplated the cool, clear pool of water in front of him. Then he dove in, completely submerging himself.

A moment later, Bud surfaced with a fat river trout in his mouth. He clambered to the stream's edge and gave himself a vigorous shake. The air suddenly sparkled with a cloud of gold flakes.

Bud lumbered off into the woods with his catch. The flakes floated above the water.

Then the gold flakes sank down into the water and disappeared forever into its depths.

# ROAD TRIP TIPS

1. If you read the Road Trip Tips in *A Very Woodsy Murder,* you know I'm a firm believer in paper maps. Why? GPS is brilliant for getting you from point to point, but much tougher on giving an overview of an entire trip. Plus, you never know when you'll lose cell reception, so a good old-fashioned paper map could save the day.
2. Keeping with the paper map theme, if you're embarking on a road trip with your kids or grandkids, involve them in the planning of it. Give them a paper map and have them chart the route. They can go online to research interesting places to visit on your vacation, but let them take in the whole picture of your trip via the paper map. I have a really good sense of direction and I'm sure I developed it through the mapping of family trips I did as a kid.
3. Let technology be your friend! This may seem antithetical to tips 1 and 2, but it's not. Apps are out there that can enhance a road trip. On a visit to friends in Tahoe Donner, we decided to make the drive part of the vacation by taking Route 395 on the eastern side of the Sierras. Our daughter downloaded a map that identified points of interest along the way. We had a wonderful time spotting each one and learned much more about the road and its sights than we would have otherwise.

# BONUS RECIPE

## Nutty Almond Date Bars

The Golden Motel Mysteries are set in California, the almond and date capital of America, which makes this recipe a perfect match for the new Golden Motel Mystery series.

*Ingredients:*
*Crust:*
½ cup brown sugar
⅔ cup softened butter
½ cup light corn syrup
1 tsp. almond extract
2 cups all-purpose flour
1 egg
½ tsp. salt

*Filling:*
⅓ cup brown sugar
⅓ cup corn syrup
¼ cup butter
¼ cup heavy cream
1 tsp. almond extract

*Nut and date mixture:*
1 cup unsalted, slivered, dry-roast almonds
1 cup chopped dates

*Drizzle:*
1 cup melting white chocolate
½ to 1 tbsp. vegetable oil (optional)

***Directions:***

Heat oven to 350°F.

Line a 13" x 9" sheet pan with aluminum foil. In a large bowl, cream ½ cup brown sugar, ⅔ cup butter, and ½ cup corn syrup. Add 1 teaspoon almond extract and the egg and mix well. Slowly add the flour and salt, mixing well to combine into a dough. Spread the dough in pan, pressing to the edges. Bake 18 to 20 minutes or until a light golden brown.

While the crust is baking, heat ⅓ cup brown sugar and ⅓ cup corn syrup over a low heat in a medium saucepan, stirring constantly until the sugar is dissolved. Stir in ¼ cup butter and the whipping cream. Raise heat to medium, and heat mixture until it boils. Remove it from the stove and stir in the teaspoon of almond extract.

Sprinkle the almonds and dates over the crust, making sure they're evenly distributed. Pour the cooked mixture over the nuts and dates, making sure to spread it evenly over the almonds and dates.

Bake 15 to 20 minutes or until light brown and set. Cool about halfway, then melt the white chocolate by following the directions on the bag. (Add ½ tablespoon to a full tablespoon of vegetable oil to thin the white chocolate if necessary.)

Use a spoon to drizzle or drop the white chocolate onto the uncut bars. Put the tray into the refrigerator to finish cooling and to harden the white chocolate.

Once the uncut bars are completely cool, use a sharp knife and carefully cut them into 16 bars or 24 squares.

# BONUS CARTOON

"Somebody be a pal and get me another Mojito."

# ACKNOWLEDGMENTS

A huge thank-you to everyone at Kensington for giving me this amazing opportunity, and massive thanks to my agent Doug Grad for connecting me to this fantastic publisher and my wonderful editor, John Scognamiglio. I must also give a shout-out to Larissa Ackerman and the incredible marketing, digital, cover design, and promo teams. You all rock!

Huge love and thanks for my fellow blogmates at Chicks on the Case, my group mates at the Cozy Mystery Crew Facebook page, and my Fearless Foursome. A special thank-you to fab authors Julia Bricklin and James J. Cudney for their beta reads and notes. I owe you all. And to Angel Trapp and her darling daughter, Addison Rose, thanks for letting me turn you into twins straight out of *The Shining*, lol! And for your generous bid at the Malice Domestic live auction.

I've said it before, and I'll say it again: To all the rangers and workers at Columbia State Historic Park, the residents of California thank you for your dedication to such an important part of the state's history. I hope you get a kick out of my tongue-in-cheek take on what is an amazing and inspiring site. And the same gratitude goes to the rangers and staff at Yosemite National Park, which is the obvious inspiration for Majestic National Park in this series.

As always, a ton of love and gratitude to my husband,

Jerry, and my daughter, Eliza, for their patience and endless support. I truly couldn't do this writing thing without you. And to my late mom and dad, two voracious readers who passed on their passion for books to all three of their children. Mom passed away while I was writing the first draft of this book. She was the angel on my shoulder helping me work through the grief and still mine humor for the draft.

And finally, a special thank-you to my late aunt Molly. I hope you knew how much you meant to me.